THE WHITE WOLF TRILOGY

THE LOST

AMANDA GEISLER

The White Wolf Trilogy book 2: The Lost

Published by Ouroborus Book Services
www.ouroborusbooks.com

Visit Amanda at
www.amandageisler.com

Cover design by Sabrina RG Raven: www.sabrinargraven.com

The Stray
Amanda Geisler

Thank you to my loving husband for always pushing me to keep going, even though it feels endless sometimes. I love you Kieren xoxo

TOBY DAVIS

It had been almost a month since Rya was taken. There had been no sign of her. Colby and Damien expected us to go on as normal while they did what they could to find her. Would they find her? We didn't even know who had her. Zac's father claimed he had nothing to do with her disappearance, and for some reason the others believed him. Like he had ever given us any reason to trust him before.

For the most part the humans left us alone now, except for Zac. He was still a bit of a poster boy for becoming a werewolf. Obviously, none of us wanted him to be that and he definitely didn't want it but he couldn't seem to get away from it.

The girls at school were always getting asked if they could turn someone. Since Rya disappeared, all the younger generation had turned, most likely because of the emotional upset her disappearance caused. This meant that there were multiple young werewolves in town that caused a potential risk... I wanted to say for exposure but we all knew that went out the window months ago... No, these days it was only causing a risk to safety.

For now, that training was being left to the parents but none of them, except the warrior class, were skilled enough to teach them more than the basics. So this made it difficult to make sure that all the new werewolves weren't going to have a problem at school. With Rya missing, everyone was on edge. I think the only reason nobody had lost control yet was because the humans had been leaving us alone. I wondered how long that would last.

'Toby!' my mother shouted through the house. 'Time for school.'

Urgh. School. Why did I even still have to go? It's not like I learned anything there anymore. I forced myself to get out of bed and put on a fresh set of clothes. I grabbed my school bag from under my desk and went downstairs saying a hurried goodbye before I walked out the door. I was so looking forward to the school year being over. Just this week to go and we would be free for the summer.

After a quick walk through the forest I trudged grumpily through the school grounds and into the building to grab my things out of my locker. At least exams would be over this week. Maybe that's why I could sense the excitement in the air. The bell rang and I rushed off to my first class.

Lunch time was better because at least I got to see some werewolves. Colby had told us to close off our minds to keep ourselves better protected but with our minds closed off I couldn't communicate with anyone like I usually did during class time. It made school incredibly boring. Instead I slept through most of the classes. The teachers stopped caring what I did because I aced all my assessments and should do the same for the end of year exams.

The others were talking to Agua when I sat down with my tray of food. 'It's hard.' Agua was saying. 'I can't even get her to talk to me right now.'

'What's this?' I asked.

'My mum,' Agua responded. 'She hasn't talked to me or my dad since she found out we're witches.'

'I'm sure she will come around,' I said to her. 'Everyone else did.' But even I knew it would take time. The human loved ones had known about the werewolves already.

She grimaced. 'I know,' she said. 'I'm hoping to go see her on the holidays and try to clear the air.'

I looked around the room. Zac was sitting at the table with his friends, eyes on his food as his friends chatted around him. He only spoke when he was spoken to. He'd been doing this since Rya disappeared. I don't even know if anyone in the pack had spoken to him since that day.

'We can invite him over if you like,' Maya suggested.

I looked at her. 'He can do it himself,' I said. 'It's not like we told him he's not allowed.'

'No,' Agua said. 'But we didn't exactly welcome him with open arms.'

True. With Rya gone the cafeteria had gone back to the way it had been before she and Zac were together. I didn't know how I felt about it. Every part of me wanted to hate him, but really, I just felt sorry for him.

At the end of lunch I put my things away. I had a free period before my next exam, so I decided to go to the library to read the hour away. To my surprise Zac was there too. He had his chemistry textbook open and seemed be going through his notes. I could sense his stress from the bookshelf I stood at.

I had gone past him into the science section of our little library. There wasn't much but there were some things on the shelf I hadn't read yet. I grabbed one of those books and went to find my usual seat at the back of the library. I paused on my way past Zac.

I hope I'm not going to regret this, I thought to myself. I sat down at Zac's table. 'Anything I can help with?' I asked him.

Zac looked up at me, surprised for multiple reasons, I was sure. 'I'm just going over our chemistry notes.' We were in the same class. 'I just don't get any of it.'

'What part?' I leaned in closer as Zac started talking to me about the different chemical reactions in the textbook.

I spent that next hour giving him a crash course on our current science topic and everything he would need to know for the exam. When the bell rang, we both got up and went our separate ways without saying a single word to each other again.

I walked out of the exam later that day and went to my locker. I was surprised to see Zac standing there waiting for me. 'Hey, man,' he said as I approached. 'I just wanted to say thanks for your help earlier. I think I may have actually passed this subject for a change.'

'No problem,' I said, opening my locker to put things away. He started to walk away. 'Hey Zac,' I called. He turned to look at me. 'The others and I were thinking of heading out for a run later,' I continued. 'To blow of some steam. Would you like to join us?'

'Oh.' He was surprised. 'I've kind of already promised to go over to Dylan's to hang out.' He paused awkwardly for a moment. 'Raincheck?'

I smirked. 'Sure.'

He returned the smile before he turned and walked down the hallway to meet his human friend. I turned back to my locker.

'Did I just see you being nice?' Agua asked, an expression of feigned shock on her face.

I ignored her comment. 'Come on,' I said. 'Let's go.' I glanced back at Zac after we walked past him and his friend. He glanced at me and he gave me a friendly smile that I returned. Maybe he wasn't so bad after all.

*****

The next day was pretty much the same. In my free period I went to the library again. Zac was there. I had only just grabbed my book off the shelf before he walked up to me.

'Do you mind helping me with my maths?' he asked timidly.

I put my book back on the shelf. 'Sure thing.'

This became the pattern for the remainder of the week. Whenever he shared a free period with me in the library, he would ask me to help him. I didn't mind. It gave me something to do to take my mind off everything else.

Each day I helped him with the subject he was studying for. I taught him the entire topic because I knew that he would retain the information now that he was a werewolf. I wouldn't have to teach him again after this. Everything else he learned in school he would retain as well.

On Friday when we finished up our session we sat in silence.

'So how have you been going with everything?' I asked after several moments of silence.

'With what?' he responded.

'Being a werewolf,' I said. 'It can't be easy for you.'

He looked down. 'I mostly just try to forget about it.'

'How's that working out for you?'

'I think I've done okay so far,' he replied. 'I haven't hurt anybody at least.'

I managed a small smile at that. 'Always a bonus.' We fell into silence. Gosh this was awkward. 'Is there anything I else I can help you study for?' I asked after a few moments.

He shook his head. 'This is my last exam.'

'Nice.' I still had two more after lunch before I was done. 'You should come out and celebrate with us tonight,' I said to him. 'We do it at the end of every school year.'

'What do you do?' he asked.

'We go out, have some fun and just relax,' I explained. 'We need to do this right now with everything that's going on.'

He hesitated. 'Sure,' he said. 'What time should I meet you?'

'I'll come get you around dusk.' He was still living at Rya's. I honestly didn't know how he did that. It would be too much of a mood dampener for me. The bell rang just as he nodded to me. Without a word he got up and left.

At the end of the school day I felt happier than I had in a while. School was over. It had been an insanely crazy year. I was just cleaning out my locker of old notebooks so that it was tidy for next year when I heard the altercation.

'Come play soccer with us.' That was unmistakeably Jace's voice. I hated that asshole.

'No,' I heard Zac say. 'I already have plans tonight.'

'With your new werewolf pals?' Jace asked.

I heard a locker door slam.

'Jace.' Dylan's voice. 'Leave him alone. He doesn't have to play.'

'We've both seen him during free periods,' Jace said. 'In the library, talking to Toby.'

'He was helping me study,' Zac said. 'Not that it is any of your business to begin with.'

'You're my friend,' I heard Jace say. 'It is my business.'

'Well you haven't been much of a friend to me lately,' Zac retorted. *Yeah, you tell 'em Zac.* 'It's making me reconsider this friendship.' And with that the new werewolf turned and walked out of the building.

I closed my locker, slung my now heavier bag over my shoulder and started the walk home. On my way through the forest I caught scent of Zac. He didn't usually travel through the forest. It was unusual enough that I changed course and followed his scent instead of heading home.

I made no noise as I moved, taking care to be as silent as possible. When I spotted him, I moved downwind so he couldn't smell me. His bag was at the base of a tree and he was standing in the middle of a small clearing. The space was maybe big enough for three people to sit comfortably.

He had his eyes closed, focusing. Then I heard a cracking sound in his direction. He was shifting. A few cracks later it stopped. Zac's bones moved back into their original place. Zac let out a gasping breath, exhausted.

I watched silently as he tried several more times to shift. None of his attempts succeeded. I walked silently into the clearing. Zac didn't notice me until I dropped my bag next to his.

He spun around to face me at the loud *thunk* my bag made when it hit the ground. 'What are you doing here?' Zac wasn't pleased.

'You need to get angrier,' I told him.

'What?'

'To shift.' I said. 'You're a bitten. The shift won't come naturally to you like it does for us. You need to get angry.'

'But I don't want to get angry.'

'Why not?' I prodded. 'It's not like you don't have anything to be angry about.'

He seemed to think about it for a moment and I thought I saw the slightest shimmer of fur across his skin before he spoke. 'Why are you helping me?'

I shrugged. 'Honestly. I don't know. But have a go of what I said,' I told him. 'I have to get to Keith for training, but I will see you later.' I grabbed my bag and continued my walk home. I knew when I wasn't wanted.

*****

When I arrived at Rya's house at sundown it was to have Zac open the door the moment I approached the front door. Without a word he followed as I lead him to the forest. We walked in silence until we had almost reached the others. That was when I spoke. 'How did you go with what I said earlier?' I asked.

He shook his head. 'Still no luck,' Zac admitted.

I stopped walking so suddenly that Zac almost walked into me. 'Do you want me to help you?' I asked.

He seemed to hesitate for a moment. 'Sure,' he answered a little sullenly.

I sat down on the ground and indicated for him to do the same. After he was sitting cross-legged across from me, I spoke again. 'I'm going to reach into your mind.' I told him.

He nodded so I took that as consent to proceed. I closed my eyes and reached out with my own. There were no walls around Zac's mind. Nobody had really taught him how to close his mind, so it was easy enough to get into without any hesitation or blocks.

I shifted through the different areas of his mind searching for the space in the back where his wolf would be hiding. I could feel the disconnection that he was feeling as I searched through the deepest parts of his mind, not just disconnection from the humans but the pack as well. When I found what I was looking for, I stopped. 'What you need to do,' I said out loud, 'is find the wolf in the back of your mind. Then you need to pull at its power.'

'But isn't that bad?' Zac responded.

'Not at all,' I assured him. 'You don't lose control from drawing the wolf's power. You lose control if you let the wolf take control over you. You have to draw on the wolf's power so you can use its form and abilities.' I felt the realisation that Zac was having as I spoke. 'I thought Colby taught you this.'

'Kind of,' Zac replied. 'He taught me a little bit but I was only able to transform a few times.'

'Have you shifted at all since… since the last full moon?' I asked.

Zac shook his head. 'Unless you count the new moon.'

I sighed. This was going to take a bit of time. 'Okay,' I said. 'For tonight let's just get you into wolf form.' I told him. 'We can get you better at it another day.'

Zac looked shocked by this. 'You're going to help me?'

'Yes.' I nodded. 'You have a problem with that?'

I was still connected to his mind so I could still hear his thoughts and feelings as they went through him; right now, confusion. 'No,' he answered finally.

'Good. Now show me what you're doing to transform.' I honestly hadn't realised that he felt afraid to approach us. He thought that we didn't want him around even if he was a werewolf now. We had thought he just didn't want to interact with us without Rya. This was all a massive misunderstanding.

Zac started his shift, showing me what he was doing while I watched from inside his mind. I quickly worked out what the problem was. 'It's just the pain,' I announced to him.

'What?' There was sweat beading on Zac's forehead from the exertion of his failed transformations.

'The pain of the transformation. You're letting it distract you and pull you away from turning.'

'Yeah, well, it is pretty painful.'

I shook my head. 'Only for now,' I said. 'It does get easier. You just have to push through it.' After a few more tries Zac finally managed to get himself into full wolf form. Once he did, he let out huge huff of exhaustion. 'Good job,' I said. 'Now let's go meet the others. We're late.'

I quickly shifted and led the way to where we were meeting the other werewolves. I kept a slowish pace while Zac got used to his paws again. On four legs it took us next to no time to get to the clearing. The others were already there; Mira, Max, Brian, Maya and Liam.

'What took you so long?' Liam asked. Then he saw Zac. *'Oh... hey.'*

'Hey,' Zac responded awkwardly.

They got over Zac's appearance pretty quickly. *'I'm starving,'* Mira said breaking the silence. *'Let's go eat.'*

That night we went hunting. We showed Zac how to hunt and the fun parts of being a werewolf: the adrenaline rush from running so fast the world became a blur, the hunting and stalking of prey, even just the feeling of friends and family. The feeling of pack. When we said goodnight to each other at the clearing he seemed a lot more comfortable.

Before leaving Zac to himself, I took him to the pack clearing to get some clothes and showed him the way home, then I went home and crawled into bed. It was well past midnight but I was feeling a lot better than I had this morning. Rya wasn't here right now. We would find her, but for now our pack was struggling to stay together without her. We had lost our drive to keep going without her. I had to help change that. There had to be something I could do.

ZAC HALL

I woke up the following morning to a knock on the front door. Dylan. I had gotten used to recognising people over the last couple of weeks. It wasn't anything like I thought it would be. Each person had their own individual… aura… I guess. I managed to learn a lot of people's auras so that I could tell who was nearby.

I dragged myself out of bed to answer the door. 'Hey what's up?' I asked.

'Morning to you too.' Dylan smirked. 'You know it's almost midday?'

'You know I was out really late?' I shot back. I really wasn't in the mood.

Dylan put his hands in front of himself defensively. 'Hey. I'm sorry. I thought with it being the full moon you would be keen head out for the day.'

'Out where?' I looked over his shoulder to see a car in the drive. Sean and Jace were sitting in the front seats with Sean behind the wheel.

'We were going to go up the mountain to the watering hole,' Dylan said.

'Who's going?'

'A bunch of people from school.'

I thought about it. I didn't really want to go but I also didn't really want to stay here either. Waiting for the full moon tonight alone would be torture. 'Fine,' I said. 'But I have to be back by dark.'

'That's cool,' he said.

I went back inside chucked on my swimming shorts and grabbed a water bottle and some snacks from the cupboard before I left the house. I climbed into the backseat of the car with Dylan.

'Glad you could come,' Sean said. 'It's a bit last minute.'

'It's alright,' I said. 'I needed something to pass the time today.'

'Before you wolf out with your new pals.'

I snapped my head around to look directly at Jace. He was turned around, looking at me. I felt my anger flare up inside me, a stirring deep within myself. I looked back out the window, choosing to ignore rather than feed the anger inside me.

'It's fine,' Sean said. 'Dylan and I have curfew anyway.'

The rest of the hour car ride was pretty quiet, with the others only conversing when necessary. When we finally arrived, I was very keen to get out of the car. There was actually a lot of people there, almost the entire high school. None of them were from the werewolf pack. I felt myself relax. I was just hanging out with everyone from school at the start of summer holidays. I did this every year. This was my chance to get back to normal.

In the water I could see everyone just hanging out.

Up on the cliff above the watering hole there were people jumping off and into the water. Some others were near where they were landing just in case anyone needed help. Everyone was just relaxed. It felt… nice.

Jace and Sean raced up the path to the top of the cliff to jump off. I followed them up at a slower pace.

'So what are your plans for the summer?' Dylan asked me when we reached the end of the short line to jump off.

I shrugged. 'I don't really have any.'

'You should come to the city with us,' Sean said. 'My family is going to New York for a few days and they said you guys can come.' Sean's family owned a few properties in the city. They weren't as rich as the Garcia's, as I had found out, but they certainly had some decent money.

I hesitated to respond though. 'I will have to see,' I said. 'I don't know if I would be allowed.'

'By who?' Jace asked.

'Well, from what I've heard there's a pack in New York,' I answered. 'I might not be able to go there for that reason.'

'Surely they could sort something out?' Sean questioned. 'Aren't the other packs Rya's family or something?'

I shrugged. 'I don't know.'

Sean shrugged it off. 'If you can come let me know?'

I gave him a small smile. 'I'll ask.'

It was Jace's turn to jump of the cliff. We watched him take a big running leap as he jumped into the open space then he disappeared as gravity pulled him down. Sean followed once Jace had safely moved out of the way.

Then it was my turn. I stepped up to the edge and looked over it. I could see the watering hole way down there. I could see the carpark off to my right and in front of me was a great expanse of trees.

'You just going to stare at the scenery all day?' Dylan asked.

In answer to his question I took several steps back then ran for the edge. I leapt off. I felt the moment of weightlessness before I felt the pull towards the earth. I felt myself turn in the air until I was head down in a more traditional diving position.

My heart was pumping with adrenaline when I hit the water. It was cold and dark as I felt my body twist again almost through instinct as I swam up and broke the surface. I shook my head to get the water out of my eyes and swam away from the centre so that Dylan could follow me down. I found a rock to settle on near Sean and watched Dylan take his dive.

When he hit the water he was curled up in a ball and made massive splash with his cannonball. Almost everyone in the vicinity was splashed before he breached the surface again. Everyone was laughing. It was nice.

We spent hours at the watering hole, just chatting and enjoying the sunshine. I caught up with most of the soccer team while I was there. The topic of werewolves never came up and I never brought it up. It was almost like they had never been discovered and I had never become one.

I couldn't shake the nagging in the back of my head though. I would be relaxing and having fun throwing a ball that someone had brought and then this voice in the back of my mind would say, *we shouldn't be having fun. Rya is gone.* I tried my best to ignore it, but it just kept nagging at me.

I was swimming around in the water while others had gone to get food. After hunting last night with the other werewolves I wasn't all that hungry. I floated on the top of the cool water my eyes closed as I enjoyed the relaxing atmosphere.

I was thinking about last year when Rya and I had come here with everyone at the start of last summer. It had been fun then too. It had been not too long after we had started dating. I wished she was there in that moment.

A prickly feeling started to form on the back of my neck. I scratched myself and it went away and I settled back but the feeling came back again stronger this time and with a bad feeling attached to it.

I sat up and looked around. Everything looked normal. A few people had started making their way back into the water. I could see my soccer teammates milling around the communal barbeque. They were as relaxed as everyone else.

But I couldn't shake the feeling and I started scanning the trees around us. *Anything could be hiding in there,* I thought to myself.

Movement in the trees caught my eyes and my head snapped around to follow the movement. It was just a bird. But I caught sight of more movement. A person. I raised my nose to the air and sniffed.

The wind carried with it the smell of something gone rotten. *Vampire.* A voice growled in the back of my head. I knew instantly where that voice came from.

I looked around. There was no way of alerting anyone to the danger without the vampire noticing. Nobody had even noticed my change in behaviour. Did the vampire even know I was here? What could I do? I pushed out with my mind. It was harder than I thought. No matter how hard I tried though I couldn't reach out more than a few metres.

I was slightly panicking now. There were no werewolves nearby that I knew of. Nearly the entire town's teenagers were located in this one spot and there were who knows how many vampires lurking in the trees.

I flinched when the vampire I was staring at started staring back. I didn't know what to do. If the vampire didn't know I was here before, he definitely did now. There would be no mistaking my golden eyes.

'Zac,' I heard Dylan's voice. 'You okay?' Where did he go? In the split second that my attention wavered the vampire was gone. 'Zac?'

'Shoosh,' I said. 'I'm trying to listen.'

I closed my eyes and reached out again. With my mind and my ears. I drowned out the sound of laughing teenagers and reached further. With my body on alert I was able to stretch myself a bit further. Far enough to sense the three vampires moving towards the edge of the trees.

It didn't matter at all though. I was outnumbered. And even if there had only been one, I didn't know how to fight. Not like Rya. Not like Toby. They seemed to know it too. I knew this because they just waltzed right into the space like everyone had been expecting them.

My classmates seemed to look at them with confusion for a moment before they started backing away. Having noticed the unmistakeable red eyes that the vampires bore. They stopped about halfway between me and the tree line.

Everyone seemed to back away at once. The entire area became incredibly silent. I didn't know if I should back away and run or fight. But I did know that I wouldn't stand a chance in this fight. I had to try though, didn't I?

They seemed to be waiting for me to do something. In the end I spoke to them. 'What are you doing here?' I asked.

'We were looking for a snack,' the one I had seen first in the trees said. 'But then I saw you. Werewolf blood is so much better than human blood.' I could feel the disgusted expression on my face. 'You're new, aren't you?' the vampire said. 'Experienced wolves would have attacked by now. You're hesitating.'

I can help you, the voice in the back of my head whispered. I ignored the voice.

'Let's make this more motivating,' the female brunette vampire started. Within seconds she flittered out of sight and back. When she returned, she had Sean in her arms, with her extended claws at his throat.

That made me move out of the water. 'Let him go,' I said. I felt the urge to growl but I suppressed it.

'Or what?' the third vampire said.

I let my anger fuel the change. Just like Toby had told me. My anger that I was in this situation. Anger that I knew I couldn't win this fight. That I knew I couldn't reach out to the other werewolves because we were too far away. This anger fuelled my transformation to the point where I didn't even feel the pain.

'Now we're getting somewhere,' the first vampire stated as he grinned mercilessly.

I couldn't fight them. I needed help. They were closing in on me. I darted in between the right two vampires before they could catch me. Then before I even knew what was happening, I felt my chest fill up with air before I released an incredibly loud howl. So loud that my classmates had to cover their ears.

You're welcome, the voice in my head said. *Now watch out!*

I dodged the incoming vampire. I had no doubt that the voice was from the wolf side of me. I only hoped that anyone from back in town heard the call for help. I stumbled as I leapt out of the way of the female.

Unfortunately, that gave them a chance to grab me. I bit down on the arm that tried to wrap around my neck. The vampire growled in pain as they withdrew their torn-up arm. I was horrified to noticed that no blood came from the wound.

The was no time to ponder that. I had to get away from all three of them. I ducked past the male on my right and turned around, as I tried to replicate what I had seen Rya do before. I lurched around and leapt at the vampire's back.

No sooner than my jaw closing around the back of his neck, I got pulled away. I saw the vampire I attacked had begun to turn to ash. There was no time to celebrate. The vampire that had grabbed me squeezed their arms in a massively painful bear hug. I felt my bones breaking under my skin and I couldn't stop the whimper that escaped me.

I felt my wolf's energy surge through me and I forced myself free, ignoring the pain of what I thought was broken ribs. Once again, I stumbled as I landed. This time from pain, not clumsiness.

I had to jump quickly out of the way before the female attacked me again. The other vampire grabbed me from behind. I struggled but I couldn't move. I felt it as his fangs sank into the skin of my neck.

The sting of pain stopped as I was thrown away from the vampire. I rolled several times and felt it as my body became human once more. It took me a moment to realise that it wasn't the vampire that threw me. Toby. In human form was now facing off against the female vampire. He had already killed the other one.

Toby didn't have to kill the last vampire. I saw Mira's wolf sneak through the watchful teenagers, surprising them as she passed. She leapt at the vampire from behind and closed her grey muzzle around the vampire's throat. Within seconds only ash remained.

I watched Mira pulled back her wolf form and she morphed back to human. The bracelet on her wrist meant she was wearing clothes when she was fully human. I was suddenly so glad that I never took mine off. Otherwise I would have been completely naked in front of everyone. I glanced at mine closed around my ankle. I was still wearing my swimming shorts.

Mira came over to me, crouched down and inspected the wound at my neck. 'You'll live,' she announced. 'It's already healing.'

Toby held his hand out towards me. 'You did pretty well for your first scuffle. You even managed to kill one.' I took his hand and he pulled me to my feet.

'It nearly killed me,' I said.

He shrugged. 'Yeah, that happens.' I was about to speak again but the sound of a phone ringing came from Toby. He dug his hand into his pocket and pulled out his phone. 'Hey, Colby,' he answered.

'Did you find him?' I heard Colby's voice on the other end.

'Yeah, I did.'

'What happened?'

'Three vampires.' As if that said everything.

A pause. *'Is everyone okay?'*

'Yeah,' Toby replied. 'I haven't had a chance to sweep the area yet but these three are dead.'

'Good,' Colby praised. *'Keith and Charlie are on their way to check the area for more. I want you three kids to come back to the bunker.'*

'Are you sure?' Toby said. 'Mira and I…'

'No!' Colby said forcefully. *'I said come back here. Keith and Charlie will handle it.'*

'Okay,' Toby replied breathlessly. The phone beeped as the call was ended. He looked at me. 'We have to go back.'

'I know, I heard,' I answered. I wondered what was

up. It sounded like more than just worry about the vampires being here.

Mira had been going around to our classmates making sure everyone was okay whilst Toby was on the phone. I looked at Sean and Dylan. 'Guess I have to go,' I told them.

They shrugged. 'I'm sure everyone will be heading home now anyway,' Sean assured me.

'Probably a good idea,' Toby said in a more projected voice. 'Best to get a bit closer to town in case there's any more lurking around.' Everyone seemed more than happy to oblige as they started grabbing their things and heading back to cars.

Without another word I followed Toby and Mira into the trees the vampires had come out of. I made sure I kept up because I knew I was safer with them. A short distance into the trees I watched as Toby transformed as he ran. A few moments later Mira did the same. I did my best to focus on drawing the wolf out of me. Thankfully I was already so sore from my broken ribs that the additional pain of transforming wasn't so bad. I stumbled a little bit as I went from two to four legs but I managed to keep running as I shifted.

We ran faster on four legs. Like last night we increased our speed until the forest was a blur around us. At our speed we reached the hatch to the bunker in no time flat and soon we were sitting face to face with Colby and Damien.

Damien had stepped up to the plate while Rya was missing to help Colby run the pack. I didn't really like the idea but I trusted Colby and he seemed to be okay with the extra help. Even so. I still felt like I had just been brought to the principal's office at school.

'What happened today?' Colby asked me.

I told him. I told him that I was just having fun with all the others when the vampires showed up. What they had said about wanting a snack but finding me instead. I told them everything about the story even what happened during the fight.

'Sounds like it was a good thing you were there,' Colby said. I felt myself relax. I had thought I would get in trouble for being so far away from the other werewolves. 'I think it is better that you don't leave town alone for the time being though,' Colby told me. 'You're untrained and if you hadn't been able to call for help you could have died.'

'It's not my fault I'm untrained,' I said flatly, looking at the ground.

'You're right,' Colby said. 'It's mine. I should have had somebody continue your training.' Colby seemed to sigh, he looked exhausted. 'With everything that's going on it seems to have slipped my mind.'

'I can train him,' Toby said suddenly. 'I can train all of them.'

Colby looked at him. 'I wouldn't have thought you would want to.'

'I need something to do,' Toby replied. 'I'm not trained enough to go out with the team yet and everyone else is busy.'

'Only if you think you can handle it,' Colby said.

Toby was nodding. 'I'm pretty sure I can.'

'Okay,' Colby said. 'I expect that Zac and the others will be reasonably trained before you all go back to school in the fall.' Toby nodded. 'And Zac needs to be taught our ways.'

'Of course,' Toby said.

'We should probably think about heading to the full moon gathering.' It had been the first time that Damien had spoken since we arrived.

Colby nodded. 'Let's enjoy tonight as much as we can,' Colby told us. And with that he got up and led us out of the bunker and into the surrounding forest.

Since my first and only full moon involved the entire town at the camp out, I didn't even know how a normal full moon gathering was meant to be. I did expect to be surrounded by a couple of dozen, potentially naked, werewolves. I didn't expect to feel excluded by most of the adults. The werewolves that did acknowledge me were the other teenagers. Most of the adults just ignored me entirely.

I sat and waited with Toby for everyone to arrive as moonrise approached. Finally, Colby stood up to address everyone.

'I know we are missing Rya this full moon,' he said. 'I can tell you that every werewolf in the country is currently looking for her. We are scouring everywhere we can think of. We will find her. It's just a matter of time.' He took a deep breath. 'In Rya's absence it has come to my attention that we have neglected our newest members of the pack. Especially Zac. He didn't ask to be one of us. It's not his fault he is now a werewolf.' He was looking at me as he spoke. 'I'm sorry, I'm still learning how to be a beta and now I have to manage alpha as well.' He turned his attention back to the pack as a whole. 'Toby has kindly offered to train our newest werewolves so that they can protect themselves should the need arise. I have accepted his offer of assistance while we work to maintain a sense of normalcy.' Colby paused for several moments before speaking again. 'I know that tonight will be hard without Rya here, but let's try and enjoy the time we have together tonight.'

When the moon finally decided to appear over the horizon, we took wolf form. This time it didn't hurt. My body slid easily into wolf form with no pain at all. Not even my broken ribs seemed to cause any pain. When my body was no longer human, I stretched out my limbs, there was no pain from the broken ribs I had from my earlier fight. I guess the full moon heals everything.

The entire pack waited until Max, Liam and Brian transformed fully. This was their first full moon. Their transformation wasn't painless, in fact it hurt a lot. I still remembered the pain from my first time, last month, I felt my canine body quiver at the memory.

I decided it was best to follow Toby and Mira's lead. They had been werewolves their whole lives and obviously knew how things worked. I followed them as we ran through the trees towards where I knew the deer would be for tonight's dinner.

I helped them hunt, causing the distraction while Toby went for the painless kill. The adults killed another three deer. Toby and Brian pulled our kill over to the centre of the small grove.

Nobody moved except Colby now. From what I knew, since he was standing in for Rya he got to eat first. Then Damien grabbed some food. Then everyone else except the teenagers went to get their food. Toby had followed them since he was no longer classed as the kid. I remembered he had been made a full member of the pack last full moon.

Finally, when they had all chosen their food. Mira indicated to me that we could eat now. Honestly, there wasn't much left. We really only got to pick at any remaining meat. This made me glad that I had eaten properly the night before with the other kids. Maybe that's why they did that. They knew they wouldn't get much on the full moon.

The rest of the night was spent playing together. It was strange to see what the town thought of as big buff werewolves play chasey in the forest. They really weren't as threatening as the human population made them out to be.

Finally, when midnight had well and truly passed, we all made our way back to the clearing to curl up and sleep. I found my own soft patch of grass and was mildly surprised when Maya, Mira and Brian curled up around me, Maya's head resting across my back. I felt myself flinch slightly at the unexpected sentiment but I quickly felt myself settle as I got comfortable enough to fall asleep.

The following morning when I woke up it was to find three quarters of the werewolves still asleep. All of them were in human form. Some were naked, others weren't, like me. I could see the clothing bracelet on some of their wrists or ankles. I still found it hard to believe that Rya invented them – they were certainly useful. Especially to a newly bitten werewolf that didn't want to be caught naked in front of his friends.

I thought about waiting for one of the others to wake up before leaving, but in the end I decided to go home to get some proper sleep. I got up and left the sleeping werewolves to their slumber, slowly making the trek home.

I don't know how I managed to get home. I just kind of knew the way back without actually knowing where I was going. It was like a part of me just instinctually knew the way. When I arrived, I locked the doors, closed the blinds and climbed into bed for a more comfortable sleep than the one in the forest.

*****

The day after all the full moon stuff I woke up to Toby banging on my front door. When I rolled over and looked at the clock I groaned. It was six o'clock. In the morning. I dragged myself out of bed and went to let him in.

'What do you want?' I said grumpily. 'It's six AM.'

'First day of training.' He seemed a little too happy about waking me up. 'Get dressed, let's go.'

I swung the door at him, and turned and walked back to the bedroom. A part of me wanted to slump back into bed, but the other part knew that I wouldn't be allowed to sleep any more that day. Instead I did as I was told and got dressed into some exercise clothes. For me that was black gym shorts and a red singlet shirt.

Even though I hated the earlier start I was somewhat excited about training, though I would have preferred learning from Rya instead of Toby. I still wasn't buying that Toby was warming up to me. He had seemed to hate me so much.

Toby took me to the bunker. He hadn't spoken to me all the way there. He took me through a door I hadn't been through before. The room was empty. It had cement walls and wooden floors.

Toby flicked on the lights and closed the door behind him. I still wondered how they had power down here without it getting detected. Maybe they had someone controlling that side of things or maybe they had their own power.

'Transform,' Toby said to me.

For the next two hours Toby had me transforming over and over again. At first it was really difficult. Without the motivation from the day before at the watering hole it was a lot harder to make myself transform. But he made me do it until every muscle in my body screaming and sweat was dripping from my face and onto the floor.

I felt like I was going to collapse from exhaustion but it didn't end there. Toby started teaching me basic self-defence and fighting techniques. Pretty much basic blocks, holds and offensive moves. We did that for about another hour until he finally let me go and I made the long walk home again. This time by myself.

I didn't get to rest like I wanted though. Dylan was at the front door when I got back. After I had a shower and got cleaned up, we went over to Kraze to meet with the guys for lunch and a couple of games of soccer. Afterwards we went back to Dylan's to play some games on his PlayStation. That night I pretty much fell into bed and went straight to sleep.

That was the pattern the next two weeks took on the lead up to the dark moon. Toby came and got me every morning at six. He was never late. He would then put me through three hours of intense training. As much as I hated it, I was already seeing a difference in my strength and stamina. I was getting to the point where I could transform with only a moment's thought. My fighting skills were getting better to the point where I could hold my own against Toby going easy on me.

Every day after training at least one of the guys would be waiting for me, they never asked me where I had been or what I had been doing and I never told them. Every day we would go and have lunch then afterwards we would play soccer for most of the afternoon. Some nights I would manage to get to myself but others I would end up spending playing video games with the guys.

The day before the new moon Toby told me that there would be no training for the next two days. I actually got really excited for that prospect. But then the idea of the new moon dampened my elated mood. I was going to have to go through that again. This was my third dark moon. I hadn't had Rya there for any of them.

On the dark moon morning I found myself waking up at six. I sighed when I looked at the clock. I had woken up at this time every day and now my body was thinking that was normal. That is not what I wanted to happen.

In the end I couldn't get back to sleep so I got up to go for a run. As much as I didn't like being a werewolf, running had to be the best feeling ever. I liked the way the wind would sweep through my fur and across my face.

Instead of training I spent the morning running in wolf form. Weaving in and out of trees without stopping. It wasn't as intense as Toby's training but it was fun and I think it helped me with my running in wolf form and my overall agility.

As usual, when I got back home, Dylan was there. I went to lunch with him but I didn't eat. I wasn't that hungry. I just sat quietly while the guys talked to each other. I took another sip of my coke, pretty much zoned out until I noticed my father sitting in a seat by the entrance to the café, alone.

I hadn't seen him for over a month. Not since before Rya had disappeared. I contemplated ignoring him. But I couldn't stop glancing at him. I sighed in defeat and excused myself from the table with my friends.

I could feel them watching me walk over. I was glad I was in public at least. These days I had no idea what my father would do. He seemed genuinely surprised when I sat in the seat across from him.

'Hey,' I said after a moment of silence.

He smiled his soft warm smile I remembered. It had always been my welcome home from school. 'Hey buddy. How have you been?'

'Yeah alright,' I answered truthfully. 'It's been a bit full on lately.'

'And how are you dealing with all of this werewolf stuff?'

'I'm not telling you anything about them,' I said sternly. I could feel the look of mistrust on my face.

He held up in his hands in defence. 'That's not what I meant,' he said quickly. 'I wanted to know how *you* were managing with it all.'

'Oh... Sorry. I guess I'm doing okay. Some parts are hard, others are fun. It's just a bit strange to me. I don't know what to do with myself anymore. Like I don't know who I am anymore.'

'I'm sorry to hear that,' my father said. 'I'm sure you will figure it out. You're a smart kid.' There was silence between us for a moment, neither of us looking at each other. 'Are they taking care of you properly?'

'As best as they can, I guess,' I said. 'They started training me last week. That's been crazy.'

'I can tell.' I gave him a confused look. 'You've always been athletic, don't get me wrong, but you just seem leaner. More aware. Stronger.'

'Why did you come here today?' I asked.

'I heard that you and your friends have been here every day since the holidays started. I needed to talk to you. Needed to see that you're okay.'

'What did you want to talk about?'

'That fight. The one that happened just before Rya got taken.'

I felt my guard go up. 'What about it?'

'Who was it that attacked Rya?'

I shook my head. 'We don't know,' I said truthfully. 'All I know is that he killed Rya's parents when she was younger.' He seemed to sigh. 'Do you know him?'

He shook his head. 'No, but I have seen him before.' His eyes seemed to glaze over. Like he was reliving a bad memory. 'He killed your mother.'

I wasn't expecting that. 'What!' I sensed several people turn their heads to look at us. I lowered my voice so they couldn't hear me. 'You told me she died in an accident.'

'I lied,' he said. 'You were just a baby when it happened.' I held back the anger I was feeling. 'And I didn't think anybody would believe me at the time.'

'What happened?' I asked. My anger had dissipated a little at his words.

He took a breath. 'I didn't always study the paranormal. I used to be an archaeologist, so did your mother. We met in college you see. We ended up getting sent on a couple of studies together and ended up getting together. A few years after we had you, we got asked to look into a set of ruins outside of a little town in New Jersey. We lived in New York at the time so we were the closest. There was a team on their way to help but it would take them a week to arrive.'

'We left you with our live-in nanny and came here to Wolfridge,' my dad continued. His voice was low enough that only I could hear him. 'We went out to the ruins using the coordinates we were given. What we found there was bizarre. There were paintings on the walls, of people and wolves and stories in another language that I could never translate. We found a door and after trying quite a few ways we managed to crack it open.'

'We never expected what was inside. Something moved in there. All I remember seeing was a flash of red for a moment before the door was pulled open. Then your mother was gone. I turned around and found her on the ground and that man, biting her neck. I later found out that it had been drinking her blood. I thought I was next, so I ran.' He looked kind of guilty when he said that. 'But he didn't come after me. I peeked out from the bush I was hiding in just in time to see him turn in to a white wolf, his eyes also changed from red to yellow.'

'That's why you started studying werewolves?' I asked, after there was a moment's silence between us. He nodded. 'And why you didn't trust the werewolves when they got discovered?' Another nod.

'It's okay,' I said. 'I believe you. But I think we need to tell Colby about this.' He looked up at me. 'The pack needs to know.'

'But what if they hate me for it? Our expedition is the reason their alphas were killed.' He seemed kind of scared. I'd never seen him afraid like this before.

'Just so you know, they already hate you.' He looked at me and I smirked slightly. After a moment he smiled back. 'You were doing your job,' I said. 'They should understand that at the very least.'

After calling Colby on his mobile and I explained briefly what my father had said he came right to the café to talk to him about it more. Colby went through the story and asked so many questions to get as much detail as possible. Afterwards Colby left almost as quickly as he had come.

With all of that done, I had no idea what Colby was going to do with the information. Hopefully it would help them find whoever it was that killed Rya's parents and apparently my mother too.

I looked at the time on the clock on the wall, only an hour. I had been here all afternoon. I sighed. 'Sorry, Dad,' I said. 'I have to go.' He looked at the clock as well. 'We should catch up again soon though. Talk more.'

He smiled. 'I'd like that,' he said.

I got up and looked over to the table where my friends had been. At some point they had left. I didn't even notice them leave. Probably for the best, I guess. I made the walk home. I didn't have to rush, glad I looked at the clock when I did.

While I waited for it to be time, I cleaned up a little, chucked some clothes in the washing machine, made sure the house was clean, especially since it wasn't my house. Then I just sat on the couch to wait.

When it was ten minutes from moonrise I went to the bookcase and pressed the hidden button to make it slide across. I pressed the button inside on the wall to close it as I walked down the steps into the small room.

When I was sure that the bookcase had closed properly, I closed the large metal door. According to Agua I didn't need to close it, my wolf shouldn't be able to get out of the metal bars at all, but I still did it anyway. I think it made me feel safer, knowing that I was locked in here and definitely couldn't get out. I went into the cage locked the door and sat against the wall waiting for the moon to take its effect on me.

The only way I could describe it would be that it's like there is a pressure closing in around my mind. It felt like an instinct to fight it but I forced myself to stay calm and just let it happen.

The first time I turned I fought it and it had hurt so much it had been almost unbearable. My second time I didn't fight as much I had remembered Rya saying that fighting it would make it worse. And it had been better that second time but it had still been so painful.

This time I hoped it would be easier again. When I felt the tug at my mind from the wolf that laid beneath the surface of my mind, I let it go. I didn't pull back, I didn't fight, I just gave up the power to this wolf inside me. After this the change happened pretty quickly. It hurt. I felt each bone break and get put back into place where it needed to be in wolf form. I breathed my way through it. It definitely hurt. But it wasn't as bad. By the time I was in full wolf form I felt more tugging at the edges of my mind before I felt the wolf push forward to envelope my entire being and take control. As the wolf stretched its limbs, I felt my consciousness drift away into the abyss.

RYA GARCIA

I felt myself groan as I woke up. The dark moon was a lot harder on me this time. Maybe it was due to the lack of food. I wasn't sure. I had never gone so long, eating so little. It was just enough to stay alive.

I forced my eyes to open. It had now been more than a month. The only way I was able to tell the amount of time was because of the dark moon. I had experienced a dark moon not long after I had arrived in this place.

When I had first got here, I had tried everything to get out. I tried howling as loudly as I could but nobody could hear me. At least not anybody who cared. I thought I was some place underground. The walls were lined with cement but there were cracks above me in the ceiling.

My area was kind of like a containment cell. There were three solid walls and a large thick metal door on one of them. I knew it was thick because even my wolf couldn't make it budge. I knew because my wolf had taken over in her panic when we first found ourselves in the room. The other wall was made up of thick metal bars and showed me into the next containment cell. If I looked past that one, I could see several more cells, all with big metal doors. At this stage none of the other cells had anybody in them.

My only saving grace was the toilet in the corner of the room. I am glad that it was here at least, otherwise my stay would have been so much more uncomfortable after a whole month.

There had been no contact either. The only reason I knew I hadn't been deserted is because somebody pushed one raw steak through a hatch at the bottom of the metal door every day. Just one per day. Just enough food to stay alive.

I could feel how weak my wolf was. I could see the weight I had lost that I didn't need to lose. My wolf didn't fight me, she just sulked like a naughty puppy in the back of my mind. There was no threat that she could fight for us. We couldn't fight gradual starvation.

My stomach ached from the hunger too. Making it hard to focus on anything else. I tried to distract myself by exercising but that would just make me hungrier. Instead, I would sleep to conserve any energy I could. It was the only thing I could do to pass the time.

I picked myself up from the corner my wolf had been sleeping in and leaned against the wall. Those first few days in here had been the worst. I didn't eat the food then. I thought it could have been drugged. But eventually hunger had won especially since all I could smell was the blood of the dried-out beef sitting on the floor near the door.

I soon figured out that it wasn't drugged. At least I

didn't notice any changes to my abilities. I didn't have any blank spots since eating it either. Since then I had been devouring the meat each day within seconds of it being pushed through the hatch.

An unusual *clunk* made me sit up straight and direct my attention to the sound in the cell beside me. The door to the next opened and a figure was thrown into the room I saw a glimpse of a large shadow in the doorframe before the door was once again slammed shut. The figure got up quickly, but not quick enough, the door was closed by the time he reached it.

I heard the growl of frustration as the person rammed himself against the metal door. 'It's n-no use.' My voice cracked as I called out to him, it was the first time I had spoken in weeks. 'Those doors are too strong.' My voice was raspy as I tried to clear my throat to speak better.

He ignored me and kept ramming the door. I didn't blame him; I would have ignored me too. Eventually he retreated to the back wall of the room and sat against the wall, I could have smirked at the significance of the moment, I had done the exact same thing when I got locked in Hall's cell. I saw him run his fingers through his hair as he worked to control himself.

I felt for him. I tried to reach out to him, but I couldn't stretch my mind or senses out. I was too drained. I had no idea what this guy was. 'What's your name?' I asked.

He looked up at me, red eyes gleaming in the darkened room. Vampire. 'Kai.' A glimmer of surprise crossed his face. 'You're that werewolf that everyone is looking for.' It didn't seem like a question.

'I suppose so,' I answered, now more guarded as I spoke to him.

'I'm not going to hurt you, young wolf,' Kai said. 'I don't drink from the vein. Haven't for at least two hundred years.'

That perked my interest. He was an old vampire. Most vampires were under fifty years old. 'Do you know who has us?' I asked.

'You don't know?' He seemed incredibly surprised by this.

I shook my head. 'I was unconscious when they brought me in.'

'It's Michael.'

It felt like my stomach had fallen through the cement floor beneath me. I had an inkling that it was him. If I had been taken by humans, I would have expected them to make contact sooner than this. 'Great.' I said exasperatedly.

We were silent for a little while. Despite the fact he was a vampire, he was the first contact I had had with anybody for weeks. 'So why did you get put in here?' I asked, craving the conversation.

'I finally broke free of his compulsion. So now he has thrown me in here,' Kai explained. 'My guess is he will try and take me under again.'

I grimaced. 'That sucks. Do you know why I'm here?' I asked.

'Probably for the same reason,' he responded. 'You're an alpha. If he controls you, he can control your pack.'

'I just want to know why,' I stated, half to myself,

half to the vampire.

'Can't help you there,' Kai said. 'He never told us why; it was just *do this* and *do that*.'

'Why are you so nice?' I asked. 'You're a vampire.'

He shrugged. 'So?'

'We're enemies.'

He shook his head. 'Nah, we're not. All the vampires that have been attacking you for the last decade have been under Michael's control.'

'But before that?'

'Before that attacks would have been few and far between.' Kai told me. 'We assimilated, just like you wolves. Most of us live peaceful lives, feeding from blood banks or willing humans.'

I shook my head, I found it hard to believe. That would change everything I ever knew about our world, everything we all thought. He was a vampire though. Should I even believe what he was saying right now? No. I shouldn't believe him just because of what he says. Every fibre of my wolf hated him being so close to us, but was that because he was lying or because I was raised hating vampires?

I came out of my thoughts when I heard a *clunk* behind my door. That was another different sound, but the same sound as before. After a moment the door opened. A vampire walked through the door. 'Michael will see you now,' she said.

'I'm not going anywhere,' I said boldly. Even though I was weakened I still had the strength to fight. Not really, but I would anyway.

The vampire seemed to sigh. 'It's best just to come,' she said. 'Saves effort on both our parts.'

I knew she sensed my defiance and I watched her reach out to the wall beside the door outside my cell. It was a gun. I felt my wolf rear in the back of my mind. She hated this situation. The vampire honestly looked like she hated what she was doing. She pointed her gun at me and pulled the trigger. She was ready for my dodge as she shot again. I felt the needle pierce the skin of my bicep.

I felt the drug taking effect almost immediately. I staggered but I didn't hit the ground, instead a hand grabbed me and dragged me out of the cell. I fought to stay conscious but I knew that defeat would be inevitable as I felt my mind slip into a deep slumber.

*****

I lurched my way back into consciousness but I couldn't move. I was stuck. I looked down at my body. My wrists and ankles were bound to the table I was on. I turned my head to look around the room. There was nobody in here with me. Just me, on this table, stuck and alone.

I didn't know what to do. There was nothing I could do. I was staring at the ceiling. I had no way to tell how long I had been there either. All I noticed was that there were several small cracks in the stone, and that my head was beginning to ache.

After what felt like hours the door clicked open. 'Nice of you to show up,' I said flatly as I looked at the door as much as I could when it was behind my head. It was him. To be honest I was too exhausted to get angry. But that didn't stop me from growling. 'Let me go?'

He walked silently to my side. 'I can't.' His voice was low and smooth. 'You're useful to me.'

'Like I said,' I growled, 'I will never help you.'

'You act like you will have a choice,' he said staring at me through his deep red eyes. Wait… red eyes. His eyes were yellow the last time I saw them. He put the palm of his filthy hand on my forehead. 'Now… obey!'

Within seconds daggers were piercing my mind. It hurt so much more than physical wounds. I felt his mind crushing into mine. I worked quickly to throw up my barriers to protect myself. It took time but even in my weakened state I was finally able to block him from my mind.

Then there was physical pain. I had been so focused on the battle of minds that I didn't notice the real dagger that had appeared in his hand, at least not until it was plunged into my stomach. I felt my barrier slipping as he pushed the dagger deeper, causing even more pain.

I refused to give up the power. I reached out to my wolf. If we were to stay alive it would be together. I pulled my wolf into my mind and I felt her envelope my entire being. I felt the strength of her push against the invasion and we successfully pushed him out entirely. He would not be controlling my mind. We refused.

*****

I didn't move from the spot I landed on after he threw me back into my cell. I hurt too much to move. My headache had worsened to the point where the light

44

was hurting me. I was so weak that my wounds hadn't even begun to heal.

It had not been easy to keep him out of my mind. He did everything that he could, stabbing me a several more times and breaking limbs. But my wolf was strong, she barely even budged as she kept us both safe. When he finally realised that he couldn't break through my defences he dragged me back, too injured to fight him, I had no choice but to allow myself to be dragged.

I don't know how long I laid there for. How long I waited for my wounds to heal but they weren't healing. I guess I didn't have the strength to heal at all. I could hear Kai trying to talk to me, He probably felt like I was ignoring him but really, I could only hear mumbling. I was unable to focus on the words that were coming from his mouth, and despite his story, I didn't want anything to do with a vampire right now.

What broke me out of my depressed, pain ridden state was the unmistakeable sound of my daily food. I slowly pushed myself up on wobbly arms, blood dripping to the floor as I half crawled over to grab the meat. Then I crawled to the back corner of my cell, as far away from the vampire as I could get. I ate the bloody meat in under a minute and then rested my head against the wall behind me. I stayed like that for a moment before I curled my knees up to my chest and fell asleep leaning against the wall.

I woke up to the sound of the metal door banging. I sat up quickly, ready for anything, except the pain that raked through my body. I clamped my hand to the wound on my hip, the wounds had clotted but they looked like they would take a long while to heal. There was nobody there. Just another steak sitting near the door.

'Hey sleeping beauty.' I glanced over at Kai. 'Looks like you've been asleep for an entire day.'

I watched him walk over to his door. There was a small, and I mean small, cup of a deep red liquid. He downed it in one, almost like a shot of alcohol, and it was gone. He threw the empty cup in the corner where I could see another one from the day before.

The hunger gnawing at my stomach forced me to get to my feet and grab the steak from the ground and walk back to my corner. 'So what is he?' I asked before taking a bite of the meat.

I heard Kai sigh. 'H e seems to be some kind of mix of werewolf and vampire. He can take on the characteristics of either.'

'So is he a hybrid or just a creature that can take on characteristics of multiple creatures?' I asked.

'Ahhh, kind of like a chimera.' He seemed impressed with my knowledge. 'I don't know really; we don't really get much time to think while under his control.'

'There's still the reason why he wants us dead in the first place,' I stated.

I saw Kai shrug. 'Sorry,' he said. 'I don't know the answer to that one. He could just be killing the werewolves he can't control.'

'Great, fantastic,' I said sarcastically.

He didn't respond but I didn't expect him to so I settled in to rest a while longer, I knew I was going to need it. I was just starting to relax when I heard the now familiar *clunk* of the large metal door being unlocked. It wasn't mine though. I turned my head to watch as the same woman from the day before walked into Kai's cell. But she looked even more unhappy this time.

'Let's go, Kai,' ,he said. 'Please don't fight me.' She knew him personally. *Same coven maybe*, I thought. I was vaguely surprised that Kai did what she asked. He stood up and followed her out of the room.

He didn't come back for hours. During that time I felt some of my strength returning to me, even as my wounds continued to heal, slowly, but healing all the same. When he did come back, he seemed similar to the state I had been in when I had been returned. But Kai wasn't dragged by Michael, he was helped back to his cell by the vampire that had taken him out. This was different for me to see. I had never seen a compassionate side to vampires before. Was this their human side?

After sitting Kai against the wall to rest, the other vampire seemed to walk out Kai's door, lock it then walk over to my door and unlock it. 'Come on,' she said. 'Let's go.'

I don't know why, but I just got to my feet and let her lead me out of my cell. Maybe it was because I knew I would end up back on that table again anyway. It didn't stop me from looking around every corner and tracking my whereabouts as we walked.

'It's an underground maze,' the vampire told me. 'You won't find you way out very easily.'

'Doesn't mean I won't try,' I told her.

'I know,' she said. 'I'm just telling you that you

won't be able to get out alone…' There seemed to be the slightest hint in her voice as she trailed off.

Kai. I didn't say this out loud but I knew this was what she meant. Did I really want to work with a vampire though? Did I really have a choice? *Maybe not.* My wolf whispered in the back of my mind. I suppose we could try to run for it, but I was already confused by these winding hallways and without being at my full strength, I couldn't use my senses to get out.

After walking for a little while we stopped outside a door. She pushed it open. It was the same room I had been in last time. The metal table was in the centre of the room. Nothing else except the straps.

I got myself strapped down. I knew it was inevitable. Might as well get it over with. The vampire left me alone in the room. Within minutes Michael entered the room. Before he could bombard my mind, I spoke. 'Why do you want to control us?' I demanded.

AGUA FRAY

I didn't like leaving the werewolf pack while Rya was missing. It felt wrong. While I knew that Colby and Damien would be able to manage anything that came their way, the pack just felt… wrong without Rya.

Still, there wasn't anything I could do. Both my father and I had tried using a locator spell to find her, but she seemed to be warded against us because the map we were using would just burn away completely instead of leaving her location. It meant that whoever kidnapped her had a witch on their side. And a powerful one too, especially since their spell held up against me and my father combined. I knew that they would call if they needed us and we would be right there if they did. But we had some family bridges to repair.

My mother hadn't spoken to us since she found out she had been lied to since she met my father. It probably made it even worse that I had been lying to her as well. I wonder if she would ever trust me again.

I sighed as I watched the world whizz past my car window.

'Hey.' I turned to look at my dad. 'The pack will

call if they need us.'

I shook my head. 'It's not that,' I said. 'I was thinking about Mum. What if she doesn't come around?'

He smiled a small smile. 'Everyone else did,' he told me. 'She might just need a little extra time.'

'Why didn't you ever tell her?' I asked.

'I don't know,' he said. 'Maybe it was because I didn't want her to know what was out there. She might not have felt safe anymore. Or maybe I just didn't want to risk losing her if she couldn't accept it.'

I understood that. But him keeping this from her for so long could have ruined the relationship entirely. I know I wouldn't be so quick to trust someone that hid a large part of their life for so long.

We sat in silence for pretty much the rest of the drive. My mother had been staying at her sister's house a couple of towns over. Mum didn't work because she thought that Dad earned enough money that she didn't have to. When really my father and I had access to the pack money since we support and defend the pack like everyone else.

Now that Rya was alpha it was his job to train me and assist the pack in any way they needed. Though the majority of his time was spent deciding what to teach me in our sessions together. It meant my dad was semi-retired from the pack but not until I was trained and fully able to support the pack on my own. That was where his teaching's came in.

Right now, we were taking the time to drive out to Linshore, the coastal town my Aunty lived. Now that I was on holidays my dad decided we should go out to see my mother. We needed to talk to her about all of this. So we booked a local motel, packed our bags and got in the car.

We finally arrived in the small town; it was smaller than Wolfridge but not too much smaller. There were no supernatural creatures that lived there, it was just a quaint little town that my mum had grown up in living on a cattle farm a short drive from the town.

We drove through the entrance of the farm and drove towards the house. I stared out the window at the familiar homestead I had visited so often as a child. It had a rustic, red roof, the external walls were cream in colour. The house was single storey with a porch off the front.

In the paddocks you could see a few horses grazing under the afternoon sun. Closer to the house you could see some shrubbery, this was my aunt's vegetable garden. Out behind the house were a few more paddocks, which held a few herds of cattle. Generally broken up by age and sometimes gender.

My dad pulled up into one of the makeshift spaces my family left for visitors. We quite often came out here to celebrate the holidays. The werewolves didn't celebrate them, because all of them were born as werewolves none of them have human family members. Because of my mother, we celebrated Christmas every year.

I took my seatbelt off and pushed open the door, more than ready to stretch my legs after the hour-long drive. I was the one who knocked on the door. A middle-aged balding man came to the door.

'Hey Uncle Pat,' I said cheerfully. The look on his

face was pure surprise. 'Is my mother here?' I asked.

He got over his surprise. 'No,' he said. 'She's gone into town with Sandra and the kids.' I sensed my dad come up behind me. 'Would you two like to come in and wait?' he asked.

'We'd love that.' I said.

He opened the door for us and stood aside while we went past him. I gave him a brief hug before moving to the side. 'Patrick.' My father said holding his hand out to my uncle.

'Jayden,' he responded, returning the handshake.

I looked around as we ventured into the house. The guest room was the first door that we came across. I could see some of my mother's things on the bedside of the dark timber bedroom setting. I felt a lump form in the back of my throat. I really hoped she would be coming home with us.

We continued through the house to the lounge. The house was strewn with evidence that young children lived here. There were toys in corners, children's DVDs sitting on the cabinet and half-finished food on plates at the table. My aunt and uncle had three children, all under ten-years-old.

It was about half an hour before we heard another car pull up in the driveway. A few moments later we heard the running and scuffling of feet just before the door could be heard being wrenched by a strong force. It banged on what I assumed was the brick wall and there were my cousins running down the house towards us.

They stopped when they saw me and my father. I wondered what they had heard about us. Maybe that was why my uncle seemed so awkward in his seat. This made the lump in my throat grow a little bit larger.

From the direction of the door I could hear two people entering at a much slower pace. When mum's smiling face came around the corner, I saw her notice both me and my father. The smile seemed to fade from her face. Words couldn't describe how the lump in my throat now felt. Maybe this wasn't salvageable after all.

'Come on, boys,' Uncle Patrick said. 'Let's leave these guys to talk.'

We waited silently as the three boys were ushered out of the room and deeper into the house. My aunt and uncle didn't return, but I could sense them in the next room, ready to jump in if they needed too.

We all stood in silence staring at each other. I felt like a toddler again, like I had just gotten into trouble. Despite my powers and everything that I had faced in the supernatural world this is what made me feel the most vulnerable.

Slowly I took a step towards my mum, then another, and another. I wrapped my arms around her torso and buried my face into her shoulder. For a moment she stiffened in my embrace, but I didn't pull away. I felt my lump melt away when I felt her arms wrap around me in return. It was going to be okay.

◎◎

COLBY MARTIN

'She might not even be there,' the blonde-haired werewolf on the screen told me.

'But what if she is?' I pointed out. 'We at least need to check it out.'

'I know,' Jeremy Garcia admitted. Damien had introduced me to the alpha cousin in Washington. He was the head of the Wolfen Council. 'But wait for back up, I have sent some wolves your way so you have a stronger defence as well. I don't want him kidnapping or killing anyone else.'

'Okay,' I submitted. 'I will wait. But that won't stop us from planning.'

Jeremy shrugged. 'Go ahead,' he told me. 'Just don't make a move on anything without my say so.' I could hear the hint of an order in his voice. I nodded in submission and the communication cut off.

We were getting closer. There were only so many places that Rya could have been taken. She definitely hadn't been taken into shifter territory; they would know if a werewolf crossed the border, willingly or not and Jeremy told me earlier that he had already asked their chief.

'I still can't believe that Hall is the one that released him from these ruins in the first place,' Damien said from his seat beside me. 'Shouldn't we do something about him?'

I shook my head. 'He didn't know what that place was,' I said. 'Frankly, we don't even know what this place is,' I admitted. 'The coordinates Hall sent me lead us right into the middle of the deep woods.'

'We aren't meant to go in there,' Damien said. 'It's dangerous even for werewolves.'

I met his gaze. 'What if it's not?' I asked. 'Hall was able to walk in and out of the deep woods and the only danger he mentioned was the creature from the ruins.'

'Are you suggesting a cover up?' He looked slightly intrigued.

I shrugged. 'Maybe. Apparently werewolves are good at covering things up.

*****

Jeremy had never said I couldn't research the ruins. I went to the local library and asked for any details about local ruins. I asked Hall to send me the research done on the site, but he didn't have access to it anymore.

It took the two of us a while to track down the people in charge of the dig then I got Toby to hack into the server and steal the files. Not the best way to do it, I know, but at this point I was desperate.

I even asked the entire pack to give me the books they had on our history in the area. Unfortunately for me, we had a lot of history in the area. This meant that I had several large volumes of hand-written history to read through to see if there was anything recorded about these ruins.

I was not cut out for being an alpha. The pack disliked Damien with a passion, even now they had a really had time even thinking of listening to him, and he was only helping me out right now. I needed Rya back, she always seemed to know how to handle a situation. Once we got her back, I would be able to go back to the supporting role of beta. I would be much better at that, I thought. I had only been the beta for a couple of weeks before Rya was kidnapped and now I was acting alpha.

Take a breath Colby. I told myself. I needed to get myself under control. I was really beginning to feel overwhelmed. I needed Rya. She always helped to ground me when I got antsy like this.

Damien was across from me reading another one of the history books. At least Damien was here to help me. As much as the pack hated him, I was grateful for his help right now. I took a long, deep breath and continued pouring over the book I was reading.

◯◯

AGUA FRAY

We talked and my mother listened. We took the keeping her safe route. Which was true. I was just glad that she wasn't mad at me, it was my father she was actually upset with. As I laid in the dingy hotel bed, I thought about the conversation we had with mum.

After we had broken apart, I apologised for lying to her, it just wasn't very safe for her to know since I found out after Erik took control and he was killing the humans that knew about werewolves. Otherwise I felt I would have told her.

We explained what happened after she left us. How Rya defeated Erik and has taken over the pack. But now that she had been kidnapped we had to find her so she coulkd run the pack instead of her brother.

She asked about our powers and we told her the truth. We draw our magic from the earth. Using the energy we have within us but also able to draw it from our environment. We preferred to use our own magic or use combined power together.

Did we know any other witches? No. Well except for my dad's sister. Otherwise we are pretty solitary beings. My grandmother on my father's side was the witch in the previous generation, she passed away naturally only a few years ago. It was soon after that that I began to learn the basics. I was five when my father and grandmother told me about our heritage and I was introduced to the werewolf pack a few days later.

After we said everything we could my dad asked if she could give him a chance to redeem himself. I could see her thinking incredibly hard. I could sense her feelings even as she sorted through them herself. Sad, lonely, angry, relief, and confusion. She ended up asking us to give her some time to think about it.

So that's how we ended up back here, trying to sleep in this uncomfortable bed in the dingy motel room. Unfortunately, there weren't any better options in a small town like this. But to be completely honest, I've slept better on the floor then I did in this bed.

I tossed and turned for the remainder of the night, barely getting more than an hour or two of sleep. When the alarm clock finally went off on the bedside between the two beds I rolled out of bed and went to the bathroom for a shower.

After a quick breakfast of cereal, we got in the car to drive the 20 minutes back to the farmhouse. Hopefully she would tell us she was coming home with us. When we arrived, there wasn't anybody outside but before we even got out of the car we heard the front door open.

My head whizzed around to see my mum hugging

her sister, then the kids and her brother-in-law. Then she unlocked her own car and chucked her bag in the back seat. I got out of dad's car and climbed into mum's. She didn't protest so I took it as an invitation to drive home with her.

Within minutes we were back on the road. I turned on the music with my phone and sensed my mother smile. We did this a lot when I was younger. It would be just me and her driving to and from my aunt and uncle's to Wolfridge.

She did the honours of rolling down the windows and we turned the music up. We spent the entire car ride singing along with the songs and talking like we hadn't just spent several months apart. Life was better already.

ZAC HALL

I felt almost scared as I walked towards Colby's house. I had never thought it would be this hard to ask a question. My friends had been bugging me since the new moon to ask if I could go to New York with them. I had been training really hard and I felt like I would be able to protect myself if needed to. It was just a matter of whether Colby thought I could too.

I knocked on the front door. 'Come in,' I heard Colby's voice call from inside. I opened the door and walked towards where I could sense Colby. I was surprised to find him hidden behind a table full of books. 'What's up Zac?' he asked when I walked around the room so I could see him.

'Ahh...' I hesitated. 'I was wondering if I can go on a road trip with my friends.'

He looked kind of surprised by my request. 'Where to?'

'New York,' I said. 'Sean's family is going to stay at their hotel and they invited me, Dylan and Jace along.'

He seemed to be seriously considering it. 'I'd have to check with Toby if he thinks you can handle yourself,' he said. 'I will also have to make sure the pack over there knows you're coming. That way you don't end up with a territory problem.' He seemed to be mulling it over out loud to himself more than to me. 'Let me get back to you,' he said finally. 'When are they leaving?'

'This weekend for a week,' I answered. 'The full moon is the night after we get back.' I said quickly. I had checked ahead of time.

He nodded. 'I will get back to you by tomorrow on that.'

I thanked him and retraced my steps back through the front door and out onto the street where Dylan and Sean were waiting. 'It wasn't a no,' I said cheerfully.

'Was it a yes then?' Sean asked.

I shook my head. 'He has to check a few things before he can say yes or no. But he said he will get back to me by tomorrow.'

'Cool,' Dylan responded. 'Sounds like he's not against the idea.'

We started walking down the street towards school. We had been using the soccer field to train on. Well, they had been training. I was providing them with a stronger opposing team to work against. I think it was helping them to think and move faster when they were playing. It might just bring up their game a bit more to defend their championship win next season.

Later that evening when I was walking home alone after dinner, I received a text message from Colby. *You can go*, it said. *I cleared it with the alpha. He will let his pack know to leave you alone.*

I almost jumped up and down I was so excited, it felt like something that would be really great to do while we waited for news of Rya. I quickly texted Sean to let him know I was able to come. I went home that night with a smile on my face for the first time in weeks.

*****

The rest of the week felt like it dragged on forever. Toby seemed to be in the mindset that I would not be training for an entire week so he was working me for twice as long to make up for it, but he also seemed to be working me twice as hard. He had me practicing stealth and evasion techniques on the robotic courses in the bunker for several hours before getting me to fight him one on one. By the end of the week I was even able to get the advantage over him a few times. It was Friday morning when Toby finally admitted that I had improved a lot over the past three weeks. The last thing I did before heading home that morning was hunt with Toby. I didn't know if I would be able to get the chance to do so in the city though according to Toby the New York pack could help me out if needed.

When I got home from training, Sean's car was already sitting in the driveway waiting for me. I was so glad that I packed the night before, otherwise I would have been scurrying around getting everything done with them watching over me. The only thing I needed to do was put the stupid contacts in to cover my now golden eyes. Instantly I didn't like them, I had trouble getting them in, they were just plain uncomfortable and they were obstructing my vision. Not a lot but just enough to make it annoying. It was like there was a kind of glaze over my eyes.

'Good to go?' Sean asked when I finally came back out to the car. 'We've been waiting for ages. You didn't answer your phone.'

'I don't take my phone training with me.' I answered as I climbed into the car. I hadn't told them where I was in the mornings. They just knew I was never home in the morning.

'That's what you do?' Jace asked.

I nodded. 'Toby has been teaching me since the holidays started.'

'So you know how to fight and kick butt now?' Dylan asked, getting all excited.

I half laughed at his enthusiasm. 'Kind of,' I answered. 'I still have a lot to learn.'

We spent the car ride talking, singing and playing scenery games like 'I Spy'. It was great fun and I got to relax and enjoy the car ride. None of them commented on my change of eye colour. They probably figured I wanted to fly under the supernatural radar or maybe they just hadn't noticed.

The drive from Wolfridge to New York took about two hours. So there was a lot of time to talk about things that would be happening as we headed into our senior year of high school. The one thing that ended up for discussion was college. The others all hoped to get a scholarship for soccer but they didn't really know what else they wanted to do for their subjects.

Unfortunately, soccer was out for me entirely now. The league would never allow a known werewolf to compete in the competition. I hated it but I knew that it would be unfair for me to play. Not to mention dangerous if something happened to me and I shifted by accident. I hadn't lost control of my wolf yet and I didn't plan to at all if I could help it.

But now I was left with the question. What do I want to do with my life? Eventually I redirected the college discussion and decided to focus more on our senior year of high school. We had the prom and graduation to look forward to. But without Rya here these events for the graduating class wouldn't feel right. We had to find her, I needed her. In the end I took myself out of the conversation, every avenue of that talk made me feel unhappy.

Slowly we sped closer and closer to the city. It wasn't my first time there but we could see the New York skyline from so far out and it always amazed me. We started driving past suburbs until we reached the city. But it all kind of just blurred together.

Before I knew it we were pulling into a parking space next to Sean's parents car. We grabbed our bags out and made our way to the reception where his parents and older sister were waiting for us with our room key. It was nice that we didn't have to share a room with his family. It meant that other than mealtimes it would be just us guys. Although I wasn't looking forward to spending an entire week with Jace. I at least hoped that Sean and Dylan would help buffer him a little bit. As much as he was a friend, we just didn't seem to click well.

To be really honest I was more worried about being noticed, by human or supernatural in this large city.

There are so many things that could go wrong and now that I was out here so far away from the pack, I was starting to feel a little bit anxious.

'You okay Zac?' Dylan asked once we got into the room that the two of us would share, Jace and Sean were in the second room of our apartment.

'I feel like I'm not supposed to be here?' I admitted. 'Like something is going to go wrong.'

He didn't laugh at me or brush my concern aside like Jace would. 'You said that there's another pack here right?' I nodded. 'Aren't werewolves territorial. Like you've entered another pack's territory. Maybe that's why you feel a bit off.'

I shrugged. Maybe that was it. I continued to unpack my things and place them into the drawers by the bed. My toiletries went into the bathroom cupboard for later. When I was done, I laid down on the bed to relax. It was nice to get away from home every once in a while.

We spent what little time we had left of the afternoon relaxing in the hotel room and figuring out where everything was. We had a bit of a lounge area with a tv and a few movies. There was a connector cable for a laptop to plug in and a Chromecast under the television. We had a small kitchenette with pretty much tea and coffee making facilities and that was it.

We didn't have a balcony or anything but the view from our window was okay. We could see a park down the street but mostly all we saw were more buildings. I knew that Sean's family owned a hotel but it wasn't five stars or anything; it was just an ordinary hotel.

When it started to get darker outside, we heard a knock on the door. It was Sean's sister, Casey, letting us know that it was time to head down to the restaurant for dinner. We got changed into some nicer clothes and Sean led us down to the little Italian restaurant on the ground floor of the hotel.

I was still wearing contacts so nobody looked twice at me. In fact I was pretty much ignored but staff the entire night. I enjoyed my meat topped pizza for dinner while everyone else enjoyed their chosen meals for the night.

After dinner I took a shower to help force myself to relax. I was starting to think that Dylan was right. It probably was the fact that I was in a foreign pack's territory. Even thoiugh I was dating the alpha's cousin, I had permission to be here, so my wolf should really just relax.

But he didn't relax. Even as I felt myself drifting towards sleep late that night, I could still feel the prickles on the back of my neck. While my human self slept, my wolf was wide awake and ready to react at a moment's notice.

*****

The breakfast that got sent up to us the next morning was amazing. We had a large selection of eggs, bacon, pancakes and even a few basics like cereal and toast. I helped myself to a decent helping of bacon after everyone else had grabbed some already and scoffed it down with pancakes and maple syrup. It was delicious.

After breakfast we started to head out the door for a day of exploring. 'Aren't you going to put your contacts in?' Dylan asked me.

I froze for a second. 'Shit,' I said. 'I forgot.' I had taken them out before bed the night before. I went back to the bathroom to change my eye colour to green and then re-joined the boys outside. I guess they had noticed in the car.

Sean's parents went to do some stuff for the hotel and his sister had plans to visit different areas of the city on her own. She knew her way around so nobody was worried about her. Us on the other hand ended up going for a wander around the city. Just to look around and get our bearings since the last time we were here.

Every so often I caught the scent of another supernatural, sometimes the scent was old but most times I just walked past them in the street. Occasionally they would look at me, recognise me and then keep going. Each time I would feel myself panic slightly. But none of them ever even made contact with me. I was grateful for that.

We stopped for lunch at a café in central park before going for a walk in the gardens. It was a really nice thing to do after wandering through the packed streets like sardines in a can. The others started to tire by this point which made me glad about my werewolf status, I had no issues walking everywhere anymore. But they were tired enough that they decided to catch a cab back to the hotel.

Once we got there we just relaxed for the rest of the afternoon. After the initial exhaustion wore off, we went upstairs to the rooftop pool for a swim. This is where I encountered my first face to face with a supernatural creature.

When I got into the pool, I didn't sense anything out of the ordinary. I remembered after the fact what Toby had mentioned about using water to hide your scent. It made it harder to follow the scent. But that didn't stop this guy from noticing me in my bright red swim shorts as I cannonballed into the pool. He would have smelt me the moment I entered the room.

I was lounging near the edge of the pool when he came up to me. 'What are you doing around these parts?' he asked in a gruff and guarded voice. 'You aren't a local werewolf.' Before me stood a tall man with what I thought was deep blonde hair, but I couldn't tell exactly because it was wet. His brown eyes stared accusingly at me.

There was no one else in the pool except the two of us and my friends, everyone here knew what I was. 'I'm visiting,' I stated. 'I have permission to be here.'

'You better,.' he said, warningly. 'Otherwise you'll have them wolves on your tail.'

I smiled slightly at the man's obvious concern for my wellbeing. 'I can assure you that I will not have any problems while I'm here.'

'Good.' He started to wade back to where he had been relaxing earlier.

'Excuse me?' I called out to him. 'What are you?' I asked as he turned around to look at me.

'I'm a shapeshifter,.' he said. 'But instead of animals I can turn into other humans.'

'Cool,' Sean said. 'So you can just turn into anybody?' he asked.

The stranger's skin began to ripple, almost as if

there was water bubbling under the surface. A few moments later we had two Sean's sitting in the pool with us. They were identical right down to the last freckle.

'Awesome,' Dylan said. He was completely flabbergasted by the sight in front of us.

I was pretty awed myself, and the shapeshifter seemed to realise this. Then a sense of recognition crossed his face. 'You're Zac Hall, aren't you?' he asked. I hesitated for a moment before nodding. 'What are you doing all the way out here?' he asked as he returned to his original form.

'Taking a holiday,' I said.

He seemed sympathetic now. 'I'm sure you need it at the moment, with your alpha and girlfriend going missing.'

'Yeah,' I said. 'We're hoping to find her soon.'

He moved away after that, not disturbing me now that he knew who I was and that I was allowed to be there. I just kind of relaxed in the pool while the others chatted around me about what they had just seen. After a while I excused myself and returned to the room for a shower and a nap before dinner. It had been a busy day walking around the city and now I was tired.

Dylan shook me awake when it was time for dinner and we went down to the restaurant for another nice dinner. Tonight I had a nice rare steak to enjoy with some chips.

I tossed and turned for a while before deciding to go for a walk. But before I exited the room I sensed someone follow me. I looked over my shoulder. It was Dylan.

'Where are you going?' he asked in a hushed voice.

'Just for a walk,' I replied. 'I can't sleep.'

'Do you want me to come with you?' he asked.

I shrugged. 'If you want.'

I left the room and he followed silently behind me. We didn't speak until we were out of the hotel lobby and onto the street. It wasn't even past midnight yet so a lot of places were still open.

'So what's the matter?' Dylan asked after we walked in silence for a while.

I felt myself sigh. 'I don't know,' I said. 'I miss Rya. I miss just being able to hang out with you guys and not having to worry about whether I would be noticed by supernatural creatures.' I continued to rant. 'I hate that everyone sees me so differently, and that I didn't have a choice about any of this. My entire future is just gone. I just hate everything right now.'

'Fair enough.' I looked at Dylan, he seemed oddly calm about my vent. He shrugged at my look. 'In the past few months your entire life *has* changed,' he said. 'You became a werewolf.'

'Exactly,' I said. 'And not by my choice.'

'Maybe not.' He responded. 'But if down the track Rya asked if you wanted to be turned. What would you have said?' I thought about it for a while. Yes, everything kind of sucked right now, but I loved Rya and I really didn't see myself leaving anytime soon. Even before I was turned I was accepting of her. My silence seemed to confirm Dylan's speculations. 'So yes, it sucks right now, because Rya is gone and you're still learning how to be a werewolf. But this is just for now. Isn't it?'

I shrugged. 'I guess,' I admitted. 'I'm already learning how to control everything.' I told him. 'Toby's been training me and the pack is starting to accept me.'

'There you go,' he said. 'That's a win. The rest of the world will stop treating you differently once they get over the fact that there are werewolves in the first place.'

That was true. The world was still reeling about the supernatural being real. They had no idea where the other werewolf packs were in the country. Not to mention the fact that they were now asking what else went bump in the night. To be honest I kind of wanted to know too. We hadn't gotten to that part of my learning yet. I was still making my way through the book on werewolf history.

'Thank you,' I said to Dylan.

'For what?' he asked. 'Come on, let's head back.'

I nodded and turned us around to lead the way back to the apartment. We didn't make it as far as I thought, just a few blocks away from the hotel. We snuck back through the hallways and up the elevator to our room.

The light was on and both Jace and Sean were awake in the lounge area. 'Where have you two been?' Sean asked anxiously. 'I was about to go get Mum and Dad.'

'We went for a walk,' Dylan replied. 'We couldn't sleep.'

'Sorry,' I added. 'We should have left a note or something.'

Dylan and I sat on one of the lounges. I didn't really

want to go to sleep. While I felt better about everything, I still was tired enough. Instead we put on a movie to watch from a streaming site on Dylan's phone and we settled in to watch.

TOBY DAVIS

When Colby pulled us onto the third floor of the bunker, I knew it was going to be important. I sat around the table with the other werewolves in the fighting faction of our pack. There was six of us: Lexi, Charlie, Charlotte, Keith, Colby and me. Rya would have made seven fighters.

Colby told us about what happened with Hall and the creature that he now thinks took Rya from us. Colby called it a hunch. I could believe that too. There had been supernatural creatures all over the country looking for Rya and nobody could find her. That and we had people in places that would know if she was taken by the human population.

We were waiting for a group of werewolves to arrive from Washington later today to help us scout out these ruins and save Rya if we could. Colby wanted us to be ready for them so we could make a plan and leave before dawn.

I was glad we had something to do. We actually had a lead that might take us to Rya. It would be really nice to have that win right about now. Training the newer werewolves was fun but harder than I thought. It filled up my time when I paired it with my own training. But now, with Zac out of town, I didn't have anything to do in the mornings. I needed to keep myself busy so I didn't think about what Rya could be going through if that thing had her locked up somewhere.

Colby dismissed us with instructions to rest up so that we would be awake and alert when the time came to leave. I went home and went to sleep until I felt the buzzing of my phone ringing. It was Keith. It was time to meet with the other werewolves.

I waved goodbye to my parents as I went through the front door and took off down the street, melting into wolf form as I ran. I ducked and weaved through the trees, the wind rushing through my sandy fur. At full speed I went from bed to bunker in maybe ten minutes. I was even one of the first pack fighters there, aside from Colby and Lexi, who would have come together.

'Thanks for being here so quickly, Toby,' Colby commended.

'Where are the other werewolves?' I asked.

'They're on their way here now,' he replied.

I yawned widely as I stretched out my body and rested as everyone else arrived. The new werewolves were the last to arrive. When they did, I stretched again and stayed back as Colby went to meet them.

Colby spoke to us about the plan. This time it would be purely a recon mission. Were the woods dangerous? Was there anybody at the ruins? We would have to come back another time to do more if there were hostiles there. My job ended up being just follow Keith and do what he says. I'm the newbie in this mission, and that made me the weak link.

Finally we were able to gear up and leave. I went into wolf form since I didn't have much in the way of advanced weapons training like the others. I could fight better like this if I needed to. Keith stayed in human form and armed up with a small gun with the bullets that killed everything. He also slipped a few back up weapons into his clothes… just in case.

We mostly stayed together as a group as we ran towards the deep woods, fanning out a little but not so much that we couldn't see everyone in our party if we looked around. Slowly the trees grew larger and more luscious. They were mostly untouched by humans since it was so far out.

I could feel prickles on the back of neck. But I didn't know if it was because something was out there or because of the stories we had been told as children. Despite my discomfort we didn't come across anything on our path to the ruins. I caught scent of a couple of deer and possibly a mountain lion but that was all. Dangerous my butt.

We reached a bluff that led into a small canyon of sorts. At the bottom I could see the ruins in the light of the waxing moon. The old, torn down buildings shone in the light like a beacon to us on the bluff.

I couldn't see movement at first, but maybe that was because it was dark. Or maybe there just wasn't anybody there, or it was just too far away for even our eyes to see. Unsatisfied with the bird's eye view, Colby directed us down into the canyon in single file, slowly winding our way down the narrow rock path along the wall.

When we reached the trees at the bottom of the canyon I was hit with the scent of vampires. Lots of vampires. Enough to make my wolf want to turn tail and run all the way home. I took a deep breath to control my sudden fear. I couldn't let it affect me. We still had work to do and rash movement could get us killed.

Even more on guard now, we traipsed cautiously through the trees until we came to the opening to the clearing surrounding the ruins. From here we could see the many vampires roaming around inside the buildings. But there was no sign of Rya.

I sensed Colby reach into the area with his mind. A dangerous move considering all the vampires. But I knew we had to be sure she wasn't in there. I watched Colby spread out avoiding touching the minds of the vampires inside as much as we could. But all he could sense was more vampires. The was no sign of Rya.

His search done Colby withdrew his mind from the area and back into himself. *Let's get out of here.* And we started the cautious journey out of the canyon.

I was surprised we managed to get back out without getting caught. There were so many vampires in that canyon. I couldn't imagine how Rya was going to react to a massive vampire nest like that in the middle of our territory. That was if we ever found her.

Not finding Rya there had left us all a bit miserable. We had actually gotten our hopes up that we might have found her at last. Colby went straight back to looking for her. I could see his strain. He was worried and had to keep it together so he could focus enough to keep searching. But where else could they search.

Supernatural creatures and humans alike were all looking for her, surely if someone had her somebody knew about it. They just weren't talking.

After we got back, it had been close to lunch time but I just went home to sleep. I tossed and turned though. I couldn't stop thinking about where Rya might be. Was she dead? No. I had to believe she was still alive. After everything she had been through, she couldn't just die like this.

The Washington werewolves were staying with us. We had started making plans to clear out the vampire nest on the way home but were worried about the sheer number of them in comparison to us. If they wanted to hurt us, they could overwhelm us by number alone. That wasn't a great feeling. Eventually exhaustion overtook my thoughts and I was forced into a restless slumber.

ZAC HALL

Using my contacts each day was the best way to stay under the radar. No one even batted an eye in my direction when I spoke to cashiers or people in the local stadium where we caught a soccer game. I was kind of enjoying the simple life right now.

Each morning we would head out and explore different areas of the city before coming back and eating dinner with Sean's family in the hotel. The only meal I had to pay for each day was lunch and we enjoyed exploring the different areas. One day we went over to Brooklyn and looked in all the art galleries that showed interesting pieces.

One day we went to the uptown and gawked at the large houses and expensive products in the local stores. It was in this area that I came across more werewolves than the rest of the city. I walked past several that day.

That night after dinner we had a knock on our hotel room door. Jace opened it. Outside stood a young werewolf around our age. She sported incredibly long, light blonde hair and green eyes that glittered in the light.

I was the only one that immediately knew what she was.

'Can I help you?' Jace said to the girl.

'We… I was wondering if you would like to join our party,' she said.

'Party?' Dylan said, sitting up.

She seemed to shy away from him a little. 'Not a party that your kind would be used to.' She looked at me. 'It's something we do here a few days before the full moon.'

'Like a hunting party or a party party?' I asked.

'Both… I guess.' She seemed unsure of herself.

'Oooooh.' Dylan said seeming to catch on. 'She's a werewolf.'

'SHHHHH!' Both me and the girl said at the same time.

He shrugged. 'Everyone knows.'

'Yeah, but we still don't want the attention,' the girl said. 'Alpha Rya's pack may be known to the human world but ours is not yet. At this stage only friends of the pack know of our locations.'

'So this party…' Jace started. 'Are we allowed to go?'

The girl nodded. 'It is for pack kids and friends of the pack. We do it every month here.'

Jace seemed kind of excited about this. 'When is it?' he asked eagerly.

'Tonight,' she said, sweeping her hair back over her shoulder.

Sean looked at me. 'Do you want to go?' he asked. 'This was meant to bit of a time away from the whole werewolf thing wasn't it?'

'Not really,' I said. 'It was just an advantage of it.' I looked at the girl. 'I thought you guys were asked to leave me alone.'

She went red. I don't think I'd ever seen a werewolf embarrassed before. 'We thought we would extend an invitation,' she said.

I glanced from Jace's eagerness to Sean's concern, before looking to Dylan, he shrugged. 'Guess it can't hurt to go,' I said. 'We've all got to get used to the whole werewolf side of the world now, I guess.'

'We'd best go then,' the girl said. 'Everyone will be on their way now.'

On her word we all got changed out of our touristy clothes into some fresh comfortable clothes. I opened the drawer next to my bedside and grabbed out my clothes bracelet. I hadn't seen the need to wear it whilst I had been here, but I would need it tonight. As close as I was with these guys, I didn't really want to end up naked in front of them.

When I came out the young werewolf look at my clothes. 'You know you will probably be shifting right?' she questioned.

I nodded and lifted up my wrist where I had placed the clothes bracelet for the outing. 'Courtesy of werewolf technology Wolfridge,' I joked.

She looked at it. 'Is that one of those clothes bracelets Alpha Rya designed?' I nodded. 'I've heard about them but apparently they're still in the testing phase.'

I shrugged. 'We all have them in our pack,' I told her.

'Should we get going?' Jace said eagerly.

The wolf girl looked at him then looked down. 'Yes, yes,' she said. She was a timid wolf for sure. I don't think I had ever seen such a timid werewolf before. Though this was the first werewolf I had met properly from another pack.

We quietly made our way out of the hotel. It was late but not so late that people wouldn't notice us going out. We were just about to leave when we heard a loud voice behind us.

'Hold up.' The unmistakeable sound of Sean's dad's voice sounded through the lobby. 'Where are you four off to?' he questioned.

Sean seemed to stammer for an excuse for going out so late. Instead I spoke. 'We were invited to a party with the local werewolf pack,' I told him honestly.

He cocked an eyebrow at that. 'You expect me to let you go to a party in the city?' he asked.

The girl stepped forward. 'Sorry, Sir,' she said. 'We will be heading out of the city. I can assure you that there will be no illegal human activities and these human boys will be perfectly safe among me and my pack brothers and sisters.'

Mr Green seemed to be shocked to see the young girl talking to him. He hesitated before he spoke. 'I don't know.' He looked from the girl to me, to the other three. 'I guess it will be okay.' He looked at me. 'First sign of trouble…'

I nodded as his voice trailed off. 'We will make our way back. We'll be safe, I promise.'

He seemed to deflate a little bit. 'Okay,' he said. 'Go have some fun.' The other boys all smirked at Sean's father. 'But go before your mother comes out of the restaurant.' I glanced over and could see her standing at the counter chatting casually to the cashier. I smirked and we quickly ducked out the door with the young werewolf leading us.

'So what's your name?' Sean asked catching up to the werewolf as she set a fast pace.

'Tiana,' she replied. 'Or Tia for short.'

'You know…' I looked over my shoulder at Jace. 'Not all of us are werewolves.'

Tia slowed down a bit. 'Sorry,' she said. 'I'm not used to travelling with humans.'

She took us quickly through the city at a fast pace but with my friends coming, it took a lot longer than if it was just werewolves in our group. This was the main thing I loved about being a werewolf. It didn't take me long to get anywhere.

When we reached the edge of the city we headed into the fringe of trees that stood there. I had no idea which forest it was but it was large enough for it to have an abundance of wildlife.

'This is Sundown Wild Forest,' she said, seeming to answer my thoughts. 'It's the biggest natural habitat left in this area. But we do have to be careful of human hunters.'

'I'm surprised we don't have that issue in Wolfridge,' Sean said in a breathless voice as we walked through the trees.

'We don't have enough population to worry about it,' I told him, remembering what Toby told me about it. 'We just avoid the areas they frequent but they know we're there now so as long as they don't shoot us, it isn't an issue.'

'Up until now we were reported as coyotes,' Tia told us. 'But I suppose they probably know better now.'

I shrugged. 'As long as they leave you all alone, you'll be fine.'

I could smell a campfire as we travelled further and further into the forest space. Eventually the trees got so thick that even I had difficulty navigating my way through them. We weaved through the branches and finally broke out of the tangle. What I saw in front of me was a bunch of werewolves lounging around a large fire. Some of them were in wolf form while others had stayed human. I could sense a couple of humans among the group but couldn't discern who the humans were.

Everyone looked up as Jace stumbled over the last branch and fell into the clearing with a *thud*. Tia seemed to prance gracefully through the clearing back to her pack leaving the four of us standing by ourselves.

She sat by another werewolf in wolf form. The colour of his wolf made him unmistakeably a Garcia. His fur was exactly same as Rya and Damien's. He stood and walked over to us. Returning to human form when he was about a metre in front of me, he showed no shyness in the nakedness of his human form.

I didn't meet his eyes. I knew instantly from the way he held himself that he was an alpha to be. He had the same leadership presence that I had noticed in Rya and Colby. I could feel him assessing me, sizing me up. I almost flinched when he reached his hand out to me.

'Mark,' he said.

I looked up to see his smiling face. 'Zac,' I said, briefly meeting his eyes before looking down again almost automatically.

I felt my wolf relax as the rest of the werewolves in the clearing also relaxed. I had been accepted by their future leader. There would be no trouble.

'Come,' Mark said. 'Join us.' He looked over my shoulder at my friends. 'Your friends are welcome too, of course.'

Mark walked up to introduce himself to my human friends. They seemed incredibly awkward at the werewolves fully naked state and found it difficult to look at him at all. I couldn't help but smile. Whilst I was still fairly modest as far as werewolves went, I was getting used to the nakedness around me.

Introductions done, Mark turned back into wolf form and travelled back to where he had been lazing with the other werewolves prior to our arrival. With the alpha's approval I was approached by others introducing themselves and encouraging me to sit with them around the fire. I didn't want my friends to feel left out so we sat near a group of people in human form.

But we had barely started our conversation about the reactions to humans finding out about us before Mark stood on all four legs. The clearing quietened down in an instant, waiting for him to speak.

'Let's welcome our new guests this month. Alpha Rya's mate Zac from Wolfridge.' He looked at me. 'I'm sorry that she is missing right now. My father is doing everything he can to help find her.' I smiled slightly in thanks. 'Now let's hunt,' he exclaimed excitedly.

I huffed slightly with amusement as all the werewolves stood. Many of the ones in human form stayed where they were; maybe they hadn't changed yet. I glanced at my friends. It had been days since I had hunted and I could feel a sense of eagerness from deep within me. 'Do you guys mind?' I asked hesitantly. 'I haven't eaten properly since before we got here.'

'But you eat plenty of… oh,' Jace said.

I shrugged. 'It's part of the deal. I can't live on just human food anymore.'

'Go on,' Dylan said. 'We'll be fine.' He smirked. 'Besides we don't need you wolfing out on us. That would ruin our holiday.'

I laughed. 'This close to a full moon I don't think I can *wolf out.*'

'Go,' Sean laughed. 'We'll be fine here, I'm sure.'

I got up and joined the standing group of werewolves. Slightly self-conscious of my friends watching, I changed into wolf form. I saw my new companions glance at me too but I think theirs was more for recognition purposes.

I felt a pressure on my mind and a shook out my long,

black fur. I recognised the aura of Mark's wolf and allowed him to speak to me. *'Open your mind to us.'*

I hesitated I had been keeping my mind shut as tight as I could since Toby had taught me how. Cautiously I opened my mind and felt the couple of dozen of werewolves join with me. They flinched a little at the new contact but seemed to realise it was me and let me in.

We walked slowly through the tight brambles around the clearing, it was certainly easier to navigate on four legs rather than two. Once we were in less dense areas of the forest, we broke into a run. I could feel the exhilaration of the werewolves running by my side and couldn't help but feel the same. Is this how it felt to truly hunt with the pack?

My wolf rose up out of the depths and seemed to join the ride without trying to take me over. No one spoke as we ran, everything was communicated through feelings. I knew exactly what I needed to do to help gather food for everyone. It was amazing. I felt so connected. I wondered if this is how it used to be before Erik took over the pack back home. Maybe it would become like this again when we finally found Rya and brought her back.

'It will.' I heard Mark's voice across the link. *'The pack has been through hard times. Rya will be a great alpha for the pack to succeed her father.'*

I didn't have time to feel embarrassed over the fact that all of the wolves around me had heard what I was thinking. We had reached a herd of deer and the pack quickly set to work breaking up into smaller groups.

Withing minutes we were dragging the deer

together and digging into the feast before us. I had to admit the raw deer was definitely a delightful animal to eat despite the strangeness of eating meat straight from a carcass in the first place.

I ate my share and helped everyone ferry food back to the clearing for the werewolves and humans we had left behind. When we got there, I noticed that there were now smaller fires surrounding the large one each had a couple of utensils on the ground beside it. I guess the humans would eat the cooked venison like I had the first time I had eaten with Rya and that wolf pack in the mountains.

I brought mine over to the fire where my friends sat along with Tia. One of the human werewolves took it off me and began tear into pieces with his claws. Apparently unturned werewolves still had claws. They held the chunks over the fire to cook before handing them to each person present.

I stretched as I retook human form once again and moved into a relaxed seated position. I used my hand to wipe the blood I knew ringed my mouth but gave up before a bottle of water was thrown my way from somewhere in the clearing, I caught it easily and used the water to clean my face before gulping some of it down. I could see so many water bottles flying around the clearing to people and had to catch several before they hit my friends. When it stopped raining bottles, I handed them out, catching their amused expressions.

With another stretch I spent the rest of the night relaxing with my friends. While the rest of the werewolves would probably stay the night, I was sure my friends wanted to go back to the hotel and sleep, we were heading back to Wolfridge the next day after all.

Tia offered to escort us back but I shook my head, my wolf knew the way. Everyone was quiet on the way back. They were tired. I kept a fastish pace so that we would get home by around sunrise, that would give us the morning to rest up before the drive home.

The sun had just started to rise when we reached the edge of the city suburbs. We walked through Brooklyn and towards the bridge back to our hotel. I felt a prickle on the back of my neck and looked around. I knew that feeling.

'Alone this time, wolfy?' the vampire I sensed said. He slinked out of a side alley.

'Just leave us be,' I stated through gritted teeth as two more vampires appeared from the alley. I felt my friends start to back up before the newcomers circled around to surround us.

One stepped forward to grab Dylan. I didn't give her the chance though. In an instant I transformed and dove at them, pinning them to the ground. The next moment she was a pile of ash beneath my paws.

I didn't have time to celebrate; the other two were already closing in on me. I forced myself to roll out onto the quiet road as they dove at me. I rolled out of the way again and *crash*. The large truck that had turned the corner hit them both, flattening them to the ground. I hadn't gotten out of the way fast enough though. My front paw had gotten caught under one of the wheels. The bones had been crushed to what felt like crumbs as I became human and cradled it against my chest.

The truck screeched to a halt and I heard the

growing groans from underneath its trailer. A few moments later one of the vampires came limply crawling out from under the truck. 'That was incredibly rude,' she stated, the pain evident in her voice.

Ignoring the pain I felt, I dove at her using my once again wolf maw to kill the vampire. The remaining vampire started to flee but I ran after them down the street and leapt at him, pinning him to the ground with a swift leap. Seconds later he was dust.

As they turned to dust, I forced my body back into human form, the adrenaline quickly being replaced with pain, so much pain. I was now grateful for the feed I had and the current timing of the month otherwise there would have been no hope for my control.

'Zac!' Sean and Dylan ran up to me, Jace only seconds behind.

I forced myself to stand, only then noticing that I was standing in the middle of the road. Cars had stopped all around me. I cradled my arm against my chest. It was hurting so much that the entire limb was trembling.

My friends stopped short when they got closer. 'Are you okay?' Dylan was looking at my trembling hand.

I nodded. 'It just hurts,' I said. Then I realised what he really meant. 'I'm fine.' I assured him. 'Full moon is tomorrow.' All three of them seemed to relax at my words. At least they cared about that, I guess. 'Come on,' I said. We started to walk until I noticed the two werewolves getting out of a police car. Instead I walked over to them. 'Hey,' I said when I reached them.

'You small town wolves always bring trouble with you,' one of them said.

I held up my hands defensively then regretted it. 'They attacked us,' I said, the pain thick in my voice.

'Head off before the media gets here,' they said. 'We will hopefully be able to keep you out of the news. People don't need to know you're here.'

I nodded my thanks and rushed my friends away and across the bridge. We practically ran all the way back to the hotel, despite the pain I was in. When we finally got back, Sean went to the first aid kit and retrieved a bandage. 'No,' he said firmly when I started to protest. 'It needs to be bound up.'

I raised an eyebrow at him. He shrugged. 'You might be a werewolf but that will still take a while to heal, I'm sure. After the bandaging was done, we snuck back upstairs to our room and practically fell into our beds. Sleep however seemed to elude me though, whether because of the pain or the thought that I may have just revealed the New York pack's presence to humans.

In the end I barely slept before Sean's dad came around to wake us up to leave. I felt him look at my hand but he didn't question it while I packed, favouring my right hand. Dylan took my bag for me and loaded it into the car.

Sean's dad pulled me aside as the others got into the car. 'I saw what you did,' he said. I looked up at him, surprised. 'One of the traffic cameras caught what happened. You saved them.' He put a hand on my shoulder. 'Thank you.'

I smiled up at him. 'I will never let anything happen to them,' I promised before climbing into the car. Once we were on the road, I rested my head against the glass and closed my eyes, incredibly glad that this holiday was now over.

RYA GARCIA

I honestly didn't know how I was still alive. Every day I would be taken from my cell. Every day I would ask him questions. And every day he bombarded my mind and try to take control of me.

The thing is, it's almost impossible to control a werewolf unless you are more dominant than them. I was an alpha, so the only thing more dominant then me was the alpha of the Wolfen Council. At the moment that was Jeremy and it had been him since Michael killed my father.

I had managed to get some information out of Michael though. He would only answer questions if I kept asking while he tried to break my mind. It seemed to anger him into answering the question.

So far, I knew that he was indeed a werewolf-vampire hybrid. He was born when the two species were still allies. I knew he wanted both species dead because our ancestors locked him away in an old tomb in my territory. Was that where I was now?

I don't know why he got locked away. And I don't know what he was looking for yet. It had been a few days since my last bit of information and I was hoping to get something else out of him soon.

With all the physical and mental exhaustion from our sessions, I was finding it had to think straight much less ask questions at this point. The only thing that was keeping me going was Kai. I hated to admit it but that vampire was growing on me. He hadn't had a session since that first time but even the scant amount of blood they gave him each day was starting to wear him down.

I could hear the difference in the way he spoke. I tried not to get too close to the bars just in case he decided to make a meal out of me. But he also seemed to be staying as far away from the bars between us as possible. Almost like he was afraid of the exact same thing.

I spent most of my time sleeping. The lack of food was making it really hard for my body to heal properly. My body was now riddled with half healed wounds and semi-healed scars. The scars weren't disappearing either. Were they going to stay there forever? Hopefully they would disappear once I actually got a decent meal.

For now all I had to do was stay alive until I could figure out how to get out of here. I was too weak to do more than run. But maybe Kai... *'KAI!'* I shouted internally at him. He seemed to spring alive at the internal intrusion. But he settled when he realised it was me. *'I think we can get out of here.'*

I told him my idea and what we would need to do. He had told me quite a bit about the place we were in but he couldn't tell me where it was exactly because it was in the middle of the forest. In the middle of nowhere.

'To do this I would need to be really strong,' he told me.

'I know,' I replied. *'You will be drinking my blood. It will make you stronger than you have ever been.'*

'Are you okay with that?' he asked.

I shrugged. *'I'm not okay with dying here from starvation and torture.'* That seemed to be enough for him to agree to the plan.

There were no cameras in the room, so we weren't constantly being watched. Our biggest problem would be if Michael saw any new wounds. He grabbed one of the small empty cups and brought it over to the bars. I walked over as he walked away and grabbed the cup.

I got blood from the least noticeable spot, my stomach. I was already riddled with bloody wounds it was a wonder I hadn't bled to death already. Somehow my wolf was still keeping me alive. I summoned a small amount of strength and cut deeply into the skin with the single claw I was able to summon.

When I moved my finger away, I waited for the blood to swell up and leak out of the wound and into the cup. Once full I handed the first cup through the bars to Kai.

◯◯

COLBY MARTIN

The next several days were hard. We knew that there were vampires just sitting out there. They could attack us at any time. Whether they were controlled by that thing that kept attacking werewolves or were just living there? It didn't matterthey had to go.

As soon as we had gotten back from our scouting

mission, I was on the teleconference call to Jeremy. We needed to do something about those vampires. That number of vampires could take out the Wolfridge pack with ease.

It took several days but Jeremy and Harry, the alpha in New York, sent a small army of werewolves our way to help us defeat them. Then came the coordinating and the planning. We wanted the element of surprise but we had to make sure we didn't lose any werewolves in the process, if we could help it anyway. We were stronger than vampires but there had been so many.

The werewolves that came into town came through the forest. I didn't want the humans to know what was happening. I didn't want those vampires to get a heads up if they had contact with the human world. That would cause issues with our element of surprise.

The day before the full moon we started the journey back to the ruins. We left at dawn, while vampires weren't as sensitive to the sun as legends say; they were still sensitive to the light. It gave us a little bit of an advantage over them rather than attacking at night.

We trudged through the forest, some of us in wolf form while others preferred to stay in human form. I was in wolf form. It had been a while since my last fight and with all the stress that has been happening, I was a little antsy. I was going to enjoy this.

When we reached the canyon we very careful, and quietly made our way down in single file. I hoped that none of the vampires looked up and saw us. Without the cover of darkness we were probably easy to see as we made our way into the trees below.

We managed to get down without being attacked and we spread out, starting tosurround the clearing, sneaking through the trees until we made a large circle, ready to close in with less chance of them escaping. We had Toby and the other werewolves in town, just in case any stray vampires made their way there.

I was linked to all the werewolves near me and through them I was able to reach the minds of every werewolf that surrounded the vampire nest. Once we were in position, I gave the order to move in.

RYA GARCIA

It had been a few days now since I had started feeding Kai my blood. He was stronger than ever but he was going to need as much blood as I could give him if he was going to have enough strength to break through that metal door and get us out of here. He drank as much blood as he could from my wrist without stopping me from being able to move the next day.

Thankfully, Michael hadn't paid any attention to Kai over the past few days. Instead his attention was still on me and trying to take control of me. While he hadn't yet succeeded, even my wolf's strength was beginning to fail us. I didn't even have the energy to ask more questions. We had to get out of here soon or he was going to take control of me and we wouldn't be able to stop him.

That next morning when I woke up, I knew it was

time for us to go. It was time to get out of here. My wolf wasn't going to last much longer, especially with the full moon so close, she would be weaker than normal not to mention the constant feeding of the vampire.

Kai knew we had to leave too. He was ready for it. He didn't like it though. Some of the vampires out there were a part of his coven but they were under Michael's control so they were a potential threat.

I held my arm through the bars of the cell offering my wrist to the vampire. There was no need to hide the part of my body where the blood was being drained. We were leaving today, I had to believe that.

Kai walked over to me and grabbed my wrist. I felt my wolf bristle at the vampire's contact then the brush of lips before the sting of fangs. I stopped myself from wincing as I felt the blood being drained.

He drank and drank and drank. As much as he could without causing me to pass out. For a moment I thought he wasn't going to let go, but he did. I pulled my hand away and massaged my wrist as I fought the dizziness that came with sudden blood loss.

'Was it enough?' I asked quietly. I would have only been able to restore a small amount of blood since the night before.

'Let's see.'

He walked over to the metal door and dug his hands into it. The metal crumpled beneath his strong grasp. He pulled the door off its hinges and threw it aggressively towards the wall opposite his door. Then he whizzed out of existence.

For a moment I thought he had left me here, but

then I heard the clunking of the locks on my door. I forced myself to ignore my exhaustion and walked over to the door even as Kai pulled it open. He wrapped an arm around me to support me as we made our way down the hallway.

I could sense my wolf driving me forward. We had to escape. We had to be free. We had to return to our pack. They needed us. I felt a jolt of energy spike through my muscles giving me more energy than before but with the energy I also felt my wolf leave me. I could no longer feel her.

I couldn't think about her right now. I detached myself from Kai and indicated for him to lead the way. We didn't come across any vampires through the series of hallways. Not one. It felt almost strange. I expected to be swarmed the moment Kai broke through that door. He wasn't exactly quiet.

Finally, I felt us start to move upwards. How far down in the earth were we. We took staircase after staircase. Until finally I was hit with a wave of fresh air, forest air. I took a moment to breath it in. It was so nice.

I could hear sounds of fighting as we rushed out of a tall, stone-like structure. I could see fighting but I wasn't focused on who it was, I was only focused on escaping. I was in full flight mode. We couldn't fight, we couldn't defend ourselves, we had no strength left to be spent. Our only saving grace would be getting out of here before Michael caught us, because I knew he would come after me.

I stumbled slightly when I stepped in a small hole in the ground. Kai grabbed me to stop me from falling, urging me to keep going. We were almost there.

Almost free, but then Kai was gone.

I fell to the ground, rolling over, ready for an attack that didn't come. I turned to see Kai laying on his back a blue grey wolf standing over him. The wolf lunged forward. 'Stop!' I yelled as I dove at the wolf. 'Colby, he saved me.'

'He's a vampire,' I heard Colby growl.

'I don't care,' I growled. 'You will not hurt him.' Despite my weakness, the dominance was clear in my voice.

Colby seemed to hesitate before stepping off of Kai. I was surprised Kai hadn't fought back, especially with the werewolf blood in his system, but he just got up carefully, seeming not to want to anger my protective beta wolf.

'Come on,' I said to Kai. 'Let's get somewhere safe.'

We followed the scent of Colby to the canyon wall. There was a thin narrow path, just wide enough for one person to walk along. I followed Kai up the hill, leaving the sounds of fighting werewolves and vampires behind us. Kai was quiet the entire time.

The scent led me to parts of the forest that I recognised and soon I was able to lead the way back to the bunker. I found the camouflaged hatch and jumped down into the tunnel. Kai followed me, though he seemed cautious about it. I indicated for him to follow and led the way through the training cortex and into the lower levels. Finally stopping on the residential floor. I opened the first door for Kai. 'You can rest in here,' I told him.

'Thank you,' he said.

I shook my head. 'It's no problem. You got us both

out of there.'

I closed his door. I heard an obvious clunk of the lock as I walked to the room across the hall. This was my usual room if I slept in the bunker. I had only had to a few times but it still felt like mine.

I laid down on the bed, not caring about the dried and fresh blood that clung to my clothes. I needed sleep. Then I would shower and find food. I closed my eyes. I was home. We had gotten away. Easier than expected, too. Was it luck that Colby and the other werewolves had been there? Or did they figure out where I was being held and more importantly who took me?

I took a deep breath as I began to relax for the first time in weeks. Slowly, and I mean very slowly, I felt myself drift off into a deep, dreamless sleep.

When I opened my eyes, I felt like I was back in the cell again. I was staring at a stone ceiling. I was contained in a stone room with a metal door. I felt myself take several quick breaths. I couldn't be back in there. We had escaped, I was sure of it.

I forced myself to calm down, taking deep long breaths. I was on a bed. There was no bed in that cell. There was no toilet in the corner of this room. *I'm safe*, I told myself. I'm home. But my wolf just continued to react to the enclosed space. She was panicking.

I felt my skin ripple with fur as she pushed out from underneath my skin. I reined her back, pulling with all my strength. I was weak but so was she. I took more deep breaths, forcing the air in and out of my lungs. Slowly she began to calm down. When she sank back into the pits of my mind, she pulled me with her.

The next time I woke up I was a lot calmer. I was able to sit up, difficultly, in bed. Like before there was nobody there. But now the metal door stood open. Someone must have realised what happened and opened it.

I was embarrassed that somebody saw my panic attack but grateful that they opened the door so it wouldn't happen again. I wondered who it was. I slowly got to my feet stretching out my blood-stained torso. I winced slightly as I pulled at the unhealed wounds, reopening them a little and allowing fresh, red blood to seep out of them.

My clothes were in tatters. Cuts and rips all through them from my encounters with Michael. I walked out of my room and down the hallway to the bathroom. I turned on the hot water in the shower. While it warmed up, I grabbed some clean clothes out of the vanity cupboard.

I can't tell you how good that shower felt. Keep in mind I hadn't showered for weeks. The water that ran off my body was easily grey-brown in colour. I flinched when the water touched my wounds, but slowly the water started to run clear again. I then had to start the process of washing my hair and cleaning out the wounds properly. I didn't want them to get infected.

When I finally stepped out of the shower I felt like a new person. I was clean. I didn't feel like I had been nearly starved to death in a dungeon for over a month. I was suddenly so grateful that I had even met Kai. That was something I never thought I would say about a vampire.

I wondered what he was doing. Had he left his room yet. I walked down the hallway to find his room locked tight from the outside. I hadn't noticed this on my way to the bathroom. Without thinking I unlocked it and opened the door.

Kai sat up on his bed as I opened the door. 'How long have you been locked in here?' I asked.

'Since that wolf got here,' Kai said in a disgruntled

tone. I assumed he meant Colby.

I shook my head. 'I will talk to him.'

'Don't bother,' he said. 'I need to leave anyway. I need to tell the grand master what is happening to our covens.'

'Grand master?' I was confused.

'He rules us,' Kai said. 'He and his advisors make decisions regarding the vampire race.'

'Ohh,' I said, understanding immediately. 'Kind of like our Wolfen Council. We have Lupis or Lupa.'

Kai nodded. 'Yes. I believe it is similar.'

'You're leaving then?' I asked.

'Yes,' he said. 'I must find food and then make the journey to the grand coven.' He held out his hand. 'It was nice to meet you, young alpha.'

I shook his hand. 'Thank you. It was nice to meet you as well,' I said. 'If you ever need anything, please let me know.'

'I will.' He said right before he blurred out of existence. But I knew he really just ran really quickly out of the bunker. If somebody was upstairs, they would soon be on their way down.

Sure enough as I was walking up the stairs towards the training area I ran into Colby. He grabbed me almost as soon as he saw me.

'Ouch,' I said, wincing and he pressed on my wounds.

He let me go. 'Sorry,' he said sheepishly. 'It's just so good to see you.'

I hugged him softly. 'It's great to see you guys as well.'

I followed Colby up the stairs. Next thing I knew I

was enveloped by hug after hug. All of the younger werewolves were here. Colby was the last one that hugged me again. I couldn't help but feel a little teary. There were definitely times in that cell that I thought I would never see my pack again.

There was one hug I was missing though. 'Where's Zac?' I asked, looking around for him even though I couldn't sense him anywhere nearby.

'Probably at home sleeping,' Colby said. 'He got home really late last night. Nobody has told him that we found you yet.'

'I'm going to go see him,' I announced.

I didn't hesitate from walking out of the bunker and back into the forest. I walked home. A lot of my strength had returned after my more restful sleep but I was still weak. I needed to eat.

I ignored my stomach. Just a little bit longer, then we can go hunt for food. When I reached the house, I felt my wolf fully relax. We were home after so long. The back door was locked but I forced it open and snuck inside. I found Zac in my old bedroom, fast asleep. I couldn't help but notice the tight bandaging wrapped around his hand. What had he been doing to himself?

I carefully crawled into the bed next to him and snuggled up behind him. I felt him lean into the cuddle then freeze before almost flying out of bed. He was against the wall and staring at me like I was a hallucination.

'Rya,' he said finally.

I smiled and nodded. Then, all of a sudden, I was getting the life squeezed out of me. I closed my arms around him and nuzzled my face into his neck. Once again I felt myself holding back tears. I took a shaky breath to control myself.

Zac pulled away. 'How did you get here?' he asked. Then he pulled me into another bear hug.

'I escaped,' I said. 'I met a vampire in there, and fed him my blood to make him strong enough to break us out.' I could feel the tears running down my cheeks. I buried my face into his neck again, I was so relieved to be home. 'It doesn't matter,' I sobbed. 'I'm just glad to be home.' I was just glad that Colby had been attacking from the outside of those ruins. I'm sure those were the ruins I was told about. Otherwise our escape might have been impossible.

He hugged me until I managed to get my emotions back under control. I leaned back sitting against the headboard and using it to support me. 'Who kidnapped you?' Zac asked.

'Michael,' I said. 'The creature that killed my parents.' We were silent while my words sunk in. 'Are you hungry?' I asked.

He smiled. 'I could eat.'

I got to my feet careful not to jostle my wounds too much. 'Good,' I said. 'Let's go hunt. I haven't eaten properly in weeks.

ZAC HALL

I almost couldn't believe that she was here. Rya was back. She was really skinny now and definitely had been through a lot but she was here. I took her hand as we left the house. I didn't want to let her go.

When we transformed, I was able to see the full scale of her time away. There were deep gashes in her abdomen along with many half-healed scars. She had lost so much weight that I could see the outline of her ribs under her skin. I couldn't believe she was still alive after enduring all that.

I had watched as she transformed, seemingly a little more difficult than I had previously seen her transform. It was probably the wounds. Once she was full wolf though you could barely see her wounds through her thick, white fur.

She looked back at me and I smiled. Caught checking her out. I stopped staring and focused on my own transformation. Within seconds I was in full wolf form standing beside her. I walked up to the white wolf and nuzzled into her neck. I couldn't believe she was here.

Rya didn't break into a run as we started walking towards where the herds liked to graze. Was it because of her wounds? I wasn't sure. But she definitely didn't have the same pep in her step as before. I had no idea what she had been through. I hoped she would be okay.

◎

RYA GARCIA

I kept an easy pace as the vibrations of walking on four legs jostled my wounds. When we finally found a herd of deer I slinked around the clearing. My wolf was salivating at the thought of sinking our teeth into one of those sweet, plump hides.

I knew I would need help so I silently indicated to Zac which one was my target, a young buck that looked like it would have good meat on it. We slinked around waiting for it to separate from the cluster of the herd. When it moved a few steps away to graze a different tuft of grass. Zac leapt at the deer and grabbed its attention while I snuck behind to go for the kill.

When my teeth closed down on the jugular, I felt it as the fresh blood seeped into my mouth and down my throat. I felt my wolf hum with hunger. As the deer collapsed to the ground the rest of its herd scattered and disappeared into the trees leaving only me, Zac and the corpse of the deer still sitting in my mouth.

I dropped the deer to the ground and used my claws to claw open the skin to allow me access to the muscle below. That first bite of fresh meat was one of the best I had ever tasted. Or at least that I had tasted in a long time. It was fresh, tender and delicious on my tongue. I couldn't help but dig into the delicious meat sitting in from of me. Zac was beside me eating but he stopped eating before I did. He would have eaten more recently.

I kept eating and eating. My wolf didn't want to stop. Finally when there were only small amounts of edible meat left on the corpse I stepped away from the deer.

'You were hungry.' I heard Zac comment through our minds.

I huffed slightly. I had eaten the majority of that

deer by myself. I decided not to answer. I didn't want to subject him to the knowledge of my torment these past few weeks. That would be my secret to keep. They didn't need to know how close I came to losing myself.

I walked over to the nearby stream that we had walked past on our way here. I turned back into human form and used the water to wash the blood off my face. It wasn't my cleanest kill that's for sure. But then I was hunting because I was starving, not just hungry.

I sensed Zac walk up behind me in human form. His hand grabbed mind and he spun me around to look at him. His other hand ran up my body from hip to neck until he cupped my cheek in his hand. I leaned into the touch.

I felt Zac pull me closer until I was pressing up against his body. My wolf leaned into the touch, encouraging the caress. I wrapped my arm around Zac's neck and pulled his face to mine. The familiar sensations were welcoming. It had been a while since I had been this close to Zac.

My hands ran over his torso. Noticing the difference since I had last seen him. He was more muscular, more toned. I liked it. Without realising it, I found myself on the ground at the base of the tree. All I could see was Zac's body towering over me. In this moment I felt safer than I had in weeks. I ran my hand down his chest until it rested on the back of his leg. I pulled him closer until there was no space between our bodies.

I arched my neck as Zac kissed from my shoulder

in a trail up my neck until he was nibbling on my ear. I took a deep breath and pulled Zac's lips to mine, kissing him deeply. I stretched my mind to his allowing my being to envelop his. Our minds and wolves connected as they embraced each other, like old lovers that had so spent many years apart.

*****

The afternoon sun filtered through the canopy of leaves above us. Its rays resting upon our naked bodies as we relaxed peacefully in the bed of leaves. I felt so peaceful, resting in Zac's arms.

I felt so safe, so content. The breeze licked my skin as it passed through the trees surrounding us, leaving a trail of leaves through the air as they were swept away. I looked up at Zac his eyes were closed. He looked peaceful, like he was enjoying a nice nap. But I knew he wasn't asleep.

Our wolves were entwined deep within our minds, refusing to let go now that they had been reunited. I sighed deeply, letting myself sink back comfortably into his embrace. I knew we would have to get moving soon, but I wanted to enjoy these last few moments.

Ten minutes later I forced myself to sit up, much to my wolf's displeasure. I looked down at Zac, his yellow eyes were staring back into mine. I still missed his brown eyes. I'm sure he did too. 'We should head back,' I told him.

He sighed as he sat up. 'I know.'

I gave him a quick cuddle before I stood up again. I staggered slightly at the tugging of my forgotten wounds. They were healing now that I had had some decent food. The scars were disappearing, and the wounds were closing over, but they still hurt. I guessed they wouldn't heal completely until the full moon.

'What day is it?' I asked. I knew the full moon was soon but didn't know how soon.

'Saturday,' Zac told me easily. 'Tonight's a full moon.' He seemed delighted by this information.

'Cool,' I said. 'I'll be able to heal tonight then. You too.' I looked at his bandaged hand.

He laughed, nervously and told me what happened while he was in New York. I was interested to find out that he was able to defend himself and his friends with minimal injuries. I was proud of him; despite the fact he was in such danger so soon.

'Let's go,' he finally said. 'I'm sure there are a few people that are dying to spend time with you.'

'Really?' I asked. 'I thought you were just going to keep me all for yourself.'

He smirked. 'Don't tempt me.'

I giggled and forced myself to transform, forcing my bones to crack and move under my skin until I stood as a wolf. Within seconds Zac's pitch black wolf stood beside me. I set a slow run. I wanted to move fast but I didn't want to hurt myself. There had been enough of that the past few weeks.

When we reached the house, it was obvious that someone was inside. More than one person. We shifted back into human form in the back yard, retrieved our clothes and entered through the door I had broken.

I knew who was in there before I reached the front

lounge room. 'Agua,' I said, running up to hug my witch friend. Toby was there too. He must have gone to get her after I left the bunker.

'Where have you been?' she asked me. 'We were about to go looking.'

'We went hunting,' I told her. 'I needed a lot of food.'

I sat down on the couch. It felt strange being back here. It almost felt like a dream or some new torture that Michael had cooked up. Maybe I hadn't escaped at all and Michael was now in control of my mind. *No, I told myself. This had to be real. The alternative would be too sinister. Besides, why would Michael play with my mind like that anyway? Why didn't he just kill me like he did my parents? Or maybe this was what it felt like to be controlled by him.

I sat silently while the others talked around me. I tried to be involved but this all felt so surreal. Where was the rest of my pack? Who were those other werewolves in that clearing? I know that there were more vampires there then we had in our pack. Did I miss something? The answer to that was, probably.

I took a deep breath and forced myself to remain part of the conversation, catching up with what everyone had been doing while I was away. Zac was learning quickly and had just gotten back from his holiday in New York the night before. Toby was the one training him and all the other younger werewolves. He took my job. For a moment I was upset about it, then I realised that I would be spending so much more time focussing on my alpha duties that I probably wouldn't have time anyway.

And Agua. Her mum was back. She hadn't fully forgiven them for lying to her all those years but at least she was working to understand. Agua told me that she and her mother had been doing some bonding over the past week and they were getting closer than ever. They had even showed her mum some of what she can do, introducing her to the world of magic that her husband and daughter lived in.

Before long, the sun started to set, and it was time to head out to the clearing for the full moon gathering. Agua waved to us as we disappeared into the trees at the edge of the back yard with promises to meet us for lunch and to hang out the next day.

The three of us, me and the two boys walked silently through the forest on the familiar track to the pack den clearing. I was barely able to step into the clearing before I was attacked by so many excited, happy werewolves. The next ten minutes was a blur of hugs and excitement as everyone welcomed me back. Nobody asked me where I had been or what happened and for that I was grateful. I didn't really want to talk about it.

I closed my eyes as the moonlight started to stream onto my skin. It had been so long since I felt the moonlight. As my skin began to slide, I lifted my canine head and howled out to the furthest reaches of the forest. So long since I felt the security of my pack around me. I was home.

There was peace among the trees the next morning. Last night had been amazing, being back with my pack again. I couldn't describe the feeling I got when the pack was all together, but it felt right.

The pack had slept really close together last night. I wasn't sure if it was because we were finally back together or because they didn't want me to disappear again. Maybe it was both. All I knew was that I liked it. I didn't want this safe feeling to go away.

But I knew that as soon as the naked werewolves surrounding me woke up from their full moon hangovers, they would all go home and I wouldn't have that feeling anymore. They would be all gone until next full moon.

I sensed as each and every werewolf woke up, but none of them moved. Nobody got up, nobody seemed to want to leave. They seemed to feel as content as I did resting there, with the entire pack surrounding them. Like this, we were safe. Nothing could beat us when we were together.

Slowly the sun continued to rise but we still didn't move. Finally, I decided that we couldn't stay here all day. I sat up. Everyone else seemed to have been waiting for me to move because they started sitting up now too. I realised that they must have stayed for me. I felt so loved.

I didn't stand up but everyone else started moving around. Some transformed and started back in the direction of town, everyone going separate ways. Finally, it was only me, Zac and Colby left.

'Are you okay Rya?' Colby asked from where he sat a few metres away.

I didn't answer at first. I wasn't so sure. 'I'm getting there,' I answered. 'I just don't want to be alone,' I admitted pulling my knees up to my chest. Vulnerable.

His face softened. 'You're not alone. We're all here for you,' he said. 'I'm here for you.' I looked up at him, he had moved closer while he spoke. I saw Zac stand up. He put his hand briefly on Colby's shoulder and then left the clearing in the direction of Wolfridge.

Colby sat down beside me and wrapped an arm around my shoulders, pulling me closer to him until I was wrapped into his arms. 'Tell me what happened.' Colby's voice was soft.

I told him. I told him everything. I told him about how I was alone with no contact with anyone for the majority of the time I was gone. I told him about being alone with only myself and my wolf, nearly starving to death in the meantime. I told him about Michael, about what he's told me about him, about what he was doing to me and what he was trying to do. By the end of retelling the events of the last few weeks the tears were flowing freely down my cheeks, I couldn't hold them back.

Colby just listened. He didn't ask questions; he just

slowly took in all the information I had given him. But he held me, comforting me in a way that no one else could. Nobody knew me better than Colby did.

When I finished talking, I took a deep breath trying to control myself. I hated being emotional, I was the alpha, I was supposed to be strong. 'I... I just don't want to be alone,' I told him. 'I can't be right now.'

'What do you want to do?' Colby asked me. 'We can't exactly live together, there's too many of us.'

'Harry does it,' I said. 'Jeremy does it. It works for them and they're safe under the same roof.'

'What, you want to build a big house or something?' He seemed confused.

I nodded. 'I think so.' I didn't want to be separated from my family ever again.

*****

I didn't really leave the house those first several days. I mostly stayed home or went to the bunker. I wasn't ready to see humans yet. I didn't want to be bombarded with questions. To be honest I didn't even know if the humans knew I was home yet.

I had a revolving door of Zac, Agua, Toby and Colby. One of them was always with me. Colby had started the process of finding land for a pack house. The idea was put out to the rest of the pack and we got a fairly positive response about making one. I didn't know if that was because they thought it was a good idea or if it was because they were aware how unstable I was feeling right now.

When it started nearing a week since my escape, Colby and Zac started nudging me in the direction of getting back into things, but I disagreed. I had spoken to Jeremy over our teleconference about where I had been and the things I had learned about Michael. He was very intrigued to find out that there were tunnels under the ruins. I knew that soon I would once again be summoned to the Wolfen Council. I knew that it was only a matter of time before the messenger wolf knocked on my door.

My first contact with the human world was through Zac. His friends had been playing soccer for the duration of the school holidays every afternoon. Except when they had been in New York. I couldn't believe Colby let Zac go to be honest. I probably wouldn't have, or I would have sent someone with him.

I sat on the side lines and watched them play their game of soccer. I had no desire to participate and they never asked. Zac must have told them not to question me because not even Jace asked me questions in his usual scathing tones. I really hated Jace sometimes and I really didn't want to deal with him right now.

My relationship with my wolf was different these days too. After our ordeal over the past several weeks we seemed to have come to an understanding. She was me now, I was her. I felt less human than ever before. I didn't feel like I fit in the human world anymore, but that's why I needed to get back into the human world. I couldn't spend my life sitting on the sidelines. I didn't want to become Erik.

The first few days I sat quietly and then we went home after the game. I didn't talk to them much. I guess I really didn't talk to anyone much these days. I was used to being on my own with nobody to talk to.

A few days later I would stay with them for food at Kraze. I didn't order food. I would sit silently and sip on my Coke. I was a bit more talkative with the werewolves. When we spent time with them, I would talk but not as much as I used to. It was hard. I wanted to join in, but it's like I couldn't remember how to talk to people.

Within a week Colby was able to find a large piece of land on the outside of town. It was covered in trees. We bought it. A few days later a road to it was made. A few days after that we cleared away a large clearing worth of trees. That was when Colby and I started planning the house.

We were just about to sign off on the plans that came back to us from Keith, he was an architect for his day job, when my long-awaited message arrived. The messenger wolf arrived at my house. They handed me the letter and then continued on their way. It told me to be ready to get picked up by the end of today, plan to stay for a few days.

I didn't want to go alone. But I needed Colby here to keep working on the house plans and to manage the pack while I was gone. I didn't want to leave Zac behind, and it was obvious that he wanted to come with me. So, I decided to take Zac with me to Washington. At least I figured that was where I was going.

We packed a bag each to make sure we had what we needed to stay away for a few days. A few sets of clothes and any personal items was really all we needed. After that we played the waiting game. I didn't know how they were arriving, but the letter said to wait at the house.

But in the end, it was a light knock on the door. I answered it to find a lady on my doorstep. She had brown, bushy hair, green eyes and a nose that very slightly pointed upwards. She looked to be in her forties. 'Alpha Rya,' she said, her voice formal. 'I'm here to escort you to the Wolfen Council.'

'How will we be travelling?' I asked.

She smirked at me. 'By magic of course.'

I grabbed my bag and Zac came forward with his over his shoulder. She took us both by the wrist and told us to close our eyes. Silence. Then the familiar feeling of being dragged into a black hole. We teleported, just like Agua had teleported us out of Hall's laboratory so many months ago.

When I opened my eyes, we were standing in a foyer. A large doorway stood behind us and another smaller doorway stood to our right. In front of us was a large staircase leading to upper floors.

It was a door hidden behind the staircase that Jeremy came out of. 'Rya,' he said, his voice warm and friendly. 'It's nice to talk to you in person rather than through a screen.' He hugged me closely.

'It's nice to see you too, Jerry,' I smirked using the nickname he had gained from the pack children a long time ago.

'Come,' Jeremy ordered, ignoring me. 'Gelda will take your bags upstairs to your room. The others have already arrived.'

He led us around the staircase and into the room he had come out of. In the boardroom-like space there were twenty-one werewolves seated at a long table.

There were three empty seats remaining. One at the head of the table that I knew was for Jeremy. He was the head of council. That seat belonged to him. Zac and I sat in the two remaining seats.

I looked around the table at the other alpha's; most of them were Jeremy's age. My father's generation. It was only Reina and her mate, Adam, that was from the new generation. My generation.

'It's nice to have a full table once again,' Jeremy said. 'It has been a long time since the Wolfridge alpha seats were sat in.' I hesitated slightly when he said my pack's town. 'We welcome Alpha Rya and her mate Zac.

'I want to thank you guys for coming on such short notice,' he continued. 'I sent my witch to get you all because we needed to speak urgently.' Jeremy paused looking around at us all. 'The creature that has been stalking our family now has a name. Michael. Zac.' I felt Zac flinch. 'Please tell everyone what your father told you about the ruins in the New Jersey pack territory.' What did Zac know?

He hesitated, stammering slightly at the sudden spotlight on him. He took a deep breath then told the story of his mother and father researching the old ruins and how they had accidently set Michael free. Michael had killed Zac's mother too. That was something we had in common.

'Thank you, Zac,' Jeremy said. 'This tells us roughly when Michael escaped from the ruins. It doesn't tell us what he was doing there in the first place.' I knew what was coming. 'Rya, tell us what you were able to get from Michael.'

I was a bit more used to this then Zac was, but it

was still difficult to speak to these werewolves who had been full werewolves since long before I was even a thought. 'Michael is a hybrid,' I said. 'He is half vampire and half werewolf. From what I've seen he can't take both characteristics at once; he can be a werewolf or a vampire, switching between the two at will. He was locked in the ruins by our ancestors, but I was never able to find out why,' I concluded.

All eyes turned automatically back to Jeremy when he started speaking. 'Nearly two months ago Rya here was kidnapped,' he stated. 'We now know that it was Michael that took her. He seemed to be trying to break into her mind and take control of her.' He looked at me. 'Apparently he has succeeded in this with vampire subjects.' I nodded once. Jeremy continued talking about things I had told him, relaying it to the rest of the council so that they were up to speed on the situation.

'Now that everyone is aware of the situation...' Jeremy started. 'What do we know about hybrids?' No one said a word. 'Nothing,' Jeremy said. 'What about these ruins?' Again there was silence. 'This is where we need to start.'

We spent the rest of the day reading through Jeremy's large library on the topic. We each grabbed a book off the shelf under supernatural creatures and started reading. We knew it wouldn't be anything recent, since Michael was locked away in the ruins a long time ago, judging by the age of the building anyway. We also hadn't been allies with the vampires in several hundred years.

I read through a book on Supernaturals with Greek

origins. Thinking I might be able to find something there. I learned a lot about vampire origins that I didn't know before. Like how it was the same witch that allowed us to shift at will that allowed the vampires to walk in the daylight. I also learned about how the original vampire angered the sun god, Apollo, and was turned into a vampire by him, but it wasn't the information we were looking for. I would revisit that later. I grabbed another book about when werewolves travelled to America. We met the vampires on the ship here so maybe there was something in there. None of the other alpha's questioned my change of section in the library. They probably figured that I was trying another angle, which I was.

Zac was pouring over the book that he was reading, *The Encyclopedia of American Supernaturals*. He was learning about all the different kinds of creatures that lived in America, including werewolves, vampires and Native American shapeshifters. These were the creatures with the largest populations here.

I was only just reaching the story of how we became werewolves in the first place. The story went like this…

'In the heart of Peloponnese lay a land named Arcadia. The one who ruled these lands was King Lycaon, his forty-nine sons and his single daughter. The Gods would often come down from Olympus to indulge in human delights that existed under Lycaon's reign.

Under Lycaon's ruling hand temples were built and he ordered his people to worship Zeus as the most supreme deity. After some time, however, Lycaon and his sons became lax in their offerings to Zeus.

Zeus learned of their negligence immediately and decided to test Lycaon and his faith. He came down from Olympus and, dressed as a countryman, knocked on the door of the Greek King, asking for the King's hospitality.

The intelligent and perceptive Lycaon saw through the God's disguise and welcomed him generously and accommodated him as well as he could. As an offering to the Great God, Lycaon served Zeus the roasted flesh of his youngest son, Nyctimus, attempting to show the God a testament of his faith through this horrible sacrifice.

Zeus, however, was not pleased by this offer of faith. He raged against his host, filled with the wrath of the Gods themselves. Zeus turned Lycaon and all of his children into wolves, condemned to hunger for human flesh.

The youngest son, Nyctimus, was restored to life by the wrathful God and was given the throne of Arcadia. The throne however was not enough for the youngest son. While he continued to worship Zeus, Nyctimus intended to exact revenge upon his cursed family.

Lycaon and his children were desperate to once again rule the lands of Arcadia and fought against Nyctimus' people. The God Zeus assisted the young king in his endeavour, giving him the aid of the God's own children, the demigods.

With the aid of these demigods, the young king's hunger for vengeance was possible, using the magic wielded by the children of the gods. Many were killed in this war for vengeance and power.

With his children dying before him in the battle for

power, Lycaon retreated.

He didn't want to lose any more of his children to the wrath of the gods' own children. As a pack the remaining wolves left Greece, seeking a safe refuge.

In the lands beyond Greece they found more cities and towns. There they came across a young witch practicing his magic. He was able to communicate with the wolves. After hearing what they had to say, he wished to help them.

The young witch enlisted the help of his family and together they attempted to lift the curse laid upon them by Zeus. Together they were able to turn Lycaon and his remaining children back into human form, but they were unable to lift the curse entirely. It was difficult to remove the magic of the gods.

Zeus was immediately aware of the effect on his magic. He quickly sought out and appeared to the former king of Arcadia. Instead of returning Lycaon to wolf form he allowed them to remain human, the condition being that they would twice a month return to wolf form. They would also become blood thirsty, killing anything that happens to stand in their path.

Glad to be human again, the human-wolves lived out their lives, hiding the curse that was laid upon them by Zeus. For several generations they lived in secret, living amongst the humans. Finally, one of their kind was caught, labelled a witch and was burned at the stake. Fortunately, a new land had been discovered and Lycaon's descendants put their names down to help build a new land. So they climbed about one of the first ships and sailed away, taking the secret with them.

It took several weeks at sea to reach the new land. They weren't the first settlers, but they were close. On the ship they could smell something onboard with them, but the ship was so large and crowded that it was impossible to find the source of the scent.

They were lucky that the ship left just after a new moon, otherwise the ship may not have made it all the way to America. They spent the full moon in the lower decks, hiding themselves from the humans. By then the pack had grown to about forty wolves. It was crowded and, of course, they were found.

The source of the scent had come from a Greek family. Their eyes were red when they looked upon the startled werewolves. They had thought nobody would come down this far. For a long while the two species stared at one another.

They did not know how to talk to the strange humans standing before them, but they tried anyway. The alpha, Graham Garcia, stepped forward and spoke, reaching out with his minds to the intruders of their temporary den. 'We mean you no harm,' the alpha had stated.

The Greek family seemed to be shocked. 'You are not wolves,' the eldest man of the family had said.

Graham shook his head. 'We are no more wolves, then you are human,' he replied.

'My family and I are looking for a fresh start,' the man stated. 'We were cursed by the great gods and were forced to flee.'

So over the weeks of the voyage towards the new land, the two creatures got to know each other, learning about each other. None spoke of the reasons for their curses and when the ship was delayed and they had to stay aboard over the new moon, the Richmond family made sure that they didn't break out and hurt the humans, and in return the werewolves allowed the family to drink small amounts of their blood, helping to stop the strange, blood drinkers from harming the humans on board, keeping suspicions away.

The two families were excited to have met other strange creatures. They may be differing from each other, but they weren't the only thing hiding from the humans anymore. Once they docked at the new land, they were quick to disembark – like all aboard they were keen to explore.

They used their superhuman abilities to help the humans build their new towns, in moderation of course, and the families continued to help each other. As they had no cages, they could only find secluded land, far from the settlers, to transform on the new moon nights. The Richmond family kept them from making their way back to civilisation.

For many years this was how it worked, that was until sickness came through the humans. None of the werewolves or the Richmond family got sick, and they did everything they could to try to save the humans. As a last resort the eldest man in the Richmond family fed a dying woman his blood. She still didn't survive. But before they could burn her with the other dying humans she rose, living again, and like the original family she featured blood red eyes and cold skin.

By this time the humans had built many towns, a few of them turning into cities as their population grew. The woman was still burned. Superstition caused the humans to kill her, and as she died in the flames, her body turned to ash.

The werewolves had worked out that they could turn people many years before, and occasionally they did so, but when this family of vampires found out that they could create more people like them, they began turning humans. Only a few at first, then as more were turned, the vampires were discovered.

The humans began to hunt the vampires and while trying to help their friends the werewolves were discovered too. But the vampires were too out of control, their hunger for blood too strong for the new ones to control.

The werewolves didn't turn against the vampires until a baby vampire drained the blood of the alpha and his mate, Sampson and Gertrude Garcia. The pack was angered by the death of their alphas and turned against the vampires, taking the life of the vampire who caused the deaths before starting to help control the droves of blood sucking monsters.

Many vampires and werewolves were captured by hunters and burned at the stake, causing them to sink into the shadows, leaving society, heading to the safety of the forests. The vampires were never forgiven for taking the lives of the pack alphas. With only one child to take their place the young werewolf suggested that the large pack separate, for the safety of the family.

There were five members in the original vampire family, two parents, Selene and Ambrogio, and their teenaged children, Johnathan, Esmond and Natasha. Over the years that followed the war continued to ensue between the two species, neither side would admit defeat.

Finally, when the young werewolf, Ryan, had grown, he hunted down vampires, his pack came face to face with the family. A battle ensued between pack and family, the werewolves defeated them and it was believed the family to be wiped out of existence.

Years later vampires and werewolves made their way back into society. Neither side could be near the other without wanting them dead, so they stayed away from each other. They had much to learn about the evolving society of humans, especially if they wanted to become a part of it once more.'

*****

Upon reading the end of the story. Knowing what I knew now about Michael and what he was, the story felt incomplete. But really it did just skim over the history of werewolves being created and the how they came to be in America instead of Greece. I kept reading the book as it started to go into different parts of history in much more detail.

Vampires and werewolves often grew close during the years they were allies, I read. I could only guess that it meant sexually close, but the book said nothing about a child.

As the afternoon progressed, I could feel my mind becoming more and more exhausted. Having read close to two large volumes in the time we had been sitting there, I was understandably tired.

I was almost falling asleep in my chair when I heard a ringing throughout the house. 'Dinner time,' Jeremy announced, slamming his book shut before the ringing sound had faded. 'Did anybody find anything?'

'Not much,' I commented. 'Just the history we all read as kids. But it feels like there are holes in it now.' Nobody else had found much either. A few mentions but nothing detailing anything about hybrids. It was starting to look like our ancestors didn't want us to know about Michael. Why?

Finally, after talking about what everyone had read, we followed Jeremy out of the library and back into the main hall. The library was connected to the conference room we had started in but there was also another door that took us straight back out to the foyer.

From the foyer, Zac and I followed the rest of the alphas through the doors on the side of the hall. The doors opened up to what looked like are large eating area. There were dozens of tables positioned around the room. It seemed almost like the school cafeteria back home. Except instead of the bain maries with food in them, there was a head table. These tables were covered in plates, cutlery and jugs of water.

It looked like some of the tables had been moved to make a second long table in front of the other. Both long tables had no werewolves seated at them. I followed the alphas as they filed towards these two tables. Jeremy and his mate, Sandra, sat at the shorter back table.

There were four other werewolves sitting there. Two of them I recognised as Jeremy's children. The oldest was Edward. He was four years older than his younger sister, Tia. At the other end of the table sat two adult werewolves. I assumed they were the pack beta and their mate. I wasn't even sure which one was the beta to be completely honest. Jeremy and Sandra sat in the two remaining seats at that table between the occupied seats.

The rest of the alpha werewolves shuffled down the front long table and situated themselves to sit next to their own mates. Being the last ones in the room.

Zac and I were seated at the very end of the table.

The rest of the room was filled with werewolves from Jeremy's pack. Wolves still trickled in as we sat and waited. I was honestly too tired to talk much. Zac sat in between me and Adam, Reina's mate. They were talking about their experiences with becoming werewolves.

I sat there silently watching the rest of the room. The younger werewolves all sat together at two tables pushed together. The adults were spread out across the rest of the room. Everyone was chatting peacefully. Everybody felt safe under the same roof because who in their right mind would attack a house full of at least one hundred werewolves.

Maybe ten minutes after sitting down about a dozen people came out of a door baring trays and trays of food. The trays got put down the centre of the tables with people on both sides. The alpha tables had the food placed across from them but not so far that we couldn't reach properly.

I started loading up my plate with meat from the platter in front of me. I avoided the vegetables. I might have lived with Agua's family for a long while but that didn't mean I liked my vegetables. I had really only tolerated them whilst living with my mostly human friend.

Next to me, Zac was grabbing both meat and vegetables. Exactly like Adam next to him. They seemed to be the main two that grabbed the vegetables. I wasn't sure if there were any other bitten wolves on the council. It was possible, but I only saw a few werewolves with vegetables on their plates at all.

Once dinner was cleared away and everyone had finished eating. The younger werewolves all stood up and started gathering the dishes each taking a handful into the room the food had come from which I assumed was a kitchen.

Behind us I sensed it as Jeremy stood up, gaining the attention of every werewolf in the room. 'I hope you all had a great day today,' he started. 'Today you have probably noticed that we are housing the entire Wolfen Council for the first time since the alphas of the Wolfridge pack were taken from us.' He looked at me. 'Today we have welcomed Rya and her mate Zac into our ranks as alphas of the Wolfridge pack. Please show them the same respect you would show any members of the council. As it is their first time under our roof, they may not be used to the way we do things here in the city. They may need a guiding hand at some point during their stay.' I could see the affirmation from the werewolves in front of me. I knew that any one of them would be able to help us if we needed assistance.

This was what I wanted for my pack. Living under one roof as a pack. Protecting and supporting each other in everything we do. It was how we should be. Not spread out all over town. I knew that it was important for us to do so before the human population was aware of us because it would almost be strange for us all to live together without drawing attention to ourselves. But now that we were out in the open, it wasn't necessary anymore. I wanted my pack to be around me whenever we were home together, whether it be eating, sleeping, working or studying.

After dinner, Zac and I were shown to our rooms where we could relax on our own. I was glad to finally be alone. The social strain had begun to wear on me. I still wasn't back to my usual self around large crowds, but I was beginning to be more comfortable around small groups of people. I hated that my isolating experience had affected me so much. To be honest I hadn't realised just how much until I returned home. It was causing so much anxiety.

That night I slept comfortably in my borrowed bed with Zac, it felt almost weird being away from my pack again so soon after getting back to them. I hoped that we weren't staying long because I definitely wanted to get started on building our very own pack house.

We ended up staying in Washington for two nights. We didn't get to do any sight-seeing. But we did a lot of reading. It took that for the twenty-four of us to get through most of the books that *might* have had something about Michael in there. But we found nothing. There was nothing about the merging of two dominant species to make a hybrid creature. Whenever it did happen, they wanted to make sure nobody knew about it that's for sure.

We ended up heading home with instructions to go through our own pack libraries to make sure there wasn't anything different in there. Since I would have to go through my father's office anyway when I moved it all to the new house. I didn't see an issue in going through it a bit early.

Greta the witch took us back home to Wolfridge, leaving us in the loungeroom of our house. It was exactly like we'd left it. Nothing was out of place from two days prior. I decided to make a start on the office now while I was still thinking about it.

It had been a long time since I had entered this room at the back of the house. It had been left untouched since the night my father was murdered by

Michael. I took a deep breath. It was hard seeing all my father's things again.

The first thing I did was go through his desk. I went through all the papers on top and in the drawer. I put the useless items in a pile and I left the things that could be used in or on the desk where I had found them.

They day wore on slowly as I moved about the room going through various things and adding them to the pile for trash. Zac helped me by bagging up the rubbish and taking it out to the bin, otherwise he pretty much left me alone to go through my father's things.

I found a bunch of city council documents in his filing cabinet. He was Mayor of the town for a couple of years before his death, so it was not surprising that he had these. I placed them in a new pile to take to our current mayor, Richard Fall. He would know what they were and where they needed to be stored.

When night started to fall, I was almost finished with the room, except for the books that covered and entire wall of the room. That would be a task for another day. When I closed the door at the end of my search, it was only to take a deep breath that the job was almost done.

The next few days continued uneventfully. We broke ground on our development site and the ten werewolves we had working on the build were making short work of all the tasks they had before them.

Once the ground was levelled, they put the cement layer for the base to keep the house stable. In the middle though was a small square large enough to stand in. this was going to be passageway between the new house and the bunker. That way we didn't have to trek through the forest to get there when we needed to. We weren't going to start that until the actual building had begun. For one we needed to wait several days for the cement layer to dry properly to work with.

When I wasn't overseeing the plans for the house or making decisions about furniture and the décor, I was pouring over my father's books, one at a time. Quite a few of them had been in Jeremy's library; standard books that everybody had usually. But there were some books that I had never seen before.

These I poured over more intently than the ones I had already read. Some of them were about leadership and how to lead a team. I slowly made my way through book after book after book.

On the third day back from Washington I came across a book with no title on the binder or the cover. Thinking I may have found something important opened it. It took a moment to register what I was seeing before I laughed outright.

Inside the book wasn't pages. It was hollow with solid edgings that made it look like a book. Inside the small wood box was a few envelopes with the name *Ivy* scrawled onto it. Ivy wasn't the name of a person. That much I knew. It meant ivy as in poison ivy. To humans it commonly caused a kind of allergic reaction, but for werewolves… Just the thought made me laugh.

I walked out of the office and went to find Zac in the

lounge room. He was playing some shooter game on the Playstation he had moved here while I was gone.

'Come on,' I said to him. 'Let's get Toby and the others together.'

A quick text message was all it took to bring the seven other werewolves to my backyard. 'What's up Rya?' Toby asked once everyone was there.

I didn't answer him, I just showed them all what was inside the book box I was holding. Instantly everyone laughed, except Zac and Maya. They didn't know what it was since they were both still relatively new to the pack. Everyone else though, they had grown up hearing about it. Every few years, when the wild pack would visit us, they would bring a stock of ivy with them.

To werewolves, ivy caused a euphoric effect almost how weed affected humans. Ivy was one of the only things that would be guaranteed to make a werewolf drunk. Unless they wanted to drink several litres of alcohol. I explained all of this this Maya and Zac.

'Is it dangerous?' Maya asked.

I shook my head. 'Not at all. Because of our metabolism the effects wear of within a couple of hours. We just usually use it away from humans a little bit because it can cause your eyes to start glowing.' But since humans know now it wasn't the worst thing in the world for us to be in my backyard right now.

'I can't believe our alpha is giving us drugs,' Toby muttered as I held one of the envelopes out towards my friends.

I shrugged. 'You don't have to have any,' I said,

holding the dried green leaves out to him.

He quickly snatched one out of the envelope before I could take them away. I huffed with supressed laughter and turned to Zac and Maya. They hesitated but ended up grabbing one of the leaves holding it cautiously in their hands. I grabbed one out for myself and tucked the envelope back in the book box.

Once the box was safely stashed back in the office I returned to the werewolves in my backyard. 'Let's have some fun,' I said right before I put the leaf in my mouth.

It was going to take a several minutes for it to take effect, so we started running out into the forest. Even though we didn't have to hide from the humans it would probably be more responsible for us to head into the trees. Plus, we were likely to be able to have free rein of our abilities to have a fun evening.

We were quiet as we waited for it to take effect. When it did it was kind of like getting hit in the head with a baseball bat. For a moment we staggered, but then we were hit with the adrenaline, the good thing about it is that it wouldn't affect the wolf. It brings it to the surface, yes, but it's just as calm as us.

I smirked at my friends, pulling my shirt over my head as I started my transformation. Everyone copied me. The sun was just beginning to dip over the tree line as we bolted towards the deeper part of the forest. We stopped when we caught the scent of a strong animal. I saw Toby's wolf smirk in the growing darkness.

We tracked the scent, following it to a clearing. The wolves spread out around it, Max and Liam staying back. I snapped a branch. The large, brown grizzly looked up, but I was already gone. I heard the snap of another branch across the clearing. The bear looked that way, the anxiety seeping out of it.

I bolted out towards it biting into its hind paw before bolting back into the trees. I heard the growl that followed. It turned to look at me as I disappeared. Mira bolted out to towards the bear from behind biting into the same leg that had fallen victim to me.

The bear growled in pain as she disappeared back into the trees before it could get her. It was Toby's turn, he bolted out from behind and grabbed its other hind leg. It lurched around, but he was too quick for it. Brian took the same leg. By this time the bear was moving even slower, unable to move its hind legs without pain coursing through them.

The bear was getting really distressed now. Its head was turning in all directions, confused. It knew it was surrounded by now. The six of us, including Maya and Zac, all broke out of the trees, circling around it.

I was in front of it with Toby. Brian and Mira grabbed it by the forelegs at the same time as Toby and I both slinked easily towards its throat while the two wolves at its sides distracted it. I wasn't expecting Maya to leap onto its back, the three of us grabbed the thick fur and skin in our mouths. Zac seemed to hang back observing our seemingly systematic hunt.

Between the power of three maws, we snapped the bone and tore away the skin. Maya leapt off its back as it fell, life escaping it quickly. It hit the ground with a loud thump. It was quickly followed by the sudden exhale of air.

When I saw what had happened, I couldn't help but burst out laughing as I retook human form. When the others saw, they changed back as well, Maya was the only one that didn't burst out laughing. 'You could help me you know,' Toby stated. He almost seemed annoyed.

Still quivering with laughter, Brian and I went around to the large, unmoving mass of fur. We pushed the bear just enough to allow Toby to get out from under it. 'You know that really isn't fun., Toby stated, rubbing his bare chest.

'And you're never gonna live this one down.' Brian clapped him on the shoulder. We all laughed again, even Maya.

Toby groaned. 'Let's eat before the coyotes get it,' he stated flatly. He easily retook wolf form. Apparently it didn't hurt getting landed on by a large grizzly. Probably just extremely uncomfortable.

By now it was dark, but thanks to the waning moon above us, it was easy to see. I retransformed. I could see the coyotes in the trees waiting for the chance to eat the prize of our hunt. Toby threw his head back, howling, I noticed the slightly higher pitch than usual. The others followed.

I smiled. This is exactly what I needed; a bit of fun with my friends. I lifted my head and joined the howl, I could feel the excitement in it, just like the others. I didn't even care that the people in town would be able to hear us.

In the silence that followed, we began to tear away the fur, searching for the meat that hid beneath it. The coyotes crept forward. We didn't force them away. There was plenty of meat to go around. Once we ate our fill, we left the coyotes to the remainder. They were more than happy to close in on the mass of juicy flesh.

I bolted into the trees, the others not far behind, as we made the journey back to our clothes. We changed back, dressed and used the water from a creek nearby to wipe the blood from our mouths.

I saw the look on Toby's face. I bolted. I could hear him coming after me, I could also hear the others running, trying to keep up with our practiced agility.

He dove for me, I jumped grabbing the branch above me. 'I've been a werewolf for a lot longer than you, brother,' I stated. 'There is no way you can beat me.'

He leapt at me. I didn't even bother avoiding him. I let him push us out of the tree. I rolled on impact, pushing him to the ground beneath me.

'Told you.' I grinned stepping back.

He rolled backwards to his feet. 'What about all of us?' he asked.

I smirked as the others surrounded me. I crouched down slightly. 'Do your worst,' I told them, a playful growl in my throat. Their wolves didn't react to the growl; they knew it was playful, so it didn't cause submission.

I waited for them to make their move. When they did, I jumped, they were expecting that, Mira grabbed my leg before I could flip over Brian's head. I use my free leg to push her away, I hit the ground rolling, easily finding my feet.

I turned to block Toby's blow to the side. I knocked him off his feet. Max was next, he landed on top of Toby, pushing him back to the ground. Maya jumped onto my back, grabbing me from behind.

Unable to turn I landed flat on my stomach. I winced as I landed on what was left of my wound, the wind leaving my chest. I didn't even have the chance to push her off. Mira had hold of my legs while Max and Liam grabbed my arms. I put my chin on the ground, trying to put air back into my aching lungs.

'Gotcha,' Toby said, playfully.

'What did you do?' Mira asked. 'Other than get tripped over.'

'Can you get off me?' I asked, trying to look at Maya. She was sitting on my back.

'Good thing it's not a bear,' Max stated.

'Heeeey,' Toby said, looking at him. His reaction just made us all laugh hysterically.

I took in a deep breath and sighed. Sitting down on the ground of the clearing we were in, I staredup at the stars above us, this was more like it. This was what I had always imagined my life being like before my parents were killed, before everything else that took me off this track.

One by one the others started settling down around me None of us had remember to bring our bracelets so we were completely naked, as we lay there soaking up the moonlight. Not that any of us really cared. It was late, the effect of the ivy was wearing off and I felt fatigue pulling at the edges of my brain.

I was safe, I told myself. I was surrounded by pack, by my friends. Knowing this helped my wolf and to disappear into a deep slumber. Our head was on Zac's chest and Toby was using my legs as a makeshift pillow. I was comfortable enough to be dragged into a blissful sleep.

The next few weeks came and went. I saw Richard and gave him the things I found in my father's office that should be at the council office. He thanked me and asked me how things had been since I got back. I lied. I told him that things had been really good, it had just been really busy since I got back. Which was true. Mostly.

The rest of the time was spent going through all of the books and organising things for our new house. It was coming together really quickly. I suppose when you threw a bit of money at the builders, they were more likely to push forward on the job a lot faster, especially when half the building crew were werewolves. The materials were the things we were waiting on the most.

Once the roof went up, we started digging our tunnel to the bunker. We used magic mostly, Agua and her father helped us dig a straight tunnel through the. Eventually we broke through the wall that the forest hatch dropped down into. This took us several weeks to complete and support properly along the way. We then sealed up the hatch from the inside. It only needed to be used as an emergency exit now.

We didn't include the humans in the knowledge of

the tunnel to the bunker. We didn't want any of them to know it was there. We made sure that while it was being built and covered that only werewolves were on site. We didn't need humans poking around in the bunker without our knowledge.

Slowly the house came together from the bottom up. Then the internal walls started getting put in and painted to the colours I had chosen. I honestly felt proud of how it was coming along. It was really looking incredible.

Once the house itself was built, it was big and empty. Colby and I had to get the furniture delivered next. We did it one room at a time, starting with the lower level, spending a while choosing where the furniture would go and what would work best for the pack. It took us a few days to do that. Finally, we were able to announce to the pack that the house was ready to move into.

We then had to start the process of actually moving in. I started by taking my things up to my new bedroom on the third floor, making sure each of my things had a specific place. Then I started moving my father's books into the bookcase we placed in the entertainment area. I hadn't had a chance to get through them all yet.

I was moving a book when a piece of folded paper fell out of it. Placing the book flat on the shelf and stooped down to pick up the paper. Unfolding it, staring at the words on the paper, almost as if they were lying to me.

When they didn't immediately disappear, I got up and almost ran to the new house where I was sure to find Colby. He wasn't there so I called him, and he made his way over straight away. I was in the office on the first floor when he arrived. This was going to be Colby's office.

I gave him the piece of paper I had found. On it was Michael's name at the top of what seemed to be a list of abilities. Several of which Michael had already exhibited to us.

'Your father was looking into Michael?' he asked.

I nodded. 'He also started looking into what Michael is and he figured it out.'

'It still doesn't tell us how to kill him though,' Colby said.

I sighed. 'I know. But I was thinking that my father's journals might have the answer.' All the pack alphas kept journals to help each new pack alpha learn from the achievements and failings of past alphas.

'Do you know where they are?'

I shook my head. 'My dad never got a chance to show me or Damien,' I said. 'The knowledge is usually passed down when the next alphas come of age.' For us that was full initiation into the pack. 'Damien hadn't been initiated yet.'

'Then we need to find the journals,' Colby said.

I nodded. 'I'm hoping I will find them during the move.'

Colby and I talked about a few other things before heading back to our homes to continue moving. It was my hope to be finished moving before school started again in the next few weeks. I couldn't believe it was August already.

I had spoken to the school about me missing end of

year exams. They said that I could just sit the exams on the first day of school and would be able to start my senior year. Especially since it was massively unlikely for me to fail those exams.

The thought had crossed my mind though. What were we going to do with all of the pack houses once we all moved out of them? They had werewolf features in them. And it wasn't like there were people flocking to live in Wolfridge. To humans it was the current capital of werewolves, since they didn't know where any other packs were for the moment. The town seemed kind of dangerous to humans now. I guessed they would stay empty or be knocked down and turned into other things.

It took me a week but I was finally able to strip the whole house of its contents. A lot of things just went to the trash. Other things went to the house and were placed against the wall of my room until I had time to find a space for it all. Zac moved his handful of things to his own room on the second floor. Since he wasn't really an alpha it wasn't proper for him to be living in the alpha quarters. Of course, he would probably be sleeping up here most of the time. But he at least had his own space.

Colby and Lexi were my neighbours. As pack beta Colby got a room up here on the third floor and as his mate, Lexi was able to move in with him. The rest of the werewolves took the time to move into their rooms as well. Couples lived together and everyone else had their own room. They were decent sized rooms too. I figured if we got to the point where we were running out of rooms, the children would be able to double up to make space.

The problem was. I didn't find any sign of the alpha journals during the move. I knew they would be stashed somewhere safe but I had no idea where that was, I even searched the walls and floors for hidden doorways. They had to be somewhere else in the house.

Our first night in the new house was set to be a cosy one. It was the day before the full moon again – a month since I had made it home. It had definitely been a busy month. That night we had dinner in the new dining hall. It was interesting because none of us really knew how to cook, having just eaten steak our entire lives, but we made it work by putting out raw steaks and sizzled bacon. No vegetables at this stage. We really needed to learn how to cook.

After dinner we went into the rec room. It was the recreational space that Colby and I decided to put on the ground floor behind the staircase leading upstairs. Inside, the room was broken up into two separate spaces. One side resembled a library of sorts, with bookcases on the walls around the room and tables spread out around the centre for studying.

On the other side of the large room it was more casual. There was a TV with a few gaming systems, these were Zac's suggestions, and a few nice couches to sit on and relax with a book or to chat with friends. I liked the patterned, maroon wallpaper that we chose. That, coupled with the fireplace against the wall, made the room incredibly cosy.

This room hid a secret though. Remember the tunnel we dug to the bunker? That was hidden behind the fireplace. Like the bookcase back at my old house, there was a button that allowed an invisible door to click open next to the cement fixture. There were now a small set of stairs that led the way into the tunnel.

I relaxed on a couch with a book about establishing pack hierarchies that I had found on my father's shelf. Everyone was doing their own thing. Some were reading books. Maya and Mira had pulled a game out and were eagerly playing Jenga. Zac was introducing Brian and Max to the world of video games on the television while several adults watched on in amusement as they worked around the controls. In one of the racing games Zac kept coming first while the other two werewolves were sitting around tenth place.

It was nice to see the pack together. There was an air of contentment around the room as pack members came and went. When I finally went to bed that night it was to the very comfortable mattress that Colby and I had chosen for everyone. I was content. I was happy.

*****

I sat down and the rest of the pack followed suit, crossing their legs so we sat in a large circle.

'Tonight is a special night of the year,' I said, looking around at each member of my pack. Even Edith and her pup, Sophie, were here. They didn't usually attend full moon gatherings but they made the exception for this time of year. 'For our newest members I will explain what will be happening over the next couple of months.

'First of all, tonight we will welcome young Sophie

into our ranks officially as a human pup of the pack. I have convinced Edith to move into the pack house and raise her daughter alongside the rest of the pack.' There were a lot of happy faces at this news. 'Tomorrow morning when the moon sets over the horizon, Sophie will take human form for the first time and will remain so until she comes of age and becomes a werewolf of the pack.'

'Pup's once born wolf to their mother spend their first year as a wolf, their mother stay a wolf alongside them. Then once they reach a year old, both return to human form, Sophie will be roughly the size of a five-year-old human.

I paused and met the young pup's gaze from in between her mother's paws. 'Tonight also marks the beginning of our breeding season.' I glanced at Zac, Maya and Matthew, the three new werewolves I was explaining this for. 'For the next month it will be possible for female werewolves to become pregnant and introduce a new addition to the pack. If you have any questions, please feel free to ask anyone or me personally if you would prefer.'

'On that note,' I continued, 'tonight, is also a time for us to feel closer as a pack and form bonds as a family and as friends, especially since we have not been able to experience this properly for a while now. I invite you all to now open your minds to each other as we spend tonight rekindling the bond that has been strained for so many years. Tonight we will not worry about the future, tonight we will not concern ourselves with the past, we will just stay in this moment as a pack, as a family.'

I felt the familiar tug of my wolf and, as I transformed, I opened my mind to the world surrounding us. I felt each member of the pack entwine their minds with mine. Opening up their thoughts and feelings until we could feel and sense everything.

That night we hunted, we played, we chased and we enjoyed each other's company like I had never seen or felt before as a full werewolf. I could feel the contentment across the pack. I could see everyone, feel everyone. We were welcoming the start of a new path. One that we had been waiting for for so long.

The next morning we woke up in a dog pile. None of us were wearing clothes. Even Zac hadn't worn his bracelet. It felt more natural this way. I was nestled in Zac's arms, the steadiness of his breath brushing the back of my neck.

Looking around I could see Lexi snuggled up against Colby's chest. The now human Sophie with her short black hair that all werewolves had when they first took human form. Her facial features were so bright and beautiful, and I knew that she was the first of the new generation of werewolves after so long without children being born to our pack.

Once everyone had awakened, we walked our way back to the house in groups. I could see Edith getting shakily onto the human legs – she had not walked on for a year. Colby assisted her to stand and I helped Sophie. She had never been in human form before so she seemed to want to use her arms as extra legs. I took her hand and helped her to stand on two legs and demonstrated moving. The next few weeks would see

Edith teaching Sophie how to walk and talk like a human, meaning not using her mind, before she made her first appearance in the local elementary school for the new year in several weeks' time.

There was a closeness in the air as we walked back to the house. That day nobody disappeared with their mates like we normally did. We all went upstairs for showers before spending the day in the rec room, enjoying the carefree time as a pack, while it lasted.

Summer was over and the mad rush of back to school was causing a fluster around town. I was glad school was going back. Without wolf training I didn't have much going on. I was left with nothing but making sure our household ran smoothly.

Our transition to living together as a pack did not run entirely smooth like I thought it would. The hard part was there wasn't as much privacy as before. Colby and I made sure to insulate to walls with soundproof padding but we could still hear each other almost all around the house.

In the end I ended up bringing Agua in to put some magic on the house and improve the sound proofing. It took several days to get the spells working properly so that we had the privacy that everyone desired at least in the bedroom spaces.

After that, it was figuring out meals and cleaning. Cleaning wise I ended up organising a housekeeper to clean a different floor of the house each day. This ended up being a human but it was a human close to the pack. Charlie's wife, Diana. She had been a cleaner around town for a long time. She had always known about Charlie being a werewolf. It was fitting that we asked her to be our cleaner for a decent salary, especially since she was living with us anyway.

The other thing I had to organise was someone to cook for thirty werewolves. Lunches were easy enough. We just had a bunch of food ready to go for the adults to take to work every day. But until school went back the rest of the pack needed food for lunch if they were hungry and hadn't hunted.

In the end I asked around the pack to see if anybody wanted to change up their job. Toby's parents said no. They were always working at either their day job, a small digital security company, or they were keeping an eye on the news feed for any signs of threat to the pack. They were way to busy and we needed them to keep doing that job.

The kids were out because they would soon be going back to school, so it wouldn't be useful for them to do it. I ended up going around to everyone. The problem was that nobody knew how to cook or even what to cook for that matter.

So I outsourced the cooking job. I got in contact with Jeremy and Harry and asked them what kinds of foods they had cooked for the pack. Then I hired a chef and a kitchen hand to make a menu for us and cook fresh for us twice a day and have a stock of food prepared for lunches each day.

This ended up working very well. They also did all of the dishes that they made when preparing the food, they let me know what they would need and I had it purchased for them. They asked for several things in the first few weeks until they had everything they needed. From that point on we had meals for breakfast and dinner instead of meat and a couple of vegetables. It was a definite step up from how we had been eating in the past and I found that I didn't need to hunt anywhere near as much. I was sure the deer were happy about that.

I heard nothing from Michael in the lead up to school starting for the new year. It was both concerning and comforting. I knew that Colby and the large gang of werewolves had cleared out the majority of the vampires Michael had under his control. Very few had escaped but now that Michael had no minions, he was a lot more vulnerable than before.

I kept in touch with Jeremy, updating him on anything I found in my father's books; except I still hadn't found his journals and neither Jeremy nor Damien had any ideas about where they could be, so I just kept moving – training myself to keep fit, checking in on the training Toby was conducting with the younger werewolves, including Zac, and making sure that everyone was happy.

I was so incredibly happy when it was time to go back to school. I hadn't seen much of Agua all holidays. She and her parents were spending a lot of time working on hashing out the secrets they had been keeping all these years. I did not envy their position.

When I walked onto the campus for the first time in two months, I was more than happy to wave at everyone and find out what classes I would be taking each day. I didn't have many changes this year. AP biology, and technology this year like usual, plus a business class. I had at least one free period every day and several classes with both Zac, Agua and Toby. Although except gym class, we were never all together.

I spent an hour of the first day going through and doing all the tests from the previous year I had missed. They were so easy that I finished them quickly and handed them back in before going off to biology.

Mr Harris welcomed me when I entered the room and sat at my usual desk.

'We hadn't been expecting you until later,' he said.

I smiled genuinely at him. He was a nice teacher and principal. 'All done,' I told him. 'Thank you for letting me do the catch-up exams.'

'No worries,' he replied. 'It wasn't your fault.' Then he returned to his lesson about ocean ecosystems.

Lunch time was louder than I remembered, especially standing in a long, talkative line of students going to have lunch for the first time in the school year. I grabbed myself a burger and went to sit at the usual table.

All of the other werewolves were sitting there and so were Dylan and Sean. The rest of the soccer team was sitting at their usual table. I took my seat next to Zac and absently listened to the conversations about classes. Zac was talking to Sean and Dylan about his newfound ability – photographic memory. He was explaining that when asked about what they learned last year in multistrand science he was able to answer all of the questions on the topics learned since becoming a werewolf.

Of course, born werewolves had this ability from birth so I didn't know how hard it would be to memorise all of the information that they pushed into students' brains. But if the test scores of even my most devoted human peers were any indication. They couldn't retain all of it.

From there I started to zone out of the conversations. It wasn't so long ago that I was trapped in that cell, by myself with nobody to talk to. I felt the hairs on the back of my neck stand up as my body remembered that isolated feeling. It was a deep, cold feeling that made me feel anxious beyond anything I had ever felt before.

I flinched when a hand touched my leg. It was Zac's hand. I took a deep breath trying to settle my suddenly rapid heartbeat. The rest of the werewolves at my table continued on like nothing happened. Only Sean and Dylan glanced at me when I flinched but they were quick to look away with no comment.

At the end of lunch I went outside to relax for a while for my free period. I had it on my own and for the moment I was enjoying the peace and quiet. Seeing a vampire come running out of the forest during my quiet time kind of ruined my time out though.

He stopped short of me. I didn't attack and neither did Kai. A moment later two adult sized wolves came running out of the trees at full speed. They startled the class of freshmen even more than the vampire did.

I held my hand up for them to stop. Kai was looking them anxiously. 'Are you okay, Kai?' I asked.

'Were you serious about helping me if I needed it?' he asked. I was surprised but I nodded. 'Good. I wasn't sure. Werewolf and vampire stuff and all that.'

'It's fine,' I said. 'What do you need?'

'Not here,' he said. 'I'll get in trouble if humans hear what I have to say.'

'I...' Damn it. 'I guess I can leave now.' I looked at

Lexi and Charlotte. 'Can you take Kai back to the house please? I just need to notify people that I'm leaving.'

The two werewolves did not look happy with what I asked them to do. I didn't blame them. They had grown up despising vampires just like I did. The main thing was though that they would do as I asked, even if they didn't like it. That was the benefit of being the alpha.

I walked to the office and told them that I would not be making my final class for the day because something had come up. Kai seriously couldn't turn up in like two hours? Jeez. I had already missed so much school. Hold on. Why am I even going to school in the first place? I knew it all already.

The bell rang as I was leaving the office. The seniors had sport so the others saw me come towards the oval where they sat waiting for the teacher and saw me keep walking into the forest and away from the school.

None of them followed me and that was good. They needed to be in school for now. I didn't know why Kai was here, but it definitely warranted me leaving school early for the day. When I arrived at the house it was quiet. I could hear Harris bustling around upstairs, cleaning and the kitchen staff were cooking away but the rest of the house seemed empty, or at least nobody was in the common areas.

I went to Colby's office to find Kai sitting in a chair opposite Colby. This was the only room on the bottom floor that we had made soundproof with the upstairs areas. The room was incredibly tense I almost wanted to walk straight back out. Instead I forced myself to take a seat in the only vacant seat.

'What do you need help with, Kai?' I asked him, ignoring Colby's uncomfortable gaze.

Kai seemed to take a breath. 'I need you to talk to the Grand Master for me,' he said.

That kind of surprised me. 'Why?' I asked, completely confused.

'Because he won't listen to me,' Kai said. 'I tried talking to him about Michael but he doesn't believe him to be a threat to us. We know different.'

'So what?' Colby said. 'A lot less vampires left in the world,' he continued. 'I see that as a win.'

'Colby,' I said sternly.

'Rya, why are we even listening to this vampire?' he asked. 'I understand what you went through may have caused you to work together but I figured that ended when you escaped.'

I felt kind of shocked by his standpoint on this.

'You don't understand what I went through at all,' I growled. 'What I saw was Michael trying to break into my mind and take control of my thoughts and actions. You don't know what that's like. Every one of those vampires were under his control, the new ones and the older ones.'

'This vampire wants to take you to vampire capital and you're okay with that?' Colby asked.

'I don't know,' I said. 'But I owe it to Kai to hear him out. He saved my life.'

'I know,' Colby admitted.

I raised my eyebrows slightly. 'Then stop talking over him and listen to what he has to say.'

There was silence in the room for several minutes.

'As I was saying,' Kai put in, breaking the silence. 'I want to stop Michael from taking control of vampires and using them to create and army of baby vampires.'

'For what purpose?' I asked.

He shook his head. 'I don't know. All I know is that he really hates your family and the original vampire family.'

'There aren't any of the original vampires left, are there?' I asked.

Kai hesitated. 'There's two. The Grand Master and his daughter. They were the only survivors of the war against werewolves.'

We were led to believe that they were all gone. But maybe that's what we were supposed to believe. There were a lot of things that I was learning weren't true these days.

'If I was to meet with them. Where would I be?' I asked.

'Ohio,' he said. One of the states we don't have a werewolf pack in. I would be alone and vulnerable.

'I would have to speak with people before I can even consider going,' I told him.

He nodded. 'I understand.'

'Is there a way I can contact you?' I asked.

He gave me a mobile number and I wrote it down for later use. Then I went to escort him out of the house.

'I will escort him to the border,' Colby announced.

I rolled my eyes. 'I will be in contact,' I told Kai. He nodded a blurred away with Colby only a few steps behind.

I spoke to Colby about my decision to leave school, at least for now. To be honest I expected him to talk me out of it, but he didn't.

'You're alpha now. There is a lot of other things you should be doing with your time.'

So I started the process of leaving school. Well, not exactly leaving. I convinced the school board, through Mr Harris to allow me to take the SAT exams early. It was going to take a few days for exam papers to arrive. In the meantime, I was free from school. To be honest I didn't quite know what to do with myself.

I ended up going to see Seth. He was my father's beta so he knew more about what things an alpha needed to do to keep things going.

'Pretty much the main thing for you to do is be available for the pack to make sure they can talk to you if they need to,' Seth had told me. 'The rest of it is thinking about where you want to take the pack. How will you make a difference?'

That made me think a lot about what I wanted to do for the pack as alpha. I already built the house to make us closer together as a pack but I never really considered what I wanted to do because there had always been something in the way.

I was never meant to be alpha in the first place, then I had to deal with Erik when Damien left. Now that I was finally alpha, it had been one thing after another just to keep the pack going.

So really what were the biggest things I wanted to do for the pack? Well, first and foremost, I wanted to make it safer for us, from Michael especially, but also from the humans. Ours was still the only pack that was known to the human public so we were the face of werewolves.

That was the main thing I wanted to focus on. I couldn't do much about Michael right now. I still had to talk to Jeremy about what Kai had asked me to do, but maybe I could do something about the human side of things.

I could also set up some new security systems to make our territory more secure.. But honestly, I didn't know where to start, so instead I kept reading the books that I found in my father's library. That's what I did my first week away from school while I waited for Jeremy to get back to me.

Outside of the reading that week I didn't really have much to do. There were a couple of little things that needed handling like paying the cooks wages and making sure that they had everything they needed each day to continue feeding us which meant a daily food delivery that arrived first thing in the morning.

I also made sure to include a wage for Diana so she had money earned for cleaning the house. It was generous wage that I thought she deserved but I ended up getting a knock on my office door the next morning. She came in telling me I had paid her too much considering all her bills were being paid for already. My reasoning was that it was a hell of a task to keep a three-storey house clean, especially when it was as large as ours. In the end she left without succeeding to lower her wage.

The only other thing I dealt with was towards the end of the week. Richard came to visit the house for the first time since it had been built. I gave him a tour starting on the ground floor.

Our entrance hall wasn't as large as Jeremy's in Washington but I think it fit our sized pack. It would be a long time before we ran out of room. Our ground floor had pretty much the same layout though.

When you entered there was a set of double doors to the right that led to the dining hall. In front of us but off to the left was a standard sized staircase. The back wall had two doors leading off of it. One led to the rec room that curled around the house in its two sections the other went to Colby's office.

Upstairs on the second floor there were a few hallways going in different directions that had bedrooms lining them. Each hallway had at least ten rooms and we had five hallways. There was also the other staircase leading upstairs to the top floor. This one had another hallway of bedrooms. Enough to cater to any visiting alphas if needed. It also had Colby's room and my room. My room also had an office attached to it with a desk and my father's alpha books. The only other thing was the large boardroom on the third floor.

In all Richard had been quite impressed with the size and layout of the house. He told me so when we finally sat down in my office after the tour. 'Surely you didn't come out here for a tour?' I said, a silent question in my voice.

'I was actually wanting to talk to you about something,' he said. 'I have received word from Capitol Hill.' The government. 'They would like you to discuss with them more details about the supernatural population as a whole.'

'What does that mean?' I asked.

'They want you to go to Washington and have a series of conversations with them about werewolves, vampires and whatever else is out there.'

'Tell them to send me the details and I will look into it,' I told him. 'I can't do anything like that without council permission.' He started getting up to leave.

'I will see what I can do,' Richard confirmed.

*****

In the end I didn't get my call back that day. It wasn't until Saturday that I finally got my phone call. 'Hey, Rya,' Jeremy said when he clicked onto the screen. 'Sorry I didn't get back to you. It's been pretty crazy around here lately.'

I shrugged. 'That's fine,' I said. 'I needed to discuss a few things with you.' I took Jeremy's silence as an indication to continue. I told him all about Kai's request and now the Government's too. 'I didn't want to agree to anything without council approval.'

'That sounds like a lot is happening on your end too,' the council leader admitted. 'I understand Colby's concerns about you going to Ohio. We just got you back. For now at least I don't think it would be good for your pack for you to go. Especially since it could be a trap.' He raised his hands up in front of him, knowing I was about to jump in. 'I know that you two went through something together but we don't know if he is being controlled by Michael or if he has his own sinister plans.' He shrugged. 'The problem is we don't know.'

'I understand,' I responded.

'The humans on the other hand I say you should go for that,' he said more cheerfully. 'We don't know what they're thinking and it will be good to talk to them so we can learn more about what we can do to make it safe for all the packs to come out in the open… if their alpha chooses to that is.' He smiled. 'Right now focus on your own pack and the humans. Leave Michael to time. He will show himself again and we will find a way to stop him. Even if we shove him back in another tomb.'

'I think we should investigate the ruins,' I said suddenly. I had only just thought of it. 'He was locked up there for so long. Surely there's something there about him.'

'Maybe,' Jeremy said. 'But we have to be careful about it. We don't know if Michael is still there.'

'Maybe we should organise a scout mission,' I suggested.

'No,' Jeremy said firmly. 'For now it is too dangerous. I'll see what I can do about investigating the ruins but for now you have other things to focus on.'

I knew that was an alpha no. 'Okay,' I said. 'I will get in contact with the government and organise these talks. I will stay in a hotel so I don't draw attention to you guys.'

'Probably a good idea for now,' Jeremy agreed.

The rest of my day was spent making the arrangements. I called the contact I was given and we arranged the meetings over a few days that would be away from both full and dark moons. I didn't need the added stress of having to transform in the city if it wasn't necessary.

I booked the hotel for me only. I didn't want Zac to miss school if he didn't have to. He was still learning to be a werewolf. He had to get used to the social side of it now that he knew how to shift and his wolf was stronger.

I announced my intentions that night at dinner. To say that the pack was less than thrilled was an understatement. Their reasoning was I had only just gotten back to them. I sympathised with this but I knew that I needed to do something to help make our future easier, especially since humans knew about us now. When I explained this to them as a whole, they seemed to understand a bit better, but they definitely weren't happy about it.

The rest of the night I spent with the pack as a whole in the rec room, chatting and enjoying each other's company. I went to bed unhappy about leaving even though I knew it was the right decision to go and speak to the human leader, Tobias Fletcher. Although I may not even end up speaking to him directly, but I guess we would soon find out.

*****

Our first dark moon in the new house came and went. We ended up using the cells in the bunker. They were strong and perfectly capable of housing several werewolves in each one. The pack spread out with Damien in one of the alpha cages with his mate, Sarah and me in another one with Zac and Toby.

Then before I knew it, I was on my way to Washington. I didn't drive or fly like most people, even werewolves, would. I decided to run. I didn't want the hassle of dealing with traffic and all that stuff. Besides I could run faster than a car going the speed limit.

I packed a few sets of clothes, my phone and wallet into a small rucksack and hooked it over both of my shoulders. I could buy anything else I might need while I was there. I said goodbye to everyone in the pack, giving Zac a particularly long hug and a kiss that caused some of the others to look away. Then I waved to everyone, transformed into wolf form and ran into the trees. Heading first out of town and over the bridge before I slowly started to head south-west.

The journey was long and tiring but I made it there by mid-afternoon. I found my hotel not too far away from where I would be having the meetings over the next several days. People recognised who I was immediately upon entering the hotel and I was quietly given a key for my room.

As I walked out, I could smell the fear amongst the humans who had noticed me. I silently walked upstairs to my one bedroom, balcony apartment. It wasn't a great view. I just wanted the balcony so I could leave if I needed to. I was only on the second floor so jumping out of the window would not be an issue.

I spent the rest of that night sleeping off my travel worn exhaustion and preparing for the meet and greet that was scheduled for the next day. The bed was comfortable and the food was good, so I felt like it was going to be an enjoyable business trip. I guessed that was what I could call it.

The next morning I followed the Google map directions on my phone to the address they had given me. Turns out the address took me to the actual White House, but I guess it made sense as a lot of Government officials worked in the building during the day.

The person at the gate made damn sure of my identity and my business before they let me in. I didn't get taken straight in either. I was taken to a processing room where they checked my identity again and made sure I wasn't carrying any weapons. I actively decided not to remind them that I was a werewolf and therefore my entire body was technically a weapon.

After that was all done, I was finally allowed to follow a guard up to the main building. I tried to hide my amazement at the foyer when we entered through the front doors. It was large and not at all like the outside.

While the outside was marble white, the inside was a more traditional set of colours, using various patterns in browns and reds rather than white like I had thought it would be. The guard took me to through a door to my left and then through a series of hallways before he deposited me into a boardroom with a large, thick window that looked out to the gardens.

I sat silently while I waited. I looked down at what I was wearing. I hoped it was professional enough for what we needed. I had ducked into a store that morning to grab a nice blouse and wore it with a new pair of jeans. Thankfully the heat wasn't so bothersome for werewolves since we were able to regulate our body temperatures better than humans could.

The people that came in to meet me were two women and two men. All of them were human as far as I could tell. 'Thank you for meeting with us Rya,' the short, brown haired man said as he sat in a chair at the end of the table. 'My name is Stephen. I have been appointed as the head of a new department here,' he said, pushing his navy blue rimmed glasses back up his nose. 'This department will be handling inter-species communications and management.

'These are my colleagues,' he continued, indicating each one in turn. Zoe, was blonde with her long hair in a plait. There were several freckles speckling across her cheeks and her glasses were silver and made her pop out at me. She seemed like a person who had a colourful personality. She was either going to be really fun or really frustrating.

Then there was Collin. He had short, spiky, red hair and blue eyes. His skin was the pasty white of someone who didn't get out of the house much. He looked like he was reading my every movement and making assumptions. It was almost a calculating gaze.

The last female had short, brown hair and had an

aura that screamed business and professionalism. She was a little plumper than most but mostly looked like she never stopped thinking about work. Her name Kelly.

Finally, after introductions were made, I introduced myself. 'My name is Rya,' I said. 'But you all know that. It's nice to meet you all.'

'Thank you for coming to meet with us on short notice,' Stephen responded. 'I guess you're wondering why we wanted to speak with you.'

'Not really,' I said. 'I figured it was because now that you know there are other species of people in your country, you want to understand what and how many so you can assess if there is any danger and how to react.'

'Somewhat, yes,' Stephen stated. 'We don't think that you are a danger to us at all. Your people have been living amongst us for years without us ever knowing about it. Surely you have rules and guidelines that you all follow to cohabit with us without being a danger.'

I nodded. 'Yes, we do have our own laws and mostly we just want to continue living the same lives we always have.'

'That's good,' he answered. 'And that is mostly what we want too. There is just the little issue of all the public fighting and killing.'

'I'm sorry,' I said. 'But we are currently at war with a creature that wants to kill us. I don't know when or where he will attack and it is a problem we are dealing with.'

'We know,' Kerry said to me. 'We want you to

resolve the issue and we want to build a relationship with your people to make sure that nothing happens whilst the country is in this transition period.'

'What are you proposing?' I asked.

Stephen answered me. 'We want to make you a liaison for werewolf communications.'

'And what would that entail?'

Collin stepped in here. 'For one we would like you to answer some questions we have about the supernatural world and prepare a public statement that werewolves are no threat to the human public.'

'And then?' I questioned Collin.

'For now that is all we need. We just need to give the public peace of mind that we aren't in any danger. At least not any more than usual anyway,' Stephen told me. 'The rest we will figure out when the time comes.'

'I will have to speak to my higher up before I can tell you anything,' I told them. 'But I don't think it would be an issue.'

'That sounds reasonable,' he agreed. 'Why don't we have a break and you can speak to your superior?'

'Sure,' I said.

I nodded to them as they each left the board room and disappeared. I pulled out my phone, and I switched on the app that toby had given me that scrambled my signal, just in case somebody tried to trace who I was calling. I couldn't be too careful.

To my surprise Jeremy picked up. 'Hello, Rya,' he said. 'How's it been so far?'

I shrugged forgetting that he couldn't see me. 'They seem to want peace.'

'That's good, isn't it?'

'I think so,' I answered. 'I just haven't gotten a full feel for them yet. They offered me a job.'

'What job?' he asked, sounding curious.

'Werewolf liaison,' I said. 'I would act as a line of communication between humans and werewolves to help maintain peace in light of our revelation.'

'That doesn't sound too bad,' he said. 'It sounds like they really do want to make this work for everyone's sake.'

'Does that mean you want me to take the job?' I asked.

'I think you should seriously look into if it is something you should do.' Jeremy answered. 'I don't know what you would be expected to do. Ask for more information about the job before you agree to it but at this stage, I think it would be the right thing to do.'

'What about their questions?' I asked.

He was silent for a moment. 'Answer them. We need to be open with them if we want this to work. Otherwise the rest of the supernatural world with stay in the shadows.'

We discussed the finer details a little bit longer before we finished the phone call. Then I waited for the others to come back. I assumed that I wasn't allowed to go looking for them.

When I sensed them coming I felt myself tense. I really wasn't sure what I was getting myself into, but Jeremy wanted to see if it worked out. I just didn't really like being the poster child for werewolves across the country.

'What was the decision?' Stephen asked me.

I hid my anxiety about this; at least I think I did. 'At this stage I would like more information regarding the liaison job,' I said. 'But questions and discussions have been approved to let me answer any questions anybody has.'

'Excellent. Kelly will get you the details about the job and will discuss it with you in detail another time.' At that the all-business lady left the room. 'For now we will set up a time for us to meet over the next few days and we will go through some of our questions during that session.'

'I will need to talk to my pack about the job though,' I said. 'Especially if it involves me travelling here all the time. I can't exactly just move away.'

'I understand,' he said. Kelly came back with what looked like a small novel worth of pages. Okay, maybe I was exaggerating. But it was a lot for just job information.

After a few more formalities I was escorted back to the entrance and back through the gate. The only difference now was that there were cameras pointed at my face. I ignored them without answering any of the questions that were fired at me, not that I could make sense of what they said in all the chaos anyway, but I forced myself to press through the small crowd and leave them all behind at a fast walk.

Even then one of the reporters didn't seem to want to give up and she followed me all the way back to my hotel. the only thing that stopped her from following me in was the security guard who stepped in to block her from chasing after me.

When I finally settled onto the bed in my room, I let out a huge sigh. Great. Now I was going to have to be more careful about what I did here. By sunset my location would be plastered all over the news. I was sure of it. Hopefully this wasn't going to put me in any undue danger.

I spent the afternoon pouring over the information about the job they had given me. making sure to read every word and every clause to make sure I understood everything I was getting myself into.

Most of it was pretty straight forward; act as a go between for humans and werewolves, provide information and engage in research with a dedicated team, help in the management of werewolf affairs, arrangements, public statements and help to enforce any laws not followed in relations to werewolves.

In the end I was happy with the requirements I needed to fulfil. There were other clauses though related to travel. Talking about how most of the work could be done anywhere and the arrangements would be made. Though I would be required to present a monthly update on the situation and any further steps that needed to be made in the future. The only thing I wasn't keen on was constantly travelling away from Wolfridge and leaving my pack all the time. I wondered if they would approve the work being done in Wolfridge. I would have to ask when I went back tomorrow to speak with Kelly about all the job arrangements.

I found it harder to fall asleep that night maybe it was the prospect of all these new things. Maybe I was just missing home. I was missing Zac, missing his company. Maybe I shouldn't have left him at home. I would have liked the support while I was here. Instead I just felt alone in a strange place, and now everyone knew where I was. After tossing and turning until midnight I finally fell into a restless sleep.

The next morning I called Colby. I needed to talk to someone from home about the job offer. I didn't want my pack to feel like I was abandoning them. They had had enough bad leadership over the last decade.

'I don't know what you want me to say about it,' Colby had said.

'I want to know what you think of it,' I said. 'I'm hoping that they will be able to set me up at home in Wolfridge.'

'And if they don't?' he asked. 'What are you going to do?'

I sighed. 'I don't know,' I admitted. 'I need to talk to this person today and find out whether I can do this job from Wolfridge. All I know is that Jeremy wants me to make this work. I don't think I really have a choice in the matter.'

'He's Lupus,' Colby said. 'He should be doing the job, e specially since the job is in his territory.'

'I know,' I said. 'I just don't think I can't say no here.'

'You said that already,' Colby told me. 'I just don't like the idea of you being gone all the time. Especially with Michael still out there.'

'I am relatively safe here with Jeremy's pack. There

are so many of them that I don't think Michael is likely to attack me here.' It was true. When I entered the city all I could smell was werewolf. The city was crawling with werewolves. I had even passed a few in the street yesterday on my way to the meeting.

'Okay,' he said. 'Just be careful out there. We don't want to lose you again.'

I said my goodbyes and hung up the phone. It was time to get ready for the day. I hadn't eaten dinner last night thanks to the full moon feast but I was hungry now.

I got myself up and showered and into another blouse, this time it was a plum colour over the top of my jeans again. There was no restaurant in the hotel so I had to go to the café across the street to get some food. I wasn't aware that there would be more reporters waiting for me outside. I didn't even watch the news to see what they said last night but I figured I would hear about it at some point today.

The security guard threw a sympathetic glance my way as he pushed the door open for me to enter the madness outside. I gave him a small grimace in return and forced my way through the crowd and across the road to the large café that hosted a buffet breakfast.

I paid at the counter before grabbing a plate and slowly making my way through the buffet line grabbing some scrambled eggs, bacon and pancakes. I accompanied it with a coffee and went to find a vacant table. Unfortunately the only tables available were outside.

I sighed and sat down at a vacant two-seater. No sooner than when I started eating, did I hear a scramble of running footsteps behind me. I tensed, ready to leave if I needed to, but the footsteps ended up being two female reporters. They were pushing in front of each other until finally one of them sat in the seat across from me.

'Hi,' she said, as the other lady walked away with a disappointed look on her face. 'My name is Caroline.'

I ignored her by not responding and instead eating another mouthful pancake.

'Hello, Rya,' she said, trying to get my attention again. 'My name is Caroline.' Again I ignored her as I continued to eat.

When I had finished my plate of food, I downed the last of my coffee and put a tip on the table and got up grabbing my phone as I moved away from the table. 'Hey!' she called out after me. 'Aren't you going to talk to me?'

I just kept walking back towards the White House. She followed me all the way there and badgered me while I stood there waiting for them to let me in. When I got moved into the processing room, I was almost relieved to be away from the crazy woman. She couldn't take my ignoring for a no. Honestly, take the hint.

'I don't think we've had this much interest outside the front gates in a long time,' the guard told me as he checked me over for weapons like he had the day before.

'You do know that this search is pointless right?' I said to him.

He snickered. 'Yeah, I know,' he said. 'But if I don't

do it then I will get into trouble.'

'Fair enough.' I smirked.

Once I was given the all-clear, the guard escorted me back to the same boardroom as the day before. I wasn't alone to start with today. Kelly was in there waiting for me. I wondered how long she had been waiting.

'Good Morning, Kelly,' I said as I entered the room.

'Good morning, Miss Garcia,' she responded formally.

'Please,' I said. 'Rya is fine.'

We shook hands and I sat down in the seat beside her.

'Have you had a chance to go through the documents I gave you?' she asked me.

I nodded. 'I have. Everything seems to be fine,' I said. 'My only concern is spending too much time away from my pack. What kind of working arrangements would we be able to make for me not have to stay away for days at a time?'

'Do you have a way of travelling here fast each morning?' she asked.

'Not really,' I admitted. 'Any form of travel would take me at least three to four hours each way.'

'I would have to see what I can do about that for you,' she said. 'But I know we would be able to work out something.'

'I suppose I could see if our witch can teleport me here each day and collect me later.' I said, more to myself than to her. 'But I don't know if either of them can teleport that far.'

'If you have a look into that I can have a look into where could get situated closer to you,' Kelly told me.

I nodded. 'But otherwise you're happy to go ahead with everything?'

'Yes,' I said.

'Great,' Kelly exclaimed excitedly. 'We will get your paperwork sorted today so that you will have the necessary clearances to enter so you don't need to go through the processing centre and be escorted everywhere.'

'Cool,' I answered.

The rest of the day was spent getting shown around the areas that I had access to. I got a photo taken for my access card that would allow me into the gate and the building during approved hours.

I found out about what I was being paid. It was massive. Like six figure massive and I almost declined the amount. But I figured I should at least get something back for my time away from my alpha duties. This money at least would come back to the pack and help fund any growth in the future. The house we built had put a decent dent in the account and it would be good to be earning that back.

Just before I left, I got caught by Stephen 'Rya,' he said. 'Can I have a word?'

'Sure,' I said.

He led me into a small office that I think he had come out of. 'I heard that you accepted the job,' he said. 'That's great news.'

'Yeah,' I said with slightly fake enthusiasm. 'What do you need me for?' I asked.

'I wanted to talk to you about the reporters that have been hounding you last night and this morning.'

'What about them?'

'Is there a reason you aren't talking to them?'

I shrugged. 'Not really,' I admitted. 'I just hate reporters. They always spread lies and invade personal space just to get a story.'

'Would you talk to them?'

I shrugged again. 'If I had to,' I said.

'Good,' he said. 'Because we are looking to organise one for our questions tomorrow. It won't be them questioning you though they will be able to ask questions if you allow. Instead it will just be the questions that the higher ups want to know the answers to.'

'Sure,' I said. 'I don't mind answering their questions if they have some. I just don't like it when they get all up in my face.'

'Excellent,' Stephen said, sitting back with a satisfied smile on his face. 'I will see what I can do about them bugging you.'

I smiled at him. 'That would be amazing. Is there anything else you need me for?' I asked.

'No,' he answered. 'I just wanted to check that before I made the arrangements for tomorrow.'

I took my leave then and made my way out of the building. Some of the people looked at me as I passed but most of them didn't seem to notice me, or maybe they just didn't care that I was there.

I went back to my hotel that night and spoke to Jayden, Agua's father. I wanted to speak to him about the teleportation idea. Turns out it wasn't just a possibility. Apparently, he had teleported my father to different places all the time. Agua was capable of going short distances but wasn't strong enough yet for what I was asking. Jayden however informed me that it would be a pleasure to assist me in this new endeavour of mine.

This was great news that I could then tell both Jeremy and Colby on the phone. Colby was the happiest out of the two because it meant that it wouldn't fully affect my time with the pack. It would be like I had a day job and came home at night for the pack. It would take some changes but I was pretty sure it was going to work out. My father did both a day job and his alpha duties. Surely it would only take a bit of time to balance my pack and work life.

The next day I went downstairs expecting there to be news reporters again. Nothing. I went across the road and ate at the same buffet for breakfast. Still nobody bothered me. It wasn't until I go to work for the day that I knew where all my vultures went.

My access cards all worked nicely and got me through the gate and the processing centre without a cavity search, but I was met at the entrance to the office area by Kelly. She led me through to the boardroom where we sat down to talk.

I ended up speaking first. 'I have a family witch that is able to teleport me here and collect me when needed,' I told her.

She looked relieved. 'That's great,' she said. 'Because the higher ups didn't approve an off-site facility for you to work in.'

I felt the amusement cross through me. 'Were you thinking I would be upset at you?' I asked her.

'Maybe a little.' She smiled. 'I wasn't sure how you would react.' There was an awkward silence for a moment. 'Let me shows you to your workspace,' she said suddenly. 'Then we need to head to the auditorium.'

This place has an auditorium? I questioned silently.

Kelly led me to a glass-faced, empty office just a few doors down from the auditorium door. My name was on a little name plaque on the door. I looked around at the other offices. I could see one for each of the people I had met the other day – Kelly, Stephen, Collin and Zoe. There were also three more offices in the section, but none of them had names on them. All of them had clear class window on the side facing the boardroom walkway. The other three walls of each room were solid and white.

'We'll start loading your office with supplies later today,' Kelly told me. 'For now we need to make our way to the auditorium.'

I nodded. 'Okay, let's go then.'

She took me down multiple hallways until it felt like we were doubling back on ourselves and we came to a larger opened up hallway with several sets of double doors along one wall. One set of these doors were open and I could hear talking coming from inside.

This was where Kelly led me to, through the open doors and into a medium sized auditorium. It could probably have seated two-hundred people. There was a podium in front of the aisle that split the crowd of chairs and there were maybe fifty people there in total.

The podium didn't have anybody standing at it. On the stage was a long table that would seat ten people. All but two of those chairs were taken. Kelly led me to these and we took the remaining seats.

At the table I recognised the other department staff from the last couple of days. Then there was an unmistakeable face – Tobias Fletcher, the President of the United States of America. The other four people were unknown to me.

'Thank you for coming, Rya,' Stephen said into the microphone that sat in front of him on the table. Looking at the table in front of me I noticed that we all had one.

'Thank you for inviting me.' Not that I really had a choice. 'Would you like to catch me up to what we were talking about?'

'We were just advising our reporter audience here about the job we offered you and how you would now be working with us to make the community safer for all of America's citizens.'

'Ahhh,' I said. 'Well, please carry on.'

Stephen smiled and looked back to the crowd. 'As I was saying. Rya has agreed to take the time out of her schedule to help us build a sector of the Government dedicated to maintaining peace between the different species of America,' he said to the crowd. Looking through them, I could see a few of the reporters that had been hounding me for the last couple of days. This is where they all disappeared to this morning. 'This will entail helping us to write legislation for human and supernatural relations, providing us with access to potential research possibilities into using the technology that Rya and other werewolves can create to help make our lives easier.'

'Now,' Stephen continued, 'the senate has

compiled a list of questions that they want to ask Rya if she has the knowledge to answer them. Afterwards we will open the floor to the audience and you can come up to the podium to ask your own questions.' He looked at me. 'May I begin?'

I nodded. 'I will answer what I can,' I said into my microphone.

'You've talked many times about your pack,' Stephen said. 'We've seen the rough size of your pack to be maybe thirty of you. Is this the normal size for a werewolf pack?'

'My pack is quite small,' I answered. 'We have been through several years of difficulty where a lot of us were killed and we weren't having children. So we are definitely smaller than all the other werewolf packs.'

'How many werewolves are in a typical pack?'

I thought about it for a moment. 'City packs tend to have more than country packs, but usually at least fifty but I know one of the city packs have a couple of hundred werewolves.'

'How many werewolf packs are in America?'

'Unofficially, I have no clue,' I said. 'But there are twelve original werewolf packs.'

'What do you mean by original werewolf packs?' Stephen asked.

I took a sip of water from the water bottle in front of me. 'An original werewolf pack is one where the alpha is a descendant from the original werewolves. In this case they are a descendant of Lycaon from Ancient Greece.' I paused. 'The unofficial werewolf packs are quite often deserters or cast outs from the original packs. There could be any number of them and we cross paths from time to time. But usually don't bother one another.'

'You say that werewolves are from Greece,' Stephen said, picking at my answers. 'Why and when did werewolves come to America?'

'My ancestors were among the first to arrive in America when the Mayflower left England. We've been here since before America was even really America.' I paused to let that sink in. 'We fled Greece after we were cursed to be trapped in the form of a wolf. When we eventually arrived in England, we found a family of witches and they were able to lessen the curse to what we are now.'

'So it was a curse?' he asked.

I nodded. 'Yes,' I answered. 'The story goes that Lycaon wanted to make an offering to Zeus and thought Zeus would be appeased by a sacrifice. Zeus was angered and cursed him.' I don't know if it is true but that is what we are told as kids.'

'Yes, kids,' Stephen said. 'How are werewolves born, most myths and legends never specify a werewolf being born only being turned?'

'Well actually most werewolves are born. We rarely turn humans because of the danger it puts them and us in,' I answered. 'Bitten werewolves tend to be more vicious and can lose control easier than a born werewolf who has been prepared for the transformation from birth.'

'And how are werewolves born?'

'More typical of wolves actually. There is one season a year where female werewolves can become pregnant. Gestation is fast, lasting only for one moon cycle, so about a month,' I answered. 'If both parents are werewolves there is a high chance of the baby being a werewolf, and an even higher chance if the werewolves have older bloodlines,' I told them. 'If the mother is a human the baby will be human with maybe slightly better than normal senses. If the father is human than there is a pretty even chance for what the baby will be.'

'Do you ever offer to turn humans?'

'Sometimes,' I said. 'Usually we end up turning the human children once they've reached about fifteen, but that is their choice and they can choose to be human and we don't mind. Either way they are taught to defend themselves and are still prepared for the change if they choose to do it.' I took another sip of water. 'Humans we rarely turn. It's usually by accident and is usually someone who interacts with werewolves on a frequent basis, but there are exceptions and we do sometimes offer to turn human allies and partners.'

'How many werewolves would you say there are right now?' he asked.

I shrugged. 'I have no clue. Nobody keeps those kind of records. It's up to each individual pack to keep track of their own.'

'Now, there are vampires too?' he questioned. I nodded. 'Why do you hate each other?'

'Well, most vampires we meet try to kill us so we've just kind of learned to hate them,' I said. 'Though I did meet one recently and he was actually rather nice and he didn't try to eat me so I thought that was a win.'

'What about that other creature you've been fighting. What is he?'

'To be honest we don't fully know ourselves. We are still trying to figure it out,' I lied. I didn't want them to know what he was. 'Hopefully we will find out soon and we will be able to let you all know what we learn.' That probably wasn't going to happen.

'Okay,' Stephen said. 'That is pretty much all of the senate's questions.' He looked up and down the table. 'Do any of you have any questions?' None of them spoke. 'Right. Then we will move onto audience questions.'

There was a sudden scramble in the audience for all of the journalists to get to the panel as quickly as possible. 'Settle down everyone!' Tobias shouted. 'We have enough time for everyone to ask one question!'

The rest of the afternoon was spent answering questions for all the media representatives. Most of the questions were pretty typical, like, what do you eat, where do you live, just how dangerous can a werewolf be? Otherwise they were all pretty easy questions to answer. I honestly expected it to be much worse.

I told Stephen this when we finished up and all the reporters had left. He laughed. 'I told them that they could only be here if they left you alone. All interviews are now to be done through official channels.'

'Thank you,' I said. It really meant a lot that he did that.

He smiled at me. 'I can't promise they won't snap a picture if they see you though.'

I shrugged. 'I'll take what I can get.'

We were interrupted then.

'Miss Garcia.'

I turned around and found myself face to face with the President.

'President Fletcher?' I said. I hadn't expected him to speak to me. 'Please, call me Rya.'

He nodded. 'You can call me Tobias. It was lovely to hear that you decided to take on the job.'

'Yeah,' I said. 'I was very surprised by the job offer, considering my age. But I suppose I was the more likely candidate for you since I am the only alpha you know.'

'Yes, exactly,' Tobias answered. 'I'm sure there would be someone more qualified but I'm sure you will do the job well.'

'I will certainly do my best,' I answered. 'I am hoping that the rest of the werewolves will soon feel safe enough to bring themselves out into the open, but for now they are watching how this all turns out.'

We exchanged a few more pleasantries before Tobias was hurried away by the other people I didn't know. They were probably Government officials of some kind. I went back to my office to find it completely decorated. Complete with a picture of my own werewolf pack on the wall. I almost laughed. It was everyone including Agua and Jayden standing in front of the new house. This, more than anything, made me miss them so much.

'I got in contact with your town mayor and he was able to organise the picture for you.' I turned around to see Stephen leaning against my door frame. 'I thought you might like to have them here with you whenever you're working.'

'Thank you,' I said. That was really sweet of him to do, especially since we barely knew each other.

I looked through the rest of the things in my new office. There was an assortment of stationery and notebooks. There also seemed to be a task tray, I guess if they wanted me to do something then it would get some kind of notice in that tray.

I was shown how to log into my new email account and given details of the next meeting I needed to attend to but otherwise I was done for now and would be able to return home tomorrow. I started here full-time next week. I got weekends off unless necessary and I was given consideration for full and dark moons which I thought was really good of them to do.

That night I went to sleep in my hotel bed thinking about how excited I was to be returning home tomorrow. I was now feeling more sure of my decision to go through with this than I would have thought possible. I just hoped it didn't all blow up in my face.

My trip home the next day was uneventful. I didn't run in to any reporters trying to get my picture. I didn't run into any werewolves like I thought I would. I just had my stuff slung over my shoulders as I ran all the way home. I had more stuff now than when I had arrived in the city. It wasn't heavy, it was all just awkward to carry and keep a decent pace all the way back to Wolfridge.

When I reached the house it was to find it almost empty. The only person home was Diana who was cleaning the second floor today. I waved to her on my way up the stairs to my bedroom. Finally I dumped all my things exhaustedly onto my bed and collapsed onto the soft cloud of a mattress. The hotel mattress had been great but it wasn't as good as my own.

It was early afternoon so most of the pack wouldn't have been home for a couple of hours since they were all at work and school. I spent my time until then doing odd jobs that needed to be done. I called the school and organised to come in the next day and complete the SAT exams so I could finish high school early and more on to more important things.

I also made lists of things that I needed to do like

organise a few more sets of business-like attire and organise my schedule to allow for contact time with the pack each day. I left the house after writing out the list and went to the local store an purchased several sets of clothes that I deemed suitable for my new job. I took them home and packed them all safely away in the cupboard.

By the time I had gotten back the schoolies had come home. They weren't in the house but I could smell that they had passed through recently. I figured they had gone to the bunker to complete their daily training session. In the end I just kind of twiddled my thumbs hanging around the house. I was bored. This made me very glad that as of Monday I would have a lot of things to do to fill up my time.

That night at dinner everyone was jumping out of their seats to welcome me home after several days away. We had a delicious dinner of roasted meats with vegetables. It was delicious. Looking around the room I was surprised to see that everybody was eating vegetables. It wasn't so long ago that everyone was turning their noses up at them.

After dinner I spent some time with the pack in the rec room. I played a game of chess against Colby and versed Zac in his favourite racing car game on the PlayStation. Finally I took my leave for my room but ended up in my office with the door open.

It was surprising when I heard a knock on the door. 'Come in,' I said to Charlotte who stood at the open door.

She came in and closed the door behind her sitting down in the chair across from me. 'What can I do for you Charlotte?'

'Uhhh…' she started awkwardly. 'I was wanting to speak with you about turning Matthew.' Her human mate. 'We've been talking about it for a couple of years but I didn't want to ask Erik.'

'Does he want to be turned?' I asked.

She nodded. 'Yes. He asked me to marry him.'

That shocked me. All of a sudden, the new ring on her finger was very obvious. 'That's great!' I exclaimed. 'Congratulations.'

'Thank you,' she said. 'We were hoping we could start the process of transitioning him.'

'If he wants to, I see no issue with it,' I told her. 'You can start running him through the preparations. I would expect him to start integrating into the pack now.' I had seen him around a few times but otherwise he was still a bit of a stranger to me.

'That was the other thing I was going to ask,' she said. 'Can he move in here with us?'

I smirked. 'Of course.'

'Thanks, Rya, you're the best.' She hopped cheerfully out of her seat and back out the door.

I couldn't help but smile. Charlotte was getting married. She was going to turn him into a werewolf and we will get one more pack member. Things were starting to turn out very well for the pack right now. At some point I just knew the other shoe was going to drop.

*****

The next day I breezed through the SAT exams in the morning and returned to the house just after lunch to find Charlotte and Matthew moving boxes into the house.

'Hey, Matthew,' I said, walking over to them.

'Rya...' he said, walking up to give me a hug that I awkwardly returned. 'Thank you for letting me move in, and, you know, turn.'

'No problems,' I said. 'It's about time you were welcomed into the pack anyway. I won't lie though it will be difficult to start with.'

'I know,' he answered. 'Charlotte clued me in on the problems I could face. We will work through it.'

'Good to hear,' I said. 'Because I wouldn't be letting her do this if you weren't willing or if I thought you wouldn't be able enough.'

'It was my choice,' Matthew told me. 'I was the one that talked Charlotte around.'

'Oh,' I said, a little surprised by this piece of information.

I helped them out with moving the boxes up into Charlotte's room then went back to my office to see if there was anything to do. I spent maybe thirty minutes before I got bored and ventured down to the bunker.

Colby was at work but I found Lexi and Charlie doing some fight training together. It had been a while since I had practiced my fighting combat. Hopefully I wasn't rusty.

'Hey guys,' I said. 'Can I join you?'

*****

Before I knew it my first day of work came around. It felt kind of good to get up with a purpose. All I was doing was laying around the house and occasionally doing something, the pack had become more independent while I was gone. I had kind of lost track of things since I got back. Or maybe being alpha wasn't supposed to be crazy busy like I thought. Maybe I didn't have to micromanage everything.

Jayden met me in the foyer after I finished a breakfast of bacon and eggs and he teleported me to outside the front gates of The White House. I scanned my key card and the gate unlocked for me to enter. I closed it securely behind me; I didn't want to be the reason some crazy person got through the gate and tried to hurt the President.

To my surprise, my task tray was full of a stack of papers when I walked into my office. *No easing into it I see. Just throw me in the deep end.* Thankfully half of them were just memos about what was happening soon or what was happening in other departments.

My first task of the day was to help hire researchers for our research department. We needed a cryptozoologist, a technology specialist and a few generalised lab assistants. I had a pile of resumes on my desk for each position and had to go through and choose who would likely be successful. Unfortunately, I wasn't surprised to find Alec Hall's resume in the pile. I didn't even consider him, not after everything he had done to us. Once I had finished choosing several candidates for each position, I called them all and set up interview times, either by video call or in person, depending on where they were in the country.

After lunch I continued hacking away at the pile of jobs, first making sure nothing was urgent before going through each job individually. I didn't finish it all before the end of the day but I had a decent whack at it. I went home with a sense of accomplishment that I had never had before, like I had actually achieved something.

My life up until now had been a continuous cycle of going to school, where I remained unchallenged through the work they gave me, and the cycle of abuse I endured at home. Besides actively training the younger werewolves, there had never really been anything that I needed to do in my life.

That night I was able to go home knowing that I was working towards making the world a safer place for supernaturals to come out of the dark and that felt really empowering to me. Hopefully, someday soon, I would be able to tell all the werewolf packs that it was safe to reveal themselves.

Jayden picked me up from the same place he had left me at and took me through what I thought would be funny to imagine as my own personal black hole. I dropped my things off to the house and went down to the bunker to flex my muscles and exercise after sitting at a desk all day.

When it finally came to rolling into bed that night, I was exhausted. I had spent some time with the pack in the rec room but eventually I went up to my office to sort through a few things for the following day. I had told the pack that I would have my door open each night before bed if anybody wanted to talk to me. This was my way of giving them a chance to come speak to me as their alpha each day if needed.

That night nobody came into my office. I didn't

expect someone to come see me every day but I knew that there would be days this was needed so I wanted to make sure that they knew I was here. Instead I closed my office door and crawled into bed, glad more than ever that I had decided to leave school.

That first week in the new job had me constantly trying to get on top of the jobs that kept getting put in front of me. I needed to outline the laws and expectations that the council had in place for werewolves. These got sent to Stephen who wanted to review them before talking about what we wanted to put in place officially.

I also conducted the interviews for the job positions. The cryptozoology interviews were the worst. The candidates spent half the interview gushing about the fact that they knew werewolves were real. Only one of them didn't do this. To be honest the rest annoyed me enough that I didn't want to hire any of them to work with every day. I didn't want to put up with that, and they thought they knew everything.

When I told Stephen why I had chosen the particular candidate he laughed heartily. This drew the attention of the rest of the department and before long we were all laughing at my decision. But really, the person, Naomi, she had a doctorate in the study of myths and legends and spent her time looking for proof of the legends or at least the reason they were formed. She was more than qualified for the job they wanted from her, anything else she could learn on the job.

The rest of the positions weren't as annoying to fill. The people I was hiring weren't deeply in love with the idea of werewolves actually being real. In fact several of them were quite sure that I wasn't real and it was all some kind of elaborate prank. I would show them at some point, at least the ones I hired anyway.

With that job done by mid-week I spent a lot of time working on the new laws with Stephen. The one thing I had to get him to change was the reasoning behind certain laws. Like there was a law about a werewolf killing a human or even another werewolf. I needed to make sure there was a clause in there that didn't condemn the person for the actions if it wasn't in their control. Like being baited, trapped or hurt in some way. We ended up going back and forward several times.

There was also the discussion of werewolf containment if they did break a law. I didn't want the werewolves to be held by the government, they would be out of our reach and we wouldn't be able to do anything to stop them from taking advantage of the werewolf in captivity. Instead we compromised, well, more like I forced upon them, that the Wolfen Council would deal with the werewolves in cases involving werewolves and humans would be able to witness the sentence. That also meant incarceration and rehabilitation was up to us as well.

This opened up several job opportunities for werewolves as well, because who better to handle werewolves than werewolves. At the end of the week

I reported all of this to Jeremy. He seemed quite interested in these developments and wanted to be kept informed.

That was the scope of my job for that first week. I fell into the regular pattern of getting up at a certain time using the alarm on my phone, hitching a ride to work with Jayden, doing a day's work, then coming home for dinner and spending time with the pack before finishing the night in my office to see if anybody wanted to talk to me.

It was on Friday night that someone actually came to my office to talk to me. It was Zac.

'Hey. Is there something you want to talk about?' I asked him, taking an alpha front rather than his girlfriend. I knew that if he was coming to see me during this time that it was alpha me that he wanted to speak to.

He closed the door behind him and sat down in the chair across from me. I waited patiently. He would speak when he was ready.

'I feel lost,' he said suddenly into the silent room.

'How so?' I asked, prodding him for more.

He took a deep breath in. 'I've spent a lot of time over the summer working on getting better at being a werewolf and learning more about this new part of me but I don't know what I'm doing.' He seemed to say it all so fast I had to focus really hard to keep up. 'When I was human, I knew what I wanted to do. I wanted to get a soccer scholarship and go to college and I would figure out the rest when I got there. But now that I'm not human anymore I can't do that. It would be unfair and I don't know what I want to do and I don't know what I can do and now I don't know what I'm supposed to do anymore. I feel like I'm losing my connections to being human and everything I liked when I was human...'

I waited several moments after he finished to make sure he had finished what he had to say, but also to figure out how best to answer. It definitely wasn't an easy first meeting for me.

'You're right. You can't play soccer professionally anymore. You're not human anymore and unfortunately that has and probably will continue to change your life as you get older.' I told him. 'But you need to realise that your friends aren't going anywhere. Dylan and Sean certainly aren't they've been by your side since you became a werewolf from what I've seen. Even Jace, as much as he annoys me, he's still there hanging out with you and helping to keep you connected to your humanity.

'Being a werewolf is harder for a bitten,' I said. 'And you didn't even get to choose to be one. It helps a lot knowing that you asked for it and knowing what you're getting yourself into.' I sighed, thinking. 'I suppose the best thing for us to do to start with is figure out what you want to do after school,' I stated. 'Do you want to join one of the pack jobs or take a different avenue and contribute to our pack and the town in another way?' He seemed confused. 'You can choose to have a pack job, like security, training even a warrior. Toby's parents work security for the pack but also do paid jobs when needed in town. The other option is getting a human, day job,' I told him. 'You can go to college or learn a trade and do whatever it is you want to do.'

'I can still go to college?' he asked.

'Of course you can,' I said. 'We aren't short on money for tuition. We do have preferences for the colleges you go to because we know people and have houses nearby for these colleges for werewolves, but you might get put in a house with another werewolf from another pack going to the same school.'

'I think that would be okay,' he said.

I nodded. 'Most werewolves go to Princeton, Yale and NYU. Princeton is more common for our pack because it is on our home turf but no alpha would have an issue with you joining their pack while you're in college.'

'But what if I want to go to a different college?' he asked.

'I...' I thought about it for a moment. 'I guess we would look into that,' I said. 'You can do pretty much anything you want. Max's mum, Miranda, is a doctor. She says that she has learned the scent of different diseases in the human body and she is able to detect things a lot easier. It really all depends on what you decide to do.'

He seemed thoughtful. 'I will have a think about it.'

I smiled. 'Let me know and we can organise your application together and send it off to one of our contacts to get you where you want to go.' He nodded, got up and left the office, leaving the door open before he went back down the stairs.

I had just settled back into my chair when there was a knock on the door. I looked up to see Damien at the door.

'Come in,' I said, waving wearily before sitting up

straight. I was really tired. It had been a busy week. 'How's it going Damien?'

'Yeah, pretty good,' he said. 'I just wanted to chat to you about my place in the pack.'

I felt my defences go up. I knew he had 'stood in' while I was gone and helped Colby run things. Was he going to challenge me?

'What about it?' I asked.

'I mean…' he started. 'I just haven't really found a role to play in the pack and I don't know where I would fit.'

'Well, did you ever get fully initiated?' I asked. He shook his head. 'Then you never would have finished your training. I suppose it depends on what you want to do in the pack. You can be a fighter, we could use more, but you would have to train under one of them like Toby until you are fully in the rank. Or you can find another way to help out.'

'Like what?' he asked.

I shrugged. 'You could be a teacher,' I said. 'Be some support in the school environment. Kind of like I was before I left. That position will be open with Toby and Agua graduating this year.' I thought about it some more. 'Even medicine. I'm sure Miranda would love the help when we severely hurt ourselves in vampire skirmishes.'

'I think I could be the teacher,' he said. 'Sarah was a pre-med student when I met her so she would be more suited to that position.'

'Do you want me to get you guys set up for the college courses?' I asked.

'Sure,' he said. 'Where are you thinking?'

'Did Sarah finish her pre-med?' he nodded. 'Cool. If she can get me the transcripts I can sign you both up to Yale. They have a good med school there and a good education department too. It is really close to New York, so you could probably stay there while you finish studying..' Not so far away that they wouldn't be able to get home.

He nodded. 'With everything that's going on I guess it is best to stay close.' I nodded.

We engaged in small talk for a little while before he left to turn in for the night. I thought I should do the same when Toby came in just as I was about to leave the office. Tired, but wanting to be open I sat down to listen to him.

'I'm starting to think about what I want to do next year after…'

'Oh my god,' I interrupted. 'Did somebody suddenly go and tell you all to choose a career today?'

*****

I was so happy to not wake up to an alarm the next day. I had been up late into the night talking to Toby about the different things he could choose to do once he left school next year. Since he was already doing training for the fighting faction, he would do that most of the time but he also needed something for him to do when fighting wasn't needed. It did mean that whatever he was going to do, he needed to study nearby so he could continue his training.

The next morning I woke up feeling an itch to run and hunt. It had been a while since I'd hunted. Now that we had food cooked for us every day we didn't really need to hunt outside the full moon.

I also hadn't really stretched my wolf form out since the full moon. So when I went downstairs that morning it felt so nice to transform and stretch out all four of my canine limbs and feel my inner wolf embrace me with contentment as her mind merged with mine.

After a nice stretch, I pushed off the ground with my hind legs and propelled myself into the trees. I ran fast. The branches brushing through my fur. I could feel my tongue lolling out of my mouth like a puppy as the wind blasted my face. This was what I missed – the exhilaration, the freedom. It was all just so blissful as I raced easily through the forest, winding around trees using my tail to guide my movements.

I didn't stop running until I smelled the deer. Then I veered towards their musky scent, following it. I didn't even stop when I reached them. I took barely a second to glance around the herd before I attacked the weak link. He was an old buck with large antlers. I managed to get him by only just avoiding his attempted defence. He was dead before his body hit the ground.

I walked around the carcass choosing where to start my meal. Finally deciding on a leg I sank my teeth into the flesh and pulled away the skin and muscle to consume the prize of my hunt.

I sensed it when Zac came wandering up behind me. When he reached me he sank his teeth into the flesh of my kill and ate some of the meat. I laid down and waited for him to finish, noticing the slow progression of a pair of coyotes at the edge of my vision.

Zac came and sat down beside me and we watched silently as the scavengers slowly prowled closer and closer to the waiting meal. In the end they wouldn't eat it while we laid there so I got up and started to walk away but Zac stopped me, transforming into human, almost instinctually I did the same. He grabbed my hand and pulled me closer, pressing his lips gently to mine before pushing me back towards the large oak tree that stood behind me. I felt myself wince as the bark scraped my back but I forced myself to deal with it. Then I grabbed Zac by the shirt that had come out of his clothes bracelet and pushed him up against the tree that had been behind me only moments before.

That weekend and the dark moon that came with it on Sunday passed quickly. I enjoyed my time off knowing that I would be back to work first thing on Monday. I had an allowance for sick days around the dark moon but I didn't think I should take them. Heading in later than normal was okay to me though.

When I did show up at work that morning it was to an incredibly surprised team. It was a full team today too, we had all of our research staff on board now. I brushed off their surprise and went to my office. I had already had food that morning. Our chef's had given us a very meaty breakfast that consisted of bacon and raw steaks. I had mentioned that this was best on dark moon days.

I may have eaten but I was still tired from the night that had just passed. Charlotte's mate Matthew had made the final transition to werewolf last night; quite successfully too. Now it was up to Charlotte to train him up and get him used to his new abilities. We also spent a bit of time this morning welcoming him to the pack officially now that he had turned.

I took a sip of my coffee. I was starting to rely on this hot drink each morning to get me started. It was not a great habit for me to get into, but then I never thought I would be sitting here working a desk job either. Coffee is the only thing that made the long day of sitting down bearable. Not that I didn't like the work, I would just prefer to move around more.

I had a meeting first up that morning. I had barely sat down to look through my jobs for the day before Stephen came in and said for me to come to the meeting, since I was here. I nodded at him and he left in the direction of the boardroom. I followed him with my coffee in hand.

'What are you doing here today Rya?' Collin asked me. 'You look half asleep.'

I felt it. 'I just haven't slept yet.' I yawned. 'I used to go to school the day after the dark moon all the time. This is just my first in a while having to do that.' They had been on weekends a lot recently, meaning we could sleep through the morning.

'You don't actually have to be here,' Stephen said. 'You can go home and sleep.'

'I'll be fine once I get moving,' I told him. 'So what's on the meeting agenda today?'

They seemed to want to discuss me going home further, but in the end Stephen looked at the piece of paper on the table in front of him. 'We have our first progress meeting coming up soon,' he said. 'We need to think of some projects to work towards in our research department but also what we want to do to help inform the greater community what we are doing and also communicate our goals.'

'That's all, huh?' I said flatly. I saw a few smiles at my bluntness. 'What do you guys want to study to do with werewolves?' I asked.

There was silence for several moments. 'What about health implications?' Naomi suggested.

'What do you mean?' Stephen asked.

'Well, werewolves heal really fast don't they?' I nodded. 'Maybe we can see what implications that will have to help human health and healing.'

'We could do that,' I agreed. 'We haven't really been able to look into this field of research ourselves because we didn't have many humans that knew about us.' I frowned. 'It would have to be a male werewolf's blood though.'

'Why?' Jenny, the assistant, asked. 'We have you already.'

'Because my blood would just turn a human into a werewolf and we don't want that.' I told her. 'The werewolf it created would be really out of control too. That kind of way to be turned is really dangerous and the humans that do survive the transition will find it really hard to control their wolf.'

'Oh,' Jenny responded quietly.

'It's okay though,' I said. 'I can easily get my hands on some blood samples.'

'Really?' she said perking up again.

I nodded, slightly amused. 'Benefits of being an alpha. I usually get what I ask for.'

'How would we know it's real werewolf blood though?' Naomi said. 'Nobody has ever seen a sample of werewolf blood.'

'You can be there when it is drawn if you really want,' I told her. 'Everyone gets pretty busy though so I will have to work out a time for a few of them to give the sample and for our doctor to actually take it. I don't know my way around more than a first aid kit and a needle.'

'I would be more than happy to be there, even drawing it myself if you are unable to get your doctor in for it,' she said.

I shrugged. 'Sure.' It would be easier if she did it, at least then I wouldn't have to work around everyone's schedules. 'I will ask for volunteers tonight when I get home.'

'Are there any other research ideas?' Stephen opened up to the table.

They seemed to think about it. 'What about...' Jesse, the other assistant we hired stuttered when we all looked at him. 'What about a lifestyle look into werewolves?' he asked.

'You mean a study into how we live?' I asked.

He nodded. 'Like maybe somebody shadows you and your pack and takes notes on how werewolves live. It might normalise it all a bit.'

'Normally I would be okay with that,' I said. 'But we're in a more delicate part of the year right now and it's probably not the best time for unknown human visitors.'

That just made the cryptozoologist curious. 'What time of year?' she asked enthusiastically.

'Breeding season,' I answered bluntly. 'Until the full moon it is possible for female werewolves to become pregnant.' An awkward silence followed my response. 'It would be a bit strange to have an outsider staying with us during that month,' I added to the silence.

'What about after that?' Stephen asked.

I shrugged. 'I would have to check if everyone is okay with it first, but I see no issue with it at a later time.'

'That's great,' Stephen said. 'That's then two projects for us to be working on. One social and one scientific.'

'What about my area?' Jordan said. He was our technology specialist.

'What would you like to do?' I asked. 'What interests you to do with werewolves that you can do with technology?'

He seemed to think long and hard about his answer. 'Is there anything that I can build that would be useful for werewolves?'

I shrugged. 'I'm not sure,' I answered. 'I only designed these a few months ago.' I said slipping the bracelet off my wrist and hand it to him. 'They serve as a kind of storage system for our clothes so when we become human, we aren't completely naked.'

'Where do the clothes actually go though?' Jordan asked.

'We kind of mixed technology and magic for this one,' I admitted. 'The magic provides a pocket for the clothes to disappear into while the program we loaded into it assesses the change in the body and signals the magic to activate.'

'That's pretty cool,' he said turning it over in his hand. 'You designed it?'

I nodded. 'Is there anything that you could think to do that would have some benefit to either werewolves or humans?'

'I will probably think of something,' he said. 'Can I

have access to the magic for projects?' he asked.

'Depends on the project,' I answered. 'Bring me the ideas and I will consider the magic side of it.'

We spent the rest of the meeting discussing the things we would need to organise our projects before we all went back to our own office spaces. The researchers were off to write up research proposals for the progress meeting to be approved and I was sending messages to a few of the werewolves in the pack that would be able to help with blood. I ended up getting a couple of different kinds of blood for them. There would be mine, an alpha's blood, Mira's a normal female werewolf's blood. Then I also organised for both a born and a bitten male werewolf to donate blood too.

By the end of the day I was ready to curl up into a ball and go to sleep. I nearly did fall asleep once or twice. I had felt myself dozing off while trying to read an email on my computer and I had definitely nodded off for a few minutes during lunch when I put my head on the table.

When I got home, I was ready for bed but I knew I had to organise everything for the next few days. But more than that I also needed to allow for alpha contact time if anyone needed it.

I sat in the office and waited leaning back in my comfortable chair. Slowly I felt myself drifting to sleep. I tried to fight it and keep my eyes open but my mind was soon enveloped in sleep and I was pulled into unconsciousness.

*****

I woke up the next morning with my head on my desk with a piece of paper stuck to my face, I swiped it off with my hand as I sat up. Looking around I saw that the door was still wide open and everything was the way it had been the night before. When exactly did I fall asleep? Did anybody come looking to talk to me and found me sleeping? I hope they didn't.

I lifted myself out of the chair and went through the closed door on my right that connected to my bedroom. Despite sleeping in a chair all night I felt quite rested. I jumped in the shower and gave made myself clean before I even looked at the time. Ten o'clock. Shit. I was really late. I threw on some of my work clothes, brushed my hair, then practically ran down the stairs.

When I made it downstairs it was to find Colby and Jayden walking out of his office. 'Hey, sleepy head,' Colby said cheerfully. I just kind of groaned in his general direction, which just made him laugh. 'We decided to let you sleep,' Colby said. 'You've been working too hard lately.' I opened my mouth to argue. 'Don't worry, we already called in to let them know you would be running late. Pack emergency.'

I sighed, the stress leaving me a little. 'That means I have time for food then.' They probably shouldn't have lied for me but I did need that extra sleep.

I went into the dining hall and through to the kitchen. The kitchen staff had already gone home for the rest of their morning but on the bench I found a plate of food, wrapped in food wrap with a note on it. *Rya's*, it said.

I grabbed the plate and unwrapped it. I couldn't

help but smile. The plate was full of my usual breakfast favourites, all ready to be cooked. I put the plate in the microwave and zapped it for a few minutes until I could hear it sizzling. I sat down on the stool at the bench and stuffed my face. It was nice that they remembered to put some aside for me when I didn't come in, or maybe they were asked to do it. I don't care. Somebody did something nice for me and I appreciated it.

When I was done, I washed up my plate and put it in the drying rack next to the sink. On the note I grabbed a pen a wrote a quick *Thanks*. Then I went searching for Jayden to help me make the trip to work.

When he left me in front of the gate, I went across the road to the coffee house I always went to before work. It was almost empty now though. The barista saw me from where she was cleaning and went straight to the coffee machine while the cashier came up to ring up my order. I smiled at them both as I scanned my debit card and collected my coffee that was made lightning quick.

Entering the office I got looks as I walked through the hallway. It had probably spread that I had some unavoidable pack emergency. I had no idea what I would say if someone asked.

'Morning Rya,' Kelly said as I walked past her open office door. I responded in kind.

I sat down and started going through my files. Then something that never happened. My phone rang. Like an external phone call. The sound made me jump it was so loud. I hesitated for a moment, before picking it up. 'Good morning, you're speaking with

Rya,' I said formally.

'Hey, Rya.' It was Jeremy's voice.

'Hey,' I said, careful not to say his name. 'What's going on?' If he was calling me here, instead of my mobile, he needed something.

'Not too much. How is the work going?' he asked seriously.

I told him all about the projects we would be working on and what we were planning to do with the new government department. I ended with telling him about how one or two of the people here would be staying with my pack for a month after breeding season to make a kind of documentary on the general werewolf lifestyle.

'That sounds like this was a really good idea to go ahead with then,' Jeremy commented.

I nodded. 'I really think it is,' I assured him. 'I don't think we have anything to worry about.'

'When do you think it would be safe to reveal ourselves to the public?' Jeremy asked seriously.

'To be completely honest I would start now,' I told him. 'The longer we wait the more it looks like we have something to hide, but maybe don't all come out at once,' I advised quickly. 'We don't want to scare anyone.'

'Noted,' He said. 'I think I will introduce my pack to the world then. How do you think I should approach it?'

I thought for a moment. 'Maybe a press conference,' I suggested. 'We could organise one through our department and it will get the desired coverage, plus we will have control over how it happens.'

'I will leave you to plan it then,' Jeremy said. 'Keep me posted about when it is so I can make the time for it.'

I nodded. 'Of course. Talk soon.' I put the phone back on the holder.

'Who did you talk to that made you so serious?' I looked up startled to see Stephen standing at my open office door.

I grabbed my coffee a took a large sip. 'The head of the Wolfen Council,' I told him. 'He wanted to know if I trust the operations going on here.'

'And do you?' he asked curiously.

I nodded. 'For the most part. I can tell that everyone here is trying to make things work for the better. I would be able to tell if anyone wasn't being truthful about their motives.'

'What was that about a press conference?' he asked.

Might as well tell him, I was going to go see him about it anyway. 'He was wondering what would be the best way to introduce each werewolf pack to the public.'

'And you think press conference?'

I nodded. 'That way we can be in a controlled environment where people the reporters can ask questions. We want to do this without scaring people. There are a lot of us and we all live fairly close together.'

'How close?'

'This pack is right here in Washington.' I told him.

'Really?' he asked, completely excited. Then he realised that I read his excitement. 'Sorry,' he said, containing himself. 'I always loved reading supernatural books when I was a teen. I still get excited knowing that it is all real.'

'Big foot is a hoax,' I said cheekily. 'I think.'

He laughed. 'You think?'

'Ehh.' I shrugged. 'Anything's possible.'

'I think a press conference will be a great way to introduce the werewolf population to the world,' he said. 'We can use the same conference to release the statistics and data we record in the lead up as well.'

I nodded. 'Sounds like a plan.'

I spent the rest of the day organising the date and time for the conference and also an agenda of our discussions for the day. While I was doing it, I came up with an idea for the conference and spoke to Stephen. He liked the idea so I contacted Jeremy afterwards. He liked it too so he handled some of the organising of that part and I organised my part for each of them.

I went home that day feeling like we were going to make a difference in a week's time. Naomi came home with me and Jayden that night. She did not take the black hole very well. Vomiting on the grass outside the foyer. 'How do you stand that?' she asked.

I shrugged. 'You get used to it.'

'I do not want to get used to that,' she said flatly.

'That's okay,' I said. 'Next time you come here you'll be able to drive. Come on, let's get this done before dinner.'

I expanded my mind out through the house and called to each of the werewolves who had agreed to give blood for the research. I asked them to meet me on the laboratory level of the bunker.

Once Naomi was feeling a bit better, we went inside and past the delicious aromas that were coming out of the dining hall and into the noisy rec room. Everyone was talking, reading or playing games like usual at this time.

I nodded to Jayden and he covered Naomi's eyes while I opened the gate to the bunker. She knew this was going to happen so she didn't panic. I grabbed her by the wrist and led her down the stairs. Once we were down and the entranced sealed over Jayden allowed Naomi to see again.

I nodded for her to follow me as I started off down the tunnel, Jayden stayed behind and when he disappeared out of sight, I heard him open the fireplace again and return to the rec room. The journey to the bunker was a lot longer with a human. I usually set a fast walk by my standards, but even Namoi's fast walk was slower than my casual one.

When we finally reached the bunker, I heard Namoi gasp at the sight of our training facility. Since there was no one using it right now the lights were off but the room was slightly illuminated by the light coming from the staircase to our right.

I took her down the several floors and into the lab. They were chatting when we got there. Zac, Toby, Mira. I think they were talking about their training. It was great to see Zac fitting into the pack these days. For a while I thought they wouldn't accept him so easily.

I already had the room set up for the blood draws. There were vials and needles ready to go. 'Is there anything else you need?' I asked.

She went through the supplies I had laid out for her yesterday. 'No, I think this will do the job.'

Each of the werewolves went through the blood draw; first Toby and Mira then Zac. Each of them had three vials drawn for use in the different studies we would probably do. This saved us coming back for more so soon.

Zac was the newest of them and his wolf didn't take to kindly to being stabbed in the arm with a needle. I saw his eyes flash the moment it entered his skin and all three of us rushed to his side. Toby and Mira grabbed him by the shoulders and pushed him down. I grabbed him around the neck and pulled his head back to the chair, covering his mouth with my hand.

He struggled a bit but with Toby holding his arm down Naomi was able to draw the three vials of blood with ease. She removed the needles and backed away from the struggling werewolf.

'It's okay,' I whispered in Zac's ear, too low for Naomi to hear. 'It's all done. It's okay. You're safe.'

At my words I felt Zac's wolf relax and slowly it stopped struggling. When Zac finally relaxed under my hands I nodded to the others and we let him go. After a few deep breaths Zac wiped the sweat from his forehead and took Toby's offered hand.

'That was fun,' he stated sarcastically. We laughed. Naomi didn't.

Still smiling I grabbed the vials of Zac's blood off her and labelled them all. *Bitten.* My turn. It was over so quickly that I barely had a chance to feel it. Three vials of blood that got labelled *Alpha*. Mira and Toby's also went went through without out and issue and getting labelled, *female* and *born* respectively.

We all went back up the stairs now that this job was done. I fell back to walk next to Zac. Grabbing his hand and holding it supportively. *'Are you okay?'* I asked silently.

He nodded. *'Just haven't had that really happen before.'*

'It can be a lot the first time the wolf tries to take control,' I agreed.

When we got to the end of the tunnel Toby covered Naomi's eyes and Mira opened the doorway. Toby and I took Naomi all the way back out to the foyer before we allowed her to see again.

Jayden was waiting for us. Naomi looked unhappy about teleporting again but she allowed the witch to grab her by the wrist, the box of blood-filled vials under her other arm. We arrived back at the office. We deposited them into the safe that had a camera watching it at all times and we left. Naomi for home and I went back into the abyss of my black hole.

The week leading up to the press conference was a busy one. We had to organise people to come in and we didn't tell them what they were coming for. They just knew that they would want to be there.

I spent a lot of my time making plans and writing out what we were going to say to everyone. Jeremy even came into the office the morning of the conference to meet and go through everything with me and make any changes if he chose to. We were there early for that so there was nobody else there to interrupt or gawk at the much more alpha looking werewolf.

We were just finishing up going through everything when Stephen arrived. He walked past my office, seemed to do a double take before taking several steps back and looking through the glass at us. Our relation was pretty unmistakeable, same golden yellow eyes and light, dirty-blonde hair that every Garcia werewolf had - we weren't really sure why that was our dominant trait.

'Morning Stephen,' I said, breaking him out of his shock.

'Who's this?' he asked.

Jeremy stood up and held his hand out to Stephen.

'Jeremy Garcia,' he said. 'Alpha of the werewolf pack here in Washington and a distant cousin of Rya's.' He looked at me. 'It is still so weird to say out loud to a human,' he commented to me. 'Does that get easier?'

I nodded. 'I'm used to it now, but then pretty much everybody knows who I am. Benefit of being the first werewolf to be fully discovered I guess.'

The two men shook hands and Jeremy sat back down.

'So, you're the head of the werewolf council?' Stephen asked.

Jeremy nodded. 'I was elected when Rya's father and mother passed away. It was a shame. Their deaths were felt in all of our packs.'

I smiled grimly. 'How are Aunty Lea, Nana and Pa?' I asked him. 'My mum was born into Jeremy's pack before she met my father on one of his council duties.' I explained to Stephen in response to his confusion.

'They've been really good,' Jeremy told me, seeming to ignore my last comment. 'They were really worried about you when you went missing.'

'I wish I'd had the chance to catch up with them the last time I stayed at your place,' I said. 'I barely saw them.'

'You can come visit soon,' Jeremy told me. 'I'm sure we will meet as a council again soon. Stay for a few extra days. You and Zac are always welcome.'

Stephen made up some excuses to go do things and left Jeremy and I to continue talking about family and the press conference. All of the others did a double take like Stephen had when they saw Jeremy.

Introductions were made and pleasantries exchanged until we were nearing the arrival the reporters.

About half an hour before the start of the conference Jeremy and I went out of the gate and to the coffee house across the street. We sat down with our coffees at a large table and waited.

One by one, werewolves started entering the café and silently sitting down at the table. There were no mates today, just the Garcia's – a family reunion if you will. There weren't many people in the café but the ones that were barely looked at the occasional person coming to sit down with us. We didn't talk verbally so it didn't get noticed when I filled everyone in.

When finally all twelve alpha werewolves were in attendance we stood up and walked out of the building together and across the street. I took them to processing. Apologising to the security guards that stared at the werewolves like they had had enough of checking people in to the premises that morning.

I waited while everyone was checked and sent over to me at the other end of the processing building. Once they were all done, I took them across the grounds to the now crowded auditorium. We took the back door into the building to allow the alphas a sneaky entrance without being seen before we wanted them to be.

Once I had them waiting on some chairs backstage, I ducked out from behind the curtain to join Stephen on the stage at the lectern. The rest of our team sat at the table behind us. This table was long enough for all the alphas to sit at once it was time.

To be honest I was kind of nervous about this. Even though it wasn't live, the alphas of the werewolf packs around America have never publicly been in the same place at once. We had made sure that it wasn't live on anyone's station. We wanted to be sure that we were safe from any supernatural threats – mostly Michael.

Once the crowd quieted down, Stephen spoke into the microphone. 'Thank you for coming everyone,' he said. 'We know we have been a bit secretive to the nature of this conference but that is due to the immediate safety of the people involved. I will now pass you on to Rya Garcia who will be talking to us for the rest of today.' He put a soft hand of encouragement on my shoulder before he went to sit down at the table with the rest of our team.

I took a deep breath and began. 'Thank you for letting us organise this press conference for today, Stephen. I know even you don't know too much about what we're going to talk about.'

I turned to address the rest of the crowd. 'Over the past couple of weeks I took a position here in the new sector of the government that is dedicated to learning about and being allies with the werewolf community. They approached me because in your eyes I am a leader of my people. That isn't entirely true,' I said. 'I am an alpha of a werewolf pack, just one werewolf pack.'

'There are eleven other werewolf packs in America that are governed by their own alpha and have their own territories that they live on. Each pack alpha is responsible for the protection and growth of the land and towns that reside in their territory,' I continued. Everyone's eyes were fixed on me. 'We do that by making sure other supernatural creatures don't come in and hurt people. We make sure the people have what they need to survive the harsher seasons. In my own father's case it was take up the mantle of town mayor and help make the town more profitable, helping the citizens on a more business level.

'But we don't answer only to ourselves. We follow the laws that everyone abides by. We have our own laws and our own consequences for breaking these laws. Each of the alphas of the werewolf packs in America form our own kind of government. We call this the Wolfen Council. Between us a single alpha is elected as the head of our council and takes up the mantle of the alpha of alphas. To us they are named Lupa or Lupus, depending on their gender.'

'Today we want to introduce to you our council that have decided that it is time for the rest of the werewolf community to come out into the open.' I turned to look behind me and I could see them waiting. 'First up is Reina, alpha of the werewolf pack in Orlando.' Reina came walking out from backstage. 'Jarrod, alpha of Atlanta. Harry, alpha of New York City. Zira, from Chicago.' I went through the entire group of alphas and they all came out and sat down at the table behind me as I said their name. 'And finally...' I said. 'Our alpha of alphas or Lupus as his title, Jeremy, alpha of the werewolf pack right here in Washington.'

'For each of these twelve werewolf packs we have set up an email address to contact their local alpha if there are any concerns about supernatural activity in the area. Or even just a curious question or two and they will try to get back to you as soon as they can.'

I stopped and looked around the small crowd of people. They were furiously writing things down in their notebooks while their cameramen recorded every word I was saying. 'You might be wondering why we wanted to open up to the world in this way,' I said. 'This is because over the last few weeks since taking this job I have been assessing whether it was actually safe for the rest of our community to come out into the open. I have been reporting back to Jeremy on my findings and, as a council, we decided that it was time to open up.'

'It was my idea to open up to everyone this way as I felt that it was easier to announce where the werewolf packs are and who you can ask if you have any problems in your area rather than introduce one pack at a time.'

'We are now going to open up the floor for any questions you would like to ask of our council,' I said. I finally moved away from the lectern and took my own seat at the end of the of the long table.

Like last time, there was a kind of fight over the line at the podium that stood in front of the crowd. We spent the rest of the conference answering any questions that the reporters had for us, none of them overly exciting. The last question was from Caroline, the reporter that had tried to corner me in the café when I had first stayed here in Washington. 'What is a werewolf pack's day to day life like?' she asked. 'I mean, I'm sure you guys do mostly normal stuff like we do but is there anything that is different?'

I indicated silently to the other alphas that I would answer that one. 'It's a bit funny that you should ask that particular question, Caroline,' I said. She seemed to beam when I said her name. 'Our Cryptozoologist was asking those same questions when we first signed her on to work with us and we were going to announce that Naomi will be staying with my pack for a few weeks to report on the lifestyle of a smallish werewolf pack. Ours would be more interesting too, since we are still finding our feet after having our pack in a rough spot for several years.' I looked at the other alphas. 'Perhaps at some point there can be a study on a larger and more established werewolf pack. Since I'm still finding my feet as an alpha, we are a bit unorganised in Wolfridge at the moment.'

There were a few chuckles at my comment. 'So thank you all for coming,' I said into the microphone on the table in front of me. 'That's all we have time for tod…' I broke off as I sensed the change in the air.

Without thinking I grabbed Jeremy and pulled us both to the ground. Not even seconds later, a shiny silver dagger protruded from the cushion of Jeremy's chair. There was a big kerfuffle as werewolves got to their feet and humans scurried away from the vampires that had appeared in the auditorium.

I only had my eyes on one person though. Michael. He was the one who had thrown the dagger. I wasn't the only one that transformed then, every single one of the alpha werewolves transformed into what looked like the same white wolf but in different sizes.

I ignored the horde of vampires that Michael had created since our last meeting and went straight for him. I was focused, but he just seemed to ignore me. When I grabbed onto his arm with my teeth I tore at the skin. He grabbed me by the muzzle and pried my teeth apart, then he threw me easily across the room. I crashed into several rows of now empty chairs, the reporters had all scurried out of the way and retreated to the back of the auditorium.

When I managed to get myself back on my feet it was to see that Michael had grabbed the dagger from the chair and was looking around the room at the white werewolves that fought his dying troops.

I saw him lock eyes with Jeremy. Why was he so set on Jeremy? How did he even find out that we were all here? Again, he ignored me, throwing me aside like a ragdoll. I crashed into the wall. Jeremy's attention wavered from Michael as he was attacked by another vampire.

I galloped across the room as fast as I could, colliding with Michael from the side and knocking him to the ground just as he reached Jeremy. I looked down menacingly into the glowing red eyes of the hybrid below me.

He moved, I moved. Before I could close my fangs around his throat, I felt a sharp pain. Then he disappeared. I fell to the ground without his body beneath me, pain ripping through my body and causing me to turn back to human form.

I looked down at my torso. There was thick, red blood soaking through my shirt from the wound just below my ribcage. I put my hand on it to stop the bleeding and looked around the room.

I saw Michael materialise behind Jeremy, then watched as the blade was plunged into his back before the werewolf even had a chance to defend himself. I knew I shouted across the room, but I couldn't hear it. All I could hear was the pumping of my heart in my chest. Michael looked at me for a few seconds, smirked then he disappeared.

While the other alphas finished off the remaining vampires, I half crawled, half walked across the room. A hand to my wound, fighting to stay conscious. Part of me already knew what I was going to find but the other part was still hopeful that he was still alive.

Finally, I reached his side. I rolled him over so I could see his face. His eyes were closed, his jaw slack. He was gone. I couldn't stop the tears that streamed down my face as I pressed my forehead to his.

I felt my wolf's mournful keen build from deep within me before I lifted my head up and let her cry fill the air. Moments later several more howls pierced the otherwise silent room. They were cries of loss, of our leader, of our family and of our friend.

When the howl drifted into silence, I felt a tug on my consciousness. I looked down at my wound. The blood was pooled on the hardwood floor beneath me. My vision started to waver, my one hand shimmering into two. Then there was a sudden darkness, like the light had been taken from the world and I fell into a deep, dark abyss.

When I came to, I was in pain. So much pain. I opened my eyes and half panicked when I took in my surroundings. I had no idea where I was. I was in a sealed room and was hooked up to several machines. One of them was beeping manically at me. The door burst open and a stranger came running in. I could see their mouth moving but no sound was reaching my ears. All I could hear was the sound of rushing wind in my head. I could feel myself breathing heavily. Everything was too much. I couldn't see. I couldn't hear. What was happening to me?

Then I felt a pinch of my skin and I felt a growl rip out of my throat, but it didn't last long because I was taken over by an overwhelming feeling of drowsiness. I couldn't keep my eyes open. I tried to stay awake. It was so hard. It felt like the walls of my mind were collapsing in on me. I retreated to the back of my mind and felt myself begin to fall. I didn't stop falling.

*****

The next time I woke up I felt calmer. I opened my eyes and looked around the room. I was still in the same room with closed in walls and I was still attached to the machines, but there were two differences. The first were the chains. I was chained to the bed. There were huge clunky metal chains holding me firmly to the metal frame beneath me.

The other thing was Zac. He was sitting in a chair by the wall, his head lolled back, snoring slightly as he slept. Maybe Zac was the reason my wolf wasn't panicking. My wolf knew he was keeping me safe.

I started to sit up but ended up gasping in pain. Looking under the purple gown I was wearing I could see bandages wrapped around my torso. The memories of before I blacked out came flooding back to me. Michael targeting Jeremy, him tossing me aside and stabbing me before he stabbed Jeremy. The last thing I remember was the howling. The howl that had ripped its way from my throat and was joined by the rest of the alpha werewolves. That was the last thing I remembered.

I carefully laid back down again, careful not to jostle the wound that needed to heal. Why wasn't I healing? I rolled over onto my side as best as I could with the cuffs to see Zac watching me, when had he awoken.

'Hey,' I said, settling into a comfortable position.

'How are you feeling?' he asked me.

I took a moment to answer as I ran through it. 'Sore,' I admitted. 'Where are we?'

'Hospital here in Washington,' he told me. 'The alpha's decided it would be best to bring you here for medical attention.' He didn't seem to agree to it, I noticed.

'Jere…my?' I throat caught when I said his name.

He shook his head. 'They laid him to rest last

night,' he said. 'They wanted to wait for you to get better but they couldn't wait any longer.' I understood that. We handled our dead differently to humans and usually wouldn't wait more than a few days before their funeral. I was sad that I didn't get to be there, but I understood that they needed to proceed without me.

I looked down at my chained limbs. 'Do you think I can be set free?' I asked. 'I swear I'm not going to lose it this time.'

He stretched his arms up over his head as he got to his feet. 'I will see if I can find someone to do that.'

He walked over to the door and opened it looking out into the hallway. 'Can I help you Zac?' I heard a voice say from the hallway.

'Rya's awake,' he said. 'She's wondering if she can be freed.'

'I will have to check with the doctor first and she will want to examine Rya as well.'

'Of course,' Zac said and he closed the door to the room. He walked back to his chair and sat down, not bothering to relay the information because he knew I heard it.

I lay in silence trying to ignore the throbbing pain in my abdomen, but my mind started to wander to thoughts of Jeremy. I couldn't believe he was gone. In my mind I could see his death over and over again like a video on repeat.

I was glad when the door finally opened and a tall lady in a set of light blue scrubs came into the room. I could smell that she was a werewolf immediately. I wonder if the staff knew this.

'Rya,' she said, closing the door behind her. 'My

name is Nancy Mott.' 'I am your doctor here at the moment. Can you tell me your name and date of birth?'

'Rya Jean Garcia,' I said. 'And the 8th of December 2007.'

'Thank you.' She looked over the chart that she was holding. 'How are you feeling?' she asked.

'A bit sore,' I told her. 'But otherwise good.'

'That's great,' she said. 'What's your pain scaled out of ten, with zero being none and ten being the worst pain you can imagine?'

'Uhhh, maybe a three or four.'

'Do you want me to get you something for the pain?'

'Sure,' I said.

'I will unlock these then I will get a nurse to give you some pain relief,' she said as she put the chart over the end of my bed. She reached into her pocket and pulled out a key before she started unlocking the cuffs around my limbs. 'I'm sorry,' she apologised. 'This was necessary when you woke up and your wolf started to panic.'

I nodded. 'It's okay,' I assured her. 'I kind of remember what happened.'

I stretched out my hands and feet when once they were released to encourage the extra blood flow that was being hindered by the chains. I still couldn't get up though. I was hooked to several machines by the bed side and I had a tube going into the cannula on the inside of my wrist. The bag it was attached to read sodium chloride which was almost empty.

A few minutes later a young man in navy blue

scrubs came into the room and shut the door behind him. He was 100% human. He had a small bottle and a syringe in his hand.

'Good Morning, Rya,' he said. 'I'm Joshua. I will be your attending nurse until later this afternoon. Now, the doctor has asked me to give you some pain relief but while I get that ready can you tell me you full name and date of birth.'

'Rya Jean Garcia,' I answered. 'The 8th of December 2007.' I had already said that.

'Thank you,' he said. 'I'm just going to put this straight through your cannula. Can I get you anything to be eat?' he asked as he attached the syringe to the device on my wrist and pushed the plunger down.

'Some food would be great,' I said.

'Fantastic,' he replied. 'That pain relief should start kicking in in the next few minutes.'

'Thanks.' He nodded and walked out of the room, leaving the door open as he left, probably since I was awake.

The opening of the door introduced a lot of new sounds to my ears. I could hear an echoing beep throughout the halls from machines hooked up to other patients. There were hundreds of different conversations going on outside the room, but I couldn't focus on any of them because they all just seemed to blur together with the rest of the noise travelling throughout the large hospital. I shut my eyes and focused on putting up a wall between me and the noise that invaded my senses. I took a deep breath and opened my eyes again, most of the noise was gone.

'So, what has happened while I've been out?' I asked Zac who was watching me closely.

He seemed to shake off some thoughts as he answered my question. 'Not much.' He admitted. 'The council is waiting for you to be released from the hospital to meet and discuss the events.'

I nodded gravely. 'We have to choose a new leader,' I told him. 'We're going to have to vote between us all and then they take up the mantle of Lupus or Lupa.'

'Does it take long to do?' Zac asked.

I shook my head. 'Usually only one meeting. We all write our preferred on a piece of paper and the alpha with the most votes becomes the alpha of alphas.'

Joshua came back then with a tray of food. He grabbed the over-bed table from the side of the room and pulled it over, placing the tray on top.

'Once you finish eating I'll come in a change your dressing,' the nurse said as he removed the now empty bag of fluids from the rail above me. He unhooked it all and took it away. 'Would you like to shower this morning?' he asked.

I nodded. 'A shower would be great,' I felt gross all over.

'I will be able to assist you with that if needed when you're ready,' Joshua told me. 'Or I can get one of the female nurses to assist you if you would prefer that.'

'No, it's all good,' I told him. 'I'm happy for you to help me.'

He left me to finish eating my breakfast. It wasn't very exciting food. Just some cereal and a piece of bread with jam on it with some apple juice. I ate it all and ended up feeling even more hungry than before I ate it, if that were possible.

I lay down and rested for the several minutes before Joshua came back in and took the tray away. He returned only moments later and helped me into the shower where he helped me wash down without causing issues with the dressings on the wound after removing the bandages.

Once I was dry and back in bed, he washed his hands and put a fresh set of gloves on. He grabbed some things out of a cupboard and put them on a small metal tray. Once he had everything he needed, he brought the tray to the bedside and changed his gloves again

Joshua started to remove the dressing already on to show a small line of stitches. The skin around the stitches was purplish and had small amounts of blood smeared around the skin. Once that was clean, the doctor came in to check on it before he put a fresh dressing on. The doctor announced that it was healing slowly but nicely. The bruising should go away soon.

I spent the rest of my day resting and talking to Zac and any other visitors that came to see me. On occasion the nurse came back in and would ask me my full name and date of birth before he would give me more pain relief.

The next morning I was given the all-clear to be released. I was given pain relief in tablet form and advised to take it easy until the wound healed more but I wasn't taken home straight away. Instead a car came to collect me and I was taken through the city to a large walled gate that announced *Wolf Security* in large acrylic letters.

Once the gate opened and allowed the car through, Zac and I were taken up a long driveway to a large house at the top of the hill. Getting out of the car, a werewolf I knew came sauntering out of the large double front doors.

'Eddy,' I said walking up to him to give him a hug. 'How are you doing?'

He took a deep breath in and out. 'I think I'm okay,' he said. 'Tia and Mum are taking it really hard.' The loss of a mate is one of the hardest things a werewolf would go through, I couldn't understand Sandra's pain but I knew it would be worse than anything I had ever felt.

'I'm glad you're okay,' I said to him. 'It's not an easy thing to go through.' I knew that from experience.

'Come on in,' Jeremy's son said, leading us inside the large house into a foyer I recognised from my last visit. I hadn't been on the outside of their home before, only the inside when I had been brought by their witch for the council meeting.

He took us upstairs to the room we had stayed in last time. 'Rest up while you can,' he said. 'The council is meeting after lunch now that you're here to choose a new head.'

I nodded. I was already tired from the short journey. I had been sleeping a lot since waking up in the hospital yesterday. Zac didn't come to sleep. He stayed out of the room to let me rest and went back downstairs with Eddy. I got changed into some more comfortable clothes than the ones the hospital had found for me and crawled into bed to get some extra sleep.

I woke up several hours later to the sound of the familiar bell gonging throughout the house. Lunch was being served. I sat up carefully but quickly and practically ran downstairs for food. The hospital did not provide enough food for a healing werewolf but I guessed that was all they were able to give me since I was in a human hospital.

I wolfed down three large helpings of steak and spaghetti bolognaise from where I sat at the table next to Zac. He seemed amused by the amount of food I was eating as he watched me go back for a fourth helping of the food in the centre of the table.

I ate this much slower as I took in the room around us. There was only one head table this time. The alphas that were here were sitting around the room at the normal tables with members of the Washington pack.

Half of the werewolves of the pack weren't here, they would have been at work or school, but the werewolves that were here all had such sombre faces that we barely did more than frown into our plates. It just showed how much this pack loved Jeremy. Hopefully Eddy would make an equally great alpha.

After lunch, I followed the alpha werewolves into the boardroom we had been in last time we were here. On the table there was a small stack of paper and a bowl. Both Sandra and Eddy joined us this time. Nobody sat in Jeremy's vacant chair. Instead Sandra remained standing while Eddy sat in hers.

'Thank you all for being here,' Sandra said, the grief evident in her voice. 'Last night we said goodbye to Jeremy.' Her eyes seemed to well up at mentioning his name. 'I have decided to step down from my position on the council and as alpha of the pack. Eddy will go through the process of becoming alpha and I will continue to help guide him as we move past our grief. Thank you.' She left the room with tears running down her cheeks.

Once she had left there was several moments of silence as nobody seemed to know what to do. In the end it was Harry that stood up and spoke. 'I wish we were gathering under better circumstances,' he said. 'But with our revelation to the human world about the packs of the world, the humans are asking questions about what happens now that our leader has been kill…ed.' His voice cracked on the last word. 'I believe now that Rya has been discharged from hospital and she is on the mend that it is time for us to vote for a new Lupa or Lupus before we all head back to our homes.' There were several moments of silence while Harry grabbed the paper from the centre of the table and handed them out to all of us. 'Write who you would prefer to lead us on the piece of paper, fold it up and place it in the bowl. Then we will read and count the votes. Remember you can only vote for someone of Garcia blood and you are unable to vote for yourself.'

Everyone took Harry's silence to start the decision process. I looked around the room focussing on each of the alpha's in turn. Really the only ones I knew were Harry, Reina and Edward. Eddy didn't have any experience as an alpha yet and he was still grieving so I didn't feel like he would be a great choice at this stage. Reina was amazing at being an alpha and was the first alpha to show me support when my pack was discovered, but from what I remember she is a bit reckless in making decisions.

This left Harry. He was older and had more experience than any werewolf I knew. He was kind and supportive and cared what others thought of his decisions. He was the logical choice. I looked down at my blank piece of paper and wrote his name on it in clear letters. I leaned towards the centre of the table from where I sat and placed my folded piece of paper into the bowl.

I sat back in my chair while I waited for everyone to finish casting their vote. Finally once everyone was sitting back in their chair waiting Harry grabbed the bowl by unspoken consent and mixed the votes around with his hand. Grabbing out the first one he unfolded it and read out.

'Rya.' I was shocked. I was really new to being alpha and I was just starting to find my feet. Harry grabbed the next one. 'Rya.' Two votes! What the hell was happening?

'Harry.' I sighed with relief that someone else voted for Harry, but then I saw my handwriting on the paper. 'Harry.' I felt even more relieved. 'Rya.' Harry kept reading out the votes. They were all either Harry or me. No one voted for anybody else. Just the two of us.

Once Harry had read them all out, he started counting the two piles of papers. 'Twelve votes for Rya, eleven votes for Harry,' he finally announced. It felt like the pit of my stomach fell into the floor. I wasn't ready for this. 'Congratulations, Rya,' Harry said excitedly.

'Why me?' I asked, disbelief in my voice.

There was a mixture of answers from the alphas around the table. I would probably lead the new generation of alphas. The humans knew who I was and would be more likely to work with me. I had shown that I was capable of making good decisions in hard times. In the end I was just so flabbergasted that I had been chosen to be the new Lupa.

I took a deep breath to control my sudden uncertainty. I guess I could see why they voted for me, but still, I was shocked. I know I was the face of werewolves at the moment but surely someone more experienced should take on the seat of alpha of alphas. I just couldn't believe it.

The ceremony to take the position of Lupa was much the same as that to become alpha of my own pack back in Wolfridge. The difference being that I didn't need to choose a beta wolf. The other alphas severed as the beta wolves and the council of the leader.

The ceremony was conducted that very night in the large yard of the Washington pack house. I went through my rights, swearing to lead the werewolf race to the best of my ability and help to ensure the safety of our people. It ended with all the other alphas crouching down and bowing their heads to me in submission.

As part of passing the test to become Lupa, I was branded one again with a mark on my shoulder this one was in the shape of a howling wolf's head and it sat below my original alpha brand. This marked me as the werewolf leader.

The next day we all left Washington for home now that council business had been taken care of. Everyone would be left to process the events of the past few days and to help decide what to do next. I was already trying to figure that out. All I knew is that I was angry and once I had finished healing, I would be coming for Michael. He was going to die.

I took the rest of the week off work while I healed and processed the events of the past few days. It gave me a chance to get over the fact that I was now the leader of the entire werewolf race as well.

Rest aside though, I was already making plans about how to confront Michael. The first step was, as always, to find out more about him. To do that I wanted to go to the ruins and see if there was anything there that would tell us his story, but to do that I knew I would need more werewolves then I had at my disposal so I called Harry and asked him to send a few squads of werewolves my way after the full moon on Friday night.

I was waiting for the full moon that night so that I could finally finish healing. This wound just didn't seem to want to budge. It was healing but at a slower and more human pace and I couldn't help but feel cheated by my wolf. She had been silent since her outburst in the hospital.

When it was finally time for the moon gathering, I left the house with Zac by my side to meet the rest of the pack. Everyone was there.

'Welcome Matthew,' I said to him once the pack quieted down. It was his first full moon. He nodded to me, his eyes looking down towards my feet in respect for his alpha. Sometimes I wondered how strange that would be to go from human to werewolf.

'This month we will also draw our breeding season to a close for another year.' I glanced at our new members. 'Tonight we will find out if the pack will be expecting pups in the coming months.' Everyone's faces brightened at this happy information.

When I finally felt the tug of my wolf form creeping on me with the rise of the full moon on the horizon, I welcomed the transformation as it washed through me. I felt several twinges of pain in my stomach as my body melted into wolf form. Once I was transformed, I stretched out my body and whimpered in pain.

Every werewolf looked in my direction. Why hadn't this wound healed? The only thing I knew of that would cause slow healing was a demiblade, the weapons that children of the gods used to wield. Michael couldn't have one of those, could he?

I mentally reassured the pack, but they knew I was in pain. Instead I drew their attention back to the specialness of the night before us. The scent of two of our women had changed to signal the growing life inside them. I walked up to Charlotte, ignoring the concern on her face and nuzzled her in congratulations. Afterwards I walked over to Leah, Liam's mother, and nuzzled her too. Two more pack members. It was amazing news. I watched as the concern washed away from the rest of the pack and they all began to congratulate the new parents.

In the end Colby convinced me to hang back during the hunt and he would lead them. In too much pain to argue I agreed and walked behind the pack as everyone started running into the trees.

It felt strange being at the rear of the pack again. It almost felt like I had never become alpha and we were still ruled by Erik in his quest for power. I hung back like I was told to while the pack silently and efficiently killed enough deer for us to eat. They all stepped away and allowed me to choose my meat first before everyone else started to eat their evening meal.

I spent that night surrounded by my pack in their bid to protect me while I was injured. It seemed natural for them to protect me like this. Zac and Colby slept on either side of me. My biggest supporters and protectors. Despite my annoying injury I fell easily into restful sleep.

The next morning I woke up surrounded by naked werewolves. It seemed that nobody had worn their clothes bracelets for the full moon again. I didn't mind too much.

I looked down at the sealed wound on my stomach. The surface of the wound had healed but the inside hadn't yet. I guessed that would take longer. I pushed myself slowly up into a seated position, carefully stretching out my aching body.

Nobody else had woken up yet. All of them were sleeping soundly... except me. I didn't get up though. Instead I lay back down and allowed Zac to pull me back into his arms while stirring in his sleep. It was nice to rest so comfortably in his arms. It had been a while since I was able to stop and enjoy the moments my pack had together.

One by one the werewolves woke up and we all

seemed to snuggle in that little bit closer together as we enjoyed the first morning of what was to be an exciting couple of months. Once I was ready to get up, I sat up on my hindquarters and gazed around at the werewolves surrounding me.

Leah and Charlotte walked back to the house, their mates walking protectively close. This would usually be the time of year that the pregnant werewolves would disappear for a year. It was needed because of the fast rate which the pups grew inside them. But with the humans knowing about us already, we didn't see the need to hide them away.

When we reached the house it was to smell the scent of many other werewolves in the grounds. The hackles on the back of my neck bristled before I recognised one of the scents as Harry's.

'What are you guys doing here so early?' I asked when I saw the man waiting in the foyer with nearly two dozen werewolves.

'It's late morning, Rya.' he said in an amused tone.

I shrugged, ignoring the pain it caused. 'Yeah, but it is also the morning after the full moon. I wasn't expecting you until much later.'

'You asked us to be here today, so we're here,' Harry told me. I just shook my head and followed Mira and Sophie inside and up the stairs for a shower and some fresh clothes.

*****

Harry and his pack spent the weekend with us while we planned our move to find out more about Michael. We just hoped that Michael was no longer using the ruins as his base of operations.

On Monday when I went in to work I was met with hearty hellos and welcome backs. It was obvious that the team was happy to see me moving around. The stack of stuff to do on my desk had reached mammoth proportions and I spent the day pushing my way through it and answering questions about what had happened the week before.

I didn't have very many answers for them as I was still processing it myself. They did ask about what happened to Jeremy as well and who was going to take his place as werewolf leader. I just didn't answer that one. I wasn't ready yet.

They left me alone for most of the week except their initial questions and the interview the higher ups wanted me to do following the events of the previous week. This interview however was only for one network, chosen by Stephen, and it would be in the boardroom instead of the auditorium like the previous ones had been.

I received a quick call at my desk on Friday afternoon that the reporter was there. I went to the boardroom after telling the guard to bring her in. I was only waiting a few minutes before three people came through the door. A cameraman, a guard and Caroline. I almost groaned when I saw her. Why did it have to be her? She annoyed me.

As much as I disliked my interviewer, I sucked it up, got to my feet and shook her hand, welcoming her into the boardroom. After a moment of silence Caroline started talking.

'Rya,' she said. 'We know that a lot of things

happened last week at the press conference,' she started. 'But can you tell us what happened? Who was that man that was attacking you? Why did he kill that werewolf?'

Straight into the hard stuff. I took a deep breath and hid any emotion from my face. 'His name is Michael,' I told her. 'We don't know much about him yet, just that he is controlling the vampire population and he is attacking and killing us where he can.'

'Do you know why?'

I shook my head. 'We know bits and pieces but not enough to know his motives.'

'He killed the alpha from here in Washington, didn't he?' she asked. 'Wasn't he the leader of the werewolf people?'

I nodded. 'His name was Jeremy,' I told her quietly. 'He was the alpha here in Washington and he was what we call the alpha of alphas. With him gone, his son has risen to the place of alpha here in Washington and we have voted in a new alpha of alphas for our people.'

'Who was voted in?' she prodded.

I hesitated. I still didn't fully believe it myself. 'Me,' I told her.

'But you're so young?' Caroline said, the shock in her voice plain.

I nodded. 'I know,' I said. 'It was a surprise to me too.'

'What does this mean then?' she asked.

'Not much,' I admitted. 'It means that I am the person that gathers the council to talk about situations that need fixing. I will be the person who gives the okay on any decisions effecting the werewolf race.'

'Sounds like you've got your work cut out for you then,' the reporter commented. 'Will you be continuing your position here in the government?'

I nodded. 'This hasn't changed. It just means that now I am the one that can be spoken to about things and I don't have to get approval from anyone, though I will still seek advice while I find my feet.'

'What is Michael?' she asked me. 'Do you know?'

I nodded. 'Michael is something we didn't even know existed until recently, he is a hybrid between werewolf and vampire. We think he was born when we were still allies with the vampires, but it is difficult to be sure. Our recorded history for that time was tampered with and it seems our ancestors didn't want us to know about him.'

'So, what do you plan to do about this Michael that has been attacking you?' she asked.

I felt the anger well up inside me. 'I'm going to find him, then I'm going to kill him.'

*****

That night when I went home it was to a quiet dinner before Harry and his werewolves met the werewolves of our fighting faction in the large boardroom upstairs. It was a bit squishy in there since the room was only built for two dozen werewolves but we made it work. 'Let's go.' Harry said, hitching a backpack onto his shoulders.

We went over the plan as quickly as we could before we made our way back through the house and into the yard. Colby led the entourage of werewolves into the trees towards the ruins I had been held captive in for more than a month. I wondered how it would feel to be back there again.

My wound was mostly healed now but I was taking it easy as I followed Colby and Harry in the direction of the deep woods. We stopped at the ridge of the canyon and peered over the edge, looking for movement. We couldn't see anything moving, but apparently, they couldn't last time either so we would soon see as we made our way down.

We walked carefully under the now waning moon as it rose above our heads. We took care to walk quickly, silently and most important, carefully. We didn't want to go falling off the edge.

When we finally reached the base of the canyon the moon was well overhead. A bunch of new smells crossed our noses when we started gathering at the bottom, but so far all of them were at least a few weeks old.

Slowly and even more cautiously we pressed in towards the ruins, keeping our senses open to sense the slightest change to our safety. Nothing ever came at us. There wasn't even the slightest hint of a new scent.

When we reached the edge of the tree line we stood and waited, watching for movement, any movement. We waited for several minutes straining to hear any sign of life within the old worn out building in front of us. I didn't take much notice to look at it when I was fleeing but I did now. The building was made out of a material that I had never seen before. It seemed to be a single storey building, if it wasn't for what I knew lay underneath – labyrinth of hallways and rooms with unknown purposes. Remembering the rooms, the walls of the underground maze were made of the same marbly white material, which meant this place had been here for a long time. I had no doubt that this would be the piece of the puzzle we needed to find out where Michael came from.

We slowly crept out of the trees after we were watched making sure there was no sign of any movement or sounds from within the ruins. I had been told the story about Michael's release from Colby after I had gotten back from being captive. The doors I assumed that they opened were the two large, heavy, stone-looking doors that sat with just enough distance for a person to slip through. I remembered running out of there but I don't remember it being such a small gap. I guess I wasn't really focusing on the architecture at the time of my escape.

We spread out around the ruins searching the outside for any clues or markings on the building but there was nothing there. So we regrouped and started to head inside. Harry went first. To be honest I didn't really want to enter. I think a part of me was scared of getting trapped in there again. After Colby followed Harry I sucked in a nervous breath and followed him into the darkened space, ignoring the glances I got from the rest of the werewolves behind me. At this moment I was glad I was in human form, otherwise I was sure my tail would be half-way between my legs.

I walked up to the two werewolves that stood in the centre of the room. They were looking up at the walls. I looked up too. There were pictures and words written all over. I wasn't sure what it said but I knew it was all in Greek.

'Did you bring the camera?' I asked Harry.

He nodded and pulled it out. Once the majority of werewolves were in the small room a few of them stood at each entrance just in case anything came at us. Four werewolves at the door we came through and another four at the top of a staircase that led into the maze of hallways.

The rest of them stood protectively around Harry and I. They weren't going to let anything get to us if they could help it. Harry walked around taking photos of the walls and roof for us to take back and translate later. We didn't know whether it was Michael who wrote all this or if it was our ancestors, but we wanted to know what it said.

We were there for several minutes while we anxiously waited for Harry to finish taking pictures. Part of me wanted to move on but the other part knew we had to stick together as a group.

'We have to be careful down here,' I told everyone in a whispering voice. 'This place is a maze. Stick together and hopefully we can find out what's down there.'

We walked down the stairs, the werewolves walking around us, protecting us as we moved deeper into the labyrinth. We opened door after door after door. We went through desks and storage units and took anything that seemed important or useful before moving onto the next room. It definitely seemed like Michael was no longer staying here.

One room had a name carved into the door. Jeriah

Garcia – my several times great grandfather that Michael had mentioned. I opened the door and saw that it was much like the other offices. There were a few books on the shelf. One was a werewolf history book. It was exactly the same on the cover as the one I had at home but something was different about it. It seemed larger. I grabbed the book and gave it to one of the werewolves that was carrying the things we found. I would have a look through that later.

I think we searched for hours before we think we finally went in every direction possible. Our last direction took us down to the cells. I absolutely refused to enter the rooms. The door to Kai's cell was still shrivelled up and bent in the hallway from him breaking through it. We found the room that I was tortured in and I even refused to go in there. Instead Colby and Harry searched the room while I hung back next to the door.

I was incredibly happy when we finally started to leave the building. Nothing crossed our path on the way out of the ruins, then through the trees or even up to the top of the canyon wall. Once a safe distance away we distributed the items we looted between us and started the journey home.

Michael wasn't staying there anymore, that much was clear. Where was he holed up now? We had no idea where he was. That was going to make it difficult to strike him first, to get revenge before he killed anyone else. I would find him though. I would find him and I would make him pay.

RYA GARCIA

It was the early hours of the morning when we made it back home. Thankfully with no problems. We hadn't even seen an animal out in the forest tonight. It was kind of eerie to be completely honest.

I had the werewolves dispose of the items the found in the boardroom before sending everyone upstairs to sleep after staying awake all night. I showered before I crawled into bed next to Zac. I snuggled up behind him and he rolled over and wrapped his arms around me.

'What time is it?' he mumbled.

'Early,' I told him. 'Go back to sleep.' He didn't need to be told twice. I rolled over in his arms so that he was spooning me and I was in a more comfortable position to sleep. In his arms I nodded off quickly to the sound of his heart beating and his slow soothing breath as he slept peacefully.

I woke up several hours later to find the bed empty. Looking over at the covered window I could see light filtering through the edges of the curtains. Getting up I got dressed and made my way downstairs for... I checked the clock on the beside... lunch.

Lunch was a delicious variety of sandwiches today. The one I chose was toasted bread with steak, barbeque sauce and a mixture of salads. It was amazing. I was so grateful that the kitchen staff we hired put so much effort into giving us a variety of foods.

After lunch I went looking around the house. There was next to nobody here, despite the fact that it was a Saturday. Where was everyone? I ended up going for a walk down to the bunker to see if they were there, but they weren't there either. Only a couple of Harry's pack wolves were there making use of the training equipment.

My only other thought was that they were in town. But why would everyone go to town together. It was strange. In the end I went back to the house and settled in the boardroom to go through the things we looted from the ruins the day before. Everyone would return later in the day.

I grabbed the camera off the table that Harry used to take pictures of the walls in the ruins. I thought that if there was anything it would be on these. Unless this is what Michael did with himself for however long he was locked away in there.

I started to look through the photos on the screen on the back of the camera, but of course I couldn't really make anything out. It was too small. I contemplated grabbing the laptop but instead I made the effort of walking into town to the local print and copy shop.

There I opened the camera files on the screen and got the computer to send all of the photos Harry took to the printer. I paid for the pictures then waited nearly half an hour for them to be ready.

On my way back through town a cheer broke through the air. It wasn't super loud but it was somewhere nearby. I followed the noise to school where I found, I kid you not, at least half the town in the stands by the oval.

Looking onto the field I could see werewolves, none of the people on the field were human. And they were playing soccer. One team was made up of the local werewolves while the other team was made up of the werewolves from New York. I quietly crept forward and watched Zac steal the ball from one of Harry's wolves, before he took off up the field with the ball at full speed. He easily dodged past them and shot a goal in their net.

He was a great soccer player before. Now with his werewolf abilities he was even better. Unfortunately, that also meant he couldn't follow his dream and I knew that was a hard thing for him to face. He still hadn't come back to me since our chat the other week. It made me wonder what he was thinking of doing now that he couldn't pursue sport. I would have to talk to him about it later. For now, I sat down at the edge of the crowd of werewolves who welcomed me into the spectator stands to watch the werewolf soccer game.

Agua caught me up to where the game was at. I had sat next to her and her parents. It was nice to see them again, out and about together as a family. It made me feel like it wasn't going to be impossible to make our human-werewolf alliance work for the better.

A few minutes after I arrived, Sean, who was being the referee, blew a whistle for half-time. The werewolves came bounding off the field and sat down on the bleachers for a rest. I got up and wandered down to them.

'Hey,' I said to the sweating Zac, Toby, Colby and Harry. Zac tried to hug me but I flinched away from him that just made the boys laugh at me. 'What spurred this?' I asked.

'We were bored and you were sleeping,' Zac said breathlessly.

'And we didn't want to start looking into the stuff without you.'

I showed them the package of photos I still held. 'I got all those pictures you took printed so we could go through them,' I told Harry.

'Cool,' he said. 'We can do that when we finish up here.'

I smiled as all of them reacted to the whistle that Sean blew, startling all the werewolves and causing them to look at him.

'Let's go,' he called out. Without being asked to, I went back and sat next to Agua again to watch the game and the others ran back onto the field.

The game was going well but apparently New York pack was still one point ahead of our home team. Before long I found myself cheering on my pack and hoping they won the game.

At five minutes to the end of the game, Zac had the ball and he was running up the field and he passed it to Toby before it got stolen by a New Yorker. Toby passed it back once Zac was open, but the ball never connected with Zac instead a werewolf collided with him instead. It was one of the other team that was running looking at the ball and the two of them ran into each other.

Both of them hit the ground hard all of the werewolves in the crowd heard the cracking of bones. I was at Zac's side in a matter of seconds, barely even realising that I did so without thinking about it.

He jumped slightly when I touched him. He hadn't been expecting me. 'Are you okay?' I asked him.

He didn't answer me for a moment. All I saw was the slightest ripple of fur under his skin before he took a deep breath and nodded. 'I think so,' he said.

I grabbed his arm and inspected the positioning of the bones for a break. I noticed that Harry was doing the same thing for his wolf that got hurt. 'You'll be fine in a couple of hours,' I told him. 'It's just a fracture.' Not a break like I thought.

'Cool,' he said getting to his feet without using his arm. 'You all good?' Zac asked the other werewolf.

Both Harry and the other wolf nodded in unison. Harry helped him to his feet before he started moving back to his position on the field. Apparently they wanted to play on. I looked at Zac. 'Are you going to keep playing?' I asked him. He nodded. 'Then be careful. You don't want to make your arm worse.'

He nodded again and I walked back to the stands to sit down next to Agua once again. The rest of the game was uneventful. Zac got a penalty kick because the other player was technically at fault for running into Zac.

In the end New York beat us in the game of soccer

but instead of hating one each other like we did with the other school teams, we could accept friendly competition and a loss if they deserved to win.

Once the game was over some of the New York werewolves started to disperse but the humans stayed as the school team came out of the change rooms in their soccer gear. Was there a game today?

Zac came and sat by me, his body drenched in sweat as he stretched out his arm. 'You gonna stay and watch?' Zac asked me.

'Is there a school game?' I asked. He nodded. 'Of course I'll stay, let me go get some snacky food. I went over to the small shop on the edge of the field that opened on game days. I got Zac his favourite sports drink in a raspberry flavour and a soda for me. I also got us a bag of chips and some popcorn for us to share.

I sat down next to him on the bleachers again. It was kind of nice to be able to sit next to him and watch a game of soccer. Since he was always playing, I had never had the chance. I gave him his drink and he took several big gulps before he came up for air.

I held out some popcorn for him and he accepted a handful and leaned back against the chair rail behind him. I nestled back into the crook of his arm and got comfortable and he returned my gesture by wrapping his arm around me and pulling me closer. So we sat back and enjoyed each other's company while we waited for the game to start.

I didn't return until later that night and by that point Harry and his pack had left. It was a shame we didn't get a chance to go through all the stuff we found together but I was sure they wanted to get back to New York. Harry knew that I would call if I found anything anyway. So I wasn't too worried about him leaving.

That night I spent the time laying out the photos in the boardroom to the rough layout I remembered from the walls in the ruins. I was so focused that when the door opened it startled me.

'Are you still doing this?' Colby asked.

I nodded. 'What time is it?'

'Morning,' he said simply.

'Really?' He nodded. 'Whoops.' I laughed.

'Go get some sleep.' He practically ordered me.

I shook my head. 'I'm not really tired,' I admitted. 'I might as well keep going.'

'Suit yourself,' he said. 'But you have to go to work tomorrow and you can't fight Michael if you're sleep deprived.' He looked at me seriously. 'This will all still be here when you wake up.'

'Fine,' I said, giving in to his words of wisdom. 'I'll sleep for a few hours.'

I went to the dining hall and ate some breakfast before heading up to bed to sleep for those few hours I promised Colby. True to my word I woke up to the sound of my alarm, went downstairs to eat lunch before heading straight back into the boardroom again.

I had almost finished laying out the pictures. Now I went through the process of translating them but it was an older form of Greek, not Ancient Greek, but it was definitely an older dialect than the one I knew. Translating them took some work and I ended up with bits and pieces of the text as I went through each one.

I didn't translate the pictures in order so once I finished writing English connotations on small pieces of paper, I was able to get a kind of story from the words and the drawings that had been painted onto the wall.

The story began back around the time that the humans were burning witches in Salem. Vampires and werewolves had retreated to their underground facility only going into town to act as travellers seeking wares, sustenance and company on their journey.

Whilst living in seclusion, two of the clan members fell in love with each other. They were the werewolf, Aniyah Garcia and the original vampire, Esmond. The two clans didn't seem to have a problem with the romance at all until one year Aniyah fell pregnant. No one was aware that vampires could even have children.

On the night of the child's birth it was said that Jeriah Garcia had a vision. A vision that this child would bring about the end of both werewolves and vampires. From then on, the werewolves treated the child with suspicion and contempt. While not stopping the child from living, they were not prepared to help the child become the doom that Jeriah saw.

His mother however didn't treat him as such. Aniyah gave so much of her love to the young boy as he grew quickly from an infant to toddler in less than a year. The powers the child exhibited were extraordinary even for a child of the supernatural. He had the speed and hunger of a vampire and the stealth and cunning of a werewolf, making him the ultimate predator but also difficult to control since he was more powerful than both werewolf and vampire.

The vampires were unsure how to respond to the boy.

They were heeding the words of the werewolf alpha with a connection to the gods but they were unable to despise the fact that they now knew they could have children and wouldn't be stuck turning humans for the foreseeable future.

At two years of age the child resembled a ten-year-old human child. He could talk fluently and could read anything placed in front of him in both English and Greek, but his powers were becoming stronger and stronger, and he was finding it difficult to control the urges that came with having both the vampiric bloodlust and the murderous wolf within him. His mother and father did their best to try and teach him how to control his powers while the werewolves refused to acknowledge that he existed.

He would often play with the other werewolf children until one day a young girl fell and cut open her knee. Overcome with hunger for werewolf blood, Michael was unable to control himself and drank the blood of the young werewolf until she died. With no adults around at the time the other children were powerless to separate him from the young girl.

This child had been Maria, Jeriah's youngest daughter. This seemed to confirm the suspicions for the werewolf pack and they held a trial with their elders to figure out what to do now that Michael had killed one of their own.

In the end he was ordered to be locked away in the dark moon cells until it was believed that he could control his bloodlust enough to be reintroduced into the community. Over the next several months Michael grew into a teenager and his growth began to slow. Each day his mother and father would work with him, training him and tempting him with werewolf blood. Each time he failed to resist the urge to indulge in the blood, but since the adults were stronger than him, they were able to stop him from killing his own mother for her blood.

So he stayed in captivity until he was five. By this point he resembled a boy in his early twenties and seemed to have stopped aging for the most part, but his powers and strength still grew and he was still unable to control his vampiric urges until one day he overpowered his father and killed him.

After killing his own father, the animal within Michael sought the blood of his mother, and she was helpless to stop him now that he was stronger than her. Before anybody knew what had happened both Michael's mother and father were dead and the hybrid escaped into the forest.

Werewolves and vampires searched through the night to find him and make sure that he didn't hurt anyone else until they finally found him in a farmhouse near the local human town. He had killed and drained the blood of the farmer, his wife and their two children.

It took the strength of ten werewolves to subdue Michael and get him back into the cage. The process of deciding what to do with him then began. While Michael waited and waited and waited. He was left to himself and was only given a cup of blood each day to allow him to survive. He would cry out for them to set him free only for them to ignore him.

Then suddenly, after months of being locked away in the same dark moon cage, Jeriah came down to the dungeons and announced to Michael that both the vampires and the werewolf elders had decided that it would be best to kill Michael. He then proceeded to snap Michael's neck for what he thought would be a painless death.

But Michael didn't die. He only screamed in pain from the depths of his mind as his powers worked to heal his damaged body. That was what started several weeks of being killed over and over again as they tried new ways to kill Michael, but he never stayed dead for long.

Finally, Jeriah announced that the humans in the local town were now looking for signs of the supernatural and that it was time for the clans to move on to a safer area. It wouldn't be long before their home was found.

Jeriah told Michael that because he could not be trusted to control his urges that Michael would remain behind and locked into the underground home that had been built for them to live in. The building would be sealed with magic to prevent it from being opened for many years to come and the vampires and werewolves would move on to ensure the safety of their peoples.

A few days later Michael was alone. He had heard everyone packing and heard them as they left this home for the last time. Nobody came to see him. Nobody came to set him free. Instead he was all alone to be left by himself for centuries.

I was fairly surprised by the story. I had never heard about this side of my ancestors and never would have believed them to turn their back on a child of theirs just because he couldn't control the powers he was born with. It wasn't his fault.

Even though it told me a lot about Michael and why he wanted to kill the decedents of the werewolves who locked him in the ruins in the first place. I had a feeling it was kind of one sided, but it was interesting to know where Michael was coming from with his revenge crusade.

I spent the rest of the evening writing down the story I was able to translate from the pictures and put it in a safe file in my office. I could see why we didn't know about this. It wasn't exactly a pretty part of our history.

I didn't end up going to work the next day. I wanted to continue going through all of the things we found. Colby wasn't too happy that I was staying home, saying that I was becoming obsessed with Michael. Maybe I was, but I was just trying to get to the bottom of this mystery. Besides, could he blame me for wanting to do this? Michael killed my parents and now Jeremy too.

I spent Monday going through the history book I found in my grandfather's office. I eventually went upstairs and grabbed mine to compare it page for page, line for line. It was all exactly the same except for one chapter. The chapter where we separated from the vampires.

My book said that the vampires learned how to turn people into vampires and those new vampires lost control and killed several humans and a couple of werewolves. Grandfather Jeriah's copy was completely different to that. It went like this...

Before our people separated, us werewolves and the vampires were allies. We shared our homes and we helped to provide for each other. We were two separate species but we worked together to help ensure our mutual survival in a possibly hostile land.

We hadn't been able to explore the land as the skinwalkers told us to be careful where we went. They didn't really like us being here and at first wanted us to leave. Though they seem to have accepted that we are now living on their land we have come to the agreement that we are not to cross onto their territory.

So for many years we lived on the outskirts of human settlements. With the help of the witches we were able to interact with the European settlers with the façade of being wandering nomads that travelled through the trees and preferred to live away from civilisation.

We built our home underground in the middle of a vast canyon that was far enough from the human encampments that it would not be easily found. The journey into the canyon was also perilous to humans should they fall from the narrow path forged by the witches in the rocky sides of the great bowl we resided in.

We lived peacefully until it came to my knowledge that a werewolf and vampire were engaging in romantic relations. I didn't mind this so much as I thought it would be bound to happen with our people living so closely to one another. But then one summer Aniyah announced that she had become pregnant and claimed to not have been unfaithful to her beloved. She was expecting his child.

Until this point no one had been aware that the vampires would be able to procreate. We had planned to look into this more until we had to separate our clans, but I am already getting ahead of myself.

In the two months of werewolf child baring the child was born as a human, or so we thought. At the time of his birth, when I was welcoming our latest additions into the pack, I was hit with the most horrible vision from who I believed to be Zeus himself.

It showed me an adult man with glowing red eyes of the vampiric race. He was surrounded by the faces of unknown werewolves that were obviously of the Garcia bloodline with their light blonde hair. They were all dead. There were miles of werewolves and even a few vampires while this man stood over them with contempt on his face. Before the vision disappeared, the man's body changed into the shape of a great white wolf. His eyes were no longer red, they were now a crisp golden yellow. From that moment I believed the half-breed child to be the man in that vision. I could not ignore the vision the gods gave me and I cautioned my pack against the future that I saw.

Despite this vision I allowed the child to be raised as one of the pack. He grew quickly, very quickly. His powers surpassing the powers of an ordinary werewolf in a matter of weeks. His language skills grew until he could comprehend as well as any adult. But with his powers setting him above the other children he quickly became complacent and cocky within the realms of training and fighting techniques. He quite often refused to listen to his instructors and exercise control for his extraordinary abilities.

One such day when the children were playing by the creek, my daughter fell and cut her knee. The children were too far away for us to hear the commotion and the boy, Michael, lost control of his vampiric bloodlust and he was unable to stop himself from draining the blood of my youngest

After that, I fear I lost faith that we could stop the future I saw through careful nurturing of this boy. I had no choice but to lock him away until he could learn to control his powers. We worked with his parents, suggesting different ways that they might be able to guide his growing abilities but nothing worked and he continued to get stronger.

Then one day I had not heard from Aniyah and I went down to check on her only to find both Esmond and Aniyah unconscious on the floor. It didn't take me long to realise that the boy had killed them. He had managed to overpower the two adults and escaped into the trees.

It took us hours to find him in the forest and when we did it took many of us to stop him. After he killed a farmer and his family, he refused to go back into confinement even though we pleaded for him to leave the humans alone and return.

After his continued refusal we were forced to subdue him and drag him back to our home where we locked him away until we were able to bury the dead and discuss the consequences his actions now faced.

In the days that followed the human town, that had already been suspicious of supernatural activity, found the death of their farmers strange and began to look for the culprits.

The other elders and I discussed it at length until we finally decided that it would be best to move on from our current location and separate our two factions to prevent another half-breed child being born. It was too dangerous for us to run the risk of being discovered and burned at the stake.

In the end it was decided that we should kill the boy for what he had done. He was a danger to himself and others and he had not proven to have the ability to learn to control his urges despite our persistence on his teachings.

However when I went down into the dungeon to kill him, snapping his neck for a painless death seemed ineffective. I had to return to the elders to tell them that the attempt had been unsuccessful and we would need to find another way to kill him.'

'We tried many, many times, but all of our attempts were fruitless. The boy would not die. Finally when we ran out of ways short of ripping the poor boys throat out and giving into our bestial urges, we decreed that it was impossible to kill him and therefore decided to seal him within the confines of this building for the rest of time. We got in contact with our magical allies and they were able to seep heavy magic into the earth and the buildings surrounding the compound. Finally we all moved out and we locked the final door behind us leaving Michael to his eternal tomb.'

'Before separating, the vampires and werewolves agreed

to distance ourselves and teach our children to fear one another to stop them from forming a union and creating a child of the sun and moon.'

I couldn't believe it. In the space of two days I had two completely different versions of what happened. One painted Michael as a cocky young child that didn't take the care to learn to control his abilities. The other, Michael's paintings, showed the vampires and werewolves not showing him the proper attention due to his differences and shunning him when he couldn't control his powers.

I wanted to believe that my ancestors did the right thing but it was so long ago and I had two completely conflicting points of view. I needed to speak to someone that knew about this story. That lived it. I needed to meet with the Grand Master. Only he would be able to tell me what was true.

Much to Colby's displeasure, I got in contact with Kai and got him to see about organising an audience with the Grand Master. He said he would see what he could do but I also had a plan if he didn't respond as well. Colby didn't like that plan either.

I went to work for the rest of the week practically sitting on my phone constantly hoping to hear from Kai that I could meet with him. Finally, on Friday, I got the call. It wasn't good news. 'I'm sorry Rya,' Kai said over the phone. 'I really tried, but he still doesn't believe me about Michael.'

I let out an exasperated sigh. 'It's okay,' I told him. 'I planned for that. Does he stay connected with the media?' I asked.

'Mostly he has people to do it for him,' Kai answered. 'What are you going do?'

'I'm going to send him a message,' I said, hanging up the phone before I got a response.

Immediately I called the one reporter who I knew would be keen for the job. 'Hello,' she said.

'Caroline Vaughn,' I said. 'This is Rya Garcia. I need to borrow your station to get a message to someone that won't speak to me.'

It was the very next day that she willingly travelled the distance between Washington and Wolfridge. I knew she was keen when she agreed to meet here on a weekend. She even got her station to clear the time on air so I could be live at the time. I think Caroline knew that I wouldn't have asked if it wasn't important.

She seemed to gasp as I led her and her cameraman into the boardroom I had been working in the past several days. I couldn't blame her for being shocked. There were things everywhere. Books on the table, pictures all over the wall. It was my organised mess.

'Sorry,' I told her. 'I've been working in here for the past week. PLEASE don't move anything,' I said hurriedly as she was about to move things off a chair.

She jumped away from the chair and backed against the wall like a startled mouse.

'Sorry,' I said again. I grabbed her a different chair that didn't have anything on it. Then I got a second one for her camera man to sit on while he filmed everything.

I even managed to get a third chair and sit in front of them so I could sit there while I spoke. I made sure I had the things next to me that I needed; those were the things that were sitting on the chair that I had yelled at Caroline for.

The camera man set up the camera to face Caroline first so that she could do a short intro to lead me in.

'Okay,' her cameraman said. I just realised I had never gotten his name. 'We are live in 3, 2 and 1.' He went silent.

Less than a moment later Caroline started talking. 'Welcome to this special live piece. I received a phone call yesterday from the one and only Rya Garcia. She has a message for a particular person somewhere out there and they haven't been returning her messages. Even werewolves don't like being ignored it seems.' She seemed to stifle a laugh. 'Okay, now let's turn this camera around to Rya.'

The camera man did just that and suddenly the camera was facing me. I took a deep breath before I spoke. 'This message goes out to the Grand Master of the vampire covens here in America. Please be aware that I will not be elaborating on the content of this message to the human population at this stage,' I said, ignoring the shock on Caroline's face. 'One of your people was kept in containment with me a few months ago. We were held by an individual named Michael. We were tortured while he attempted to gain control of our minds and control each of our races. When Kai approached me about speaking to you in person, I was reluctant because of the history of our races. I haven't exactly shown my love for vampires and your people have been attacking our packs for their blood for centuries.'

I stared right into the camera. 'Recently I have learned several things about Michael and where he came from. Kai told me that you and your daughter are from the original family of vampires, the family we thought to have been killed in battle a long time ago.' I grabbed a picture showing the outside of the ruins. 'This is the place Kai and I were held hostage at,' I said. 'This is where I found access to a book in Jeriah Garcia's office that contained information different to the book I read from in the days I was learning about werewolf history as a child.' I head up the two books. 'On the outside they are identical. But on the inside one chapter is very different to what I was taught.'

'The problem with this discovery though,' I continued, 'is that I believe Michael wrote a very different view of the same time that was written in this book. It was found on the internal walls of the entrance chamber. Werewolves from mine and another pack went on a scouting mission to gain intel about this place and see whether Michael was still using it as his base of operations. The story that Michael wrote and drew on the walls, paints me a very different picture about what happened towards the end of the werewolf and vampire alliance several hundred years ago. It is making me question a lot of things I thought I knew about our history,' I admitted.

'The main reason I wish to speak with you is because I am hoping that because you were there, and lived through it, you could shed some light on the situation for me. If you truly are one of the vampires from the original family you know Michael from when he was born. You would have been a part of the process to lock him away and part of the reason that he wants us all dead or enslaved to him. Please meet with me. I would be happy to meet on neutral territory where we will only have a few close allies at our side. I need to know what happened then to stop what's happening now.' I put my stuff back down on the chair next to me. 'Please get into contact with me. I'm pretty sure the lives of both our races depend on it. You can contact me through Kai. He has my number.' I looked at Caroline. 'Thank you.'

The camera got turned back to Caroline. 'There you have it guys. This important message from Rya Garcia, now leader of the werewolf race, to an unnamed Grandmaster of the vampire covens. We probably won't get very much elaboration in the future so we have to take what we can get. We will be playing this several times throughout the day to help this message reach the intended party and hopefully Rya will get the answers she needs. Thank you very much. This is Caroline Vaughn with Washington Central News.'

*****

Things happened pretty quickly from there. Harry called me in a hurry after I got off air. He kind of knew what I was planning to do but not to the full extent of what I did. After I explained the circumstances leading up to the important message on the news channel all across the country he understood, but only if I promised that he would be a part of the group going to meet the Grand Master. I agreed immediately. I was going to invite him along anyway.

After the message aired on the news channel, a lot of other stations paid Caroline's company for the rights to air it as well. It seemed that Washington Central News was making a small packet of money out of doing me a favour. That made them very happy.

It was on Sunday that I got the phone call I wanted from Kai. I wasn't really surprised to be honest.

'You could have told me what you were doing,' Kai said.

I huffed slightly with amusement. 'I was going for dramatics,' I said. 'I needed him to listen.' Kai didn't answer. 'So, has he agreed to meet with me?'

'You're lucky he wants to meet with you and he didn't decide to kill me for telling you that he was alive,' he said seriously.

'Sorry,' I apologised. I waited an extra moment before speaking again. 'So, when and where can I meet with him?'

'Day after tomorrow. Ten o'clock. He has agreed to come to you,' Kai said. 'He needs to see all the things you have learned.'

I was kind of surprised that he was coming here. I almost would have expected to go to him or at least to the neutral ground I suggested.

'Great,' I responded. 'Will I be seeing you then too?'

'Yes,' was his response. 'Because of my connection to you and Michael, he wants me there to fill in any blanks.'

'Cool,' I said. 'I'll see you then.'

After getting off the phone and informing Colby and Harry of the future visit of the vampire Grand Master, I spent the rest of my Sunday making sure that everything was organised. Harry was making his way back here to stay for a few days. Just him this time.

I also called Stephen and informed him that I would need to take the next few days off of work for pack alpha duties. I told him to forward all of my emails to me and I would sort out anything I needed to do from home.

Then I called Caroline and informed her that she

could stop showing the replay of my message. She asked me if I had received the response I wanted and I replied to her that I had. I thanked her for her assistance and sent a cheque for the airtime she gave me to the station in the mail. I didn't tell her it was coming though. It was a special thanks to the company for helping me out when I needed it.

I spread the word amongst the pack that we would have a probably several vampires entering our territory, to identify them I made sure they knew that Kai would be with them since most of them had met or at least seen Kai after we escaped from Michael's clutches.

When the morning finally arrived Colby insisted on putting a few of our team on patrol before during and after the visit to make sure there was no danger to anyone, human or werewolf. I knew he was being cautious but I also thought he was overeating a little bit. I tried to remind myself that while I had recently made… acquittances? Friends seemed too much… that it might take a bit for everyone else to get used to talking with vampires instead of killing them. This idea kind of irked me too, but I guess it was just because we were raised to hate them and told to kill them if they enter our territory.

The morning of, I basically paced anxiously back and forward. It was a school day and Zac was so glad that he was going to school because I was making him antsy with my growing anxiety.

Finally, I got the message across the link that vampires had crossed the boundary line. One was identified as Kai. I sensed Colby and Lexi through our mind link racing towards them to flank the vampires and guide them to the house while Charlie, Charlotte and Keith continued to run the border to ensure safety.

I made sure that there weren't many werewolves in the house today. Everyone was at work and school except for those meeting with me and the three wolves running the border. I even gave the kitchen staff and Diana the day off and told them I would let them know when they could come back. I didn't want any issues so I made sure everyone was safely away for the day.

'Please stop,' Harry said. I was still pacing while I was waiting. 'I'm sure it will be fine.'

I took a massive deep breath to help relax myself. I stretched out each of my limbs in a hope of settling myself down. Just in time too. I could hear Kai talking and could sense two others with him. Just three of them.

I heard the loud knock on the door and I had to force myself to move out of the boardroom and to the front door to let them in. When I opened the door, I saw Kai smiling at me with the kind of enthusiasm I felt like smacking off his face in that moment.

One of the vampires I didn't know seemed to sense that feeling.

'Try travelling all the way here with his smug I told you so look he's got going on,' the older, balding man said in a deep, rumbling voice.

I couldn't help it. I laughed. 'I'm sure that would be very annoying.' I held out my hand to him. 'Rya Garcia,' I introduced. He took my hand and shook it once. 'This is my associate Harry Garcia.' I indicated the alpha werewolf standing behind me. 'And my beta Colby Martin.' I indicated Colby that was now standing defensively behind the vampires.'

'Yes,' the man said. 'I noticed your wolves flanking us on the way in.'

I ran my hand through my hair nervously. 'I have to apologise. My beta is feeling somewhat protective and wants to be sure there is no foul play.'

'Understandably,' he said. 'My name is Ambrogio and this is my daughter Natasha,' he said. 'And of course you know my son Kai.'

My gaze whipped over to Kai then. 'You never told me,' I accused.

He put up his hands defensively. 'I am not an original,' he said. 'I was born to a human mother about two centuries ago. When I came of age I was offered to be turned and I accepted.'

We all stood awkwardly at the door for a moment. 'Would you like to come in?' I asked them hurriedly.

'Yes,' the three vampires chorused at the same time.

Then there was the moment of me stepping back and them kind of filing awkwardly into the foyer. I couldn't believe how weird this was. As soon as they stepped over the threshold, I felt like we were being invaded. My wolf stirred at the feeling and I had to force her to quell her anxiety. *We need this.* I told her.

Colby closed the door behind everyone. I wondered where Lexi ran off to. Maybe Colby didn't want her near the big scary vampires. Honestly, I couldn't blame him, I didn't really want to be here either, but I knew that this meeting had to happen so

I sucked in a big breath and forced myself to act like the friendly host and like this was all perfectly normal.

I led them silently into the boardroom, I had managed to clean up enough since Caroline had been here that we were all able to sit on opposite sides of the table with my research spread out around us.

'You've been busy,' Ambrogio commented as he looked around the room at the walls and the ceiling.

'Yeah,' I said. 'Should I start with what I have learned?' I asked him.

He nodded, so I dove into all the information I had found. I showed him my translations from the walls in the ruins and the account that grandfather Jeriah wrote his version of the werewolf history book in. I also showed him the comparison to the copy that every werewolf family had access to to help teach children about our past.

It was nearly midday when we finally finished going through everything I had found out. 'I didn't know you did so much,' Harry said to me.

I nodded. 'I wanted to get to the bottom of it.' I looked at Ambrogio. 'So I hit a block when I found the two conflicting accounts of what happened.' I looked down at the history book in my hands for a moment before looking up at him again. 'You were there. I need to know what really happened. Can you please tell me?'

'I was there,' he said. 'But I don't think my account is what you want to hear.'

'I need to know.'

'Okay then.' And he started to tell his story…

A long time ago, maybe fifty years after we all arrived in America on the Mayflower, our community was thriving as a small town of its own. We lived separate from other settlements that had formed over the years and we mostly kept to ourselves, though we quite often wandered into town on occasion to act as travellers. Of course we didn't have contacts back then to cover the colour of our eyes so it was much harder for us to interact without being noticed.

We built our home in the base of a valley. We built small homes above it and created our own little village and had the underground facility where we would lock the werewolves away each month to transform safely. In return the werewolves would provide us with their blood to help us to survive. It was a mutually beneficial time in both our histories as we were unable to access human blood without raising suspicion and your kind needed to be watched over in case one of you escaped.

The witches lived among us but mostly kept to themselves. They were able to spend more time with the humans than we could since they didn't have an abnormal eye colour to give them away. They would often be the ones to go into town and get any items we needed like clothes and house items like bedding.

After a while I noticed that my son, Esmond, and the

werewolf, Aniyah, were courting. At first they did so quietly. I assume this was because there had not been any interspecies relations by this point and they were unsure if this were acceptable. But at the time none of the elders, werewolf or vampire, had an issue with the union as we never expected what would come of it.

When Jeriah had his vision, this was a cause of great concern. We knew that he had a connection to the gods, as many of your bloodline have had in the past, and we were concerned for the future this child would bring to our cultures.

But we felt that nothing could be done. We certainly weren't going to kill an innocent child that hadn't done anything to deserve such an early death. It was not the way of our tribes and we refused to throw away our values because a vision of what might happen.

As the boy grew, and he grew quickly, so did his powers. Whilst we tried to treat him as one of the other children, it was difficult. His different powers made it hard for him to fit in and be a child like the rest of the wolf children. He was often teased and ridiculed when he showed something new that he discovered about himself.

When he killed Jeriah's daughter though, Jeriah lost faith in the boy and insisted that he be locked away. He was grieving the loss of his daughter and, at the time, we were all fearing the worst so we agreed to lock Michael away.

However, your grandfather said that they helped to provide options for teaching the boy but the werewolves withdrew from the boys education and, following their elder's lead, the rest of the werewolves did the same, leaving Aniyah, alone, to deal with what her son was becoming.

I do understand what he did, but I fear that by ignoring

Michael the way he did that Jeriah is the reason that Michael holds so much contempt for us. Finally, when Michael killed his own parents in his bloodlust and escaped, only to kill the human farmer and his family, Jeriah was left with no choice but to sentence Michael to death. He had not proved able to be taught to control his abilities and he had drawn attention to us by killing the humans. Whilst I and the other elders didn't like it, we were forced to agree that Michael needed to be dealt with.

Because Jeriah was the one that decreed he be killed, it was Jeriah's job to take the boy's life. It was a of guideline that we followed back then. Jeriah agreed to do it and went down to the dungeon to kill Michael.

But he proved unsuccessful. That led Jeriah to go into a kind of obsession with killing Michael until he was forced to accept that Michael could not be killed through means at our disposal.

During that time the humans had become suspicious and we were forced to make the decision to leave before we were discovered. However there was the decision we needed to make regarding Michael and what we should do with him.

Some of us thought to take him with us, while Jeriah and the others felt that leaving him here would be the best option. They ended up with the majority vote and we devised a plan with the witches to lock Michael into the underground facility with no way to escape through non-magical means, or so we thought, it seems.

The witches created and embedded their spells into the land and we sealed the building shut and never looked back. When we reached a new area to start our new lives, Jeriah suggested that it would be best for our tribes to go our separate ways to prevent this from happening again.

I agreed because I felt sickened by what we had done to that child by locking him up in an eternal tomb. We agreed to tell our future generations that were used to be friends but we weren't anymore. We fabricated the war between us and wrote the deaths of each side in such a way that it could be believed that we were at war with each other.

However, as time went on and the new generations grew, the hatred between our people grew and the false war continued for centuries to follow. I wanted to stop the war but by that time it became so detrimental to our sides, the hatred was already ingrained in the minds of the young werewolves and vampires that were born. I was powerless to stop it.

When news of a powerful being attacking the werewolves reached the news several months ago, I hoped that it would be something else. But when you sent me your message, I could not ignore the truth for any longer. Michael was back, he had escaped his prison and now that he was grown, he had a hatred inside him that I knew would be released upon both vampires and werewolves alike.'

I sat back in my chair. I was kind of surprised about the story and I was also, like Ambrogio said, not very happy with the answers I got.

'So what happened after Michael got locked away in the base?' I asked.

'We buried the history of it,' he said. 'My family and yours decided that it would be best to separate our species to stop it happening again and to deter our children of making friends with each other. Then we separated and never looked back.'

'Then what happened to the rest of your family?' I asked.

'They're around,' he said. 'Some of them have moved to other countries while others have their own covens spread out around America.'

'Like the one in New York?' Harry questioned.

'Yes,' he said. 'My oldest son is the leader in that coven.'

'You knew there was a vampire coven in your territory?' I questioned him.

He nodded. 'They never really crossed paths with us and they stayed out of our way so I never had a reason to stop them,' he told me. 'We kept an eye on them of course but they never really seemed to hurt anyone. Only ever willing humans, but even then, they mostly used the blood bank they own.'

'What about the vampires that attacked Zac?' I asked.

'The vampires assured me it wasn't any of their vampires and they hadn't given me any reason to believe otherwise,' he told me.

Kai nodded at this. 'My coven was much the same before Michael enslaved us,' he said. 'We would take blood donations, keep what we needed and sold the rest to the local hospital for their needs. There were enough people donating that we were able to cater for ourselves and make a profitable business.'

'I think my head hurts,' I said putting my hands on my head. 'Vampires are fully assimilated, and we didn't even know it.'

I sensed the amusement that came from the others in the room. Colby seemed to be the only other person that got where I was coming from. I took a moment to let all this new information process before I spoke again. 'So what should we do about Michael now?'

'Maybe shove him back into the ruins,' Colby suggested. 'We should be able to get the witches to spell the doors shut again.'

'We could,' I said. 'But that wouldn't be solving the problem. It would just put the problem away for another couple of centuries and our children would need to deal with him then.' I shook my head. 'I'd rather we deal with him.'

'We could work out how to kill him,' Kai said. 'If we can work that out maybe we will be able to stop him for good.'

'We couldn't find a way before,' Ambrogio said. 'I suppose there could be something now that we could try but we don't know if it would work.'

I sighed. 'Maybe we could reach out to him,' I said quietly. 'Turns out he is family after all. Surely if we can talk to him and admit to him that what our ancestors did was wrong then he might stop and we can all move on.'

'Then what?' Colby asked me. 'We just forget everything that he has done? He killed your parents. He killed Jeremy.'

'No,' I said. 'We can't forget what he did, but we need to stop him from killing any more of us and the only way might even be making a truce with him if we can.'

'And if that doesn't work?' Harry asked me.

'Then we would have no choice but to handle him,' I said. 'In the meantime, we come up with ways that we might be able to kill him.'

'So we have a truce here, do we?' Ambrogio asked me.

'I guess so,' I nodded. 'Trust me, if we can put aside all of the hate that has built up over the last few centuries, then we will all be much safer for it.' I paused. 'Especially since there was never any reason for it in the first place. It was just a cover up to separate us all.'

Harry nodded. 'It will take some time but I think we will be able to become allies again.'

I nodded in agreement. 'We're gonna have to undo all the hatred and that may take a while.'

'We understand,' Ambrogio said. 'We will need to

do much of the same things with our own people. It will certainly be a change.'

I looked at Harry. 'I say we organise a council meeting and discuss it with the others and see how best it would be to approach this.'

He nodded. 'Would probably be the right way to go about it,' he admitted. 'They would know best how to discuss this with their own packs themselves.'

'Yeah. We will organise that later today.'

'We will do the same on our end,' Kai interjected for the first time in a while. 'We will spread the word to the covens and talk to them about the changes to our situation. That will at least take any heat off you guys with worrying about vampires as well as Michael and you would at least know that any vampires that attack you are likely to be under Michael's control.'

'Have you done much with your alpha power?' Ambrogio asked me.

I cocked my head to the side. 'Alpha power?'

'The power you used when you fought Michael the first time,' he prodded. 'The lightning?'

'Oh.' I had forgotten all about that. To be honest I didn't really remember much of that time. 'No not really,' I said. 'I haven't really had the time to think about it.'

'That's okay,' he said quickly. 'I remember Jeriah was kind of only just learning about it when we separated. I wasn't sure if it was a normal thing.'

'We haven't heard anything about it at all,' Harry said. 'Jeremy never showed any abilities like those that Rya had that day.'

'Maybe it's only something from Rya's bloodline,' he said. 'I remember that Jeriah is a direct descendant of Lycaon after he was turned into a werewolf so maybe that was how the powers were carried.'

'But my father never showed any signs of these powers, did he?' I asked Harry and Colby.

They both shook their heads.

'Maybe there was never a reason for him to need them,' Harry said. 'Before Michael started attacking us, we didn't really have many issues. We were pretty relaxed with the occasional skirmish against vampires that caused an issue.'

'That's probably it,' Kai said. 'You were under a lot of pressure in that moment. Maybe that awakened the powers in you.'

'These powers might prove useful against Michael,' Ambrogio said. 'It might be best to see if you can explore these abilities.'

'Who would know about them?' I asked Harry.

He shrugged. 'We might be able to dig out some old literature on them but I doubt it has been recorded very much and if it is particular to your line of Garcia's then any information on it would be here in Wolfridge.' He paused, looking thoughtful. 'Maybe the wild pack alpha will know about them.'

'They're due to come here in the next month,' I stated. 'I can talk to them about it then.' I looked at Colby. 'In the meantime... we can explore them on our own and see what we can figure out.' Colby nodded. At least he was on board with all of this.

'I think we're done here for now then,' Ambrogio said.

I nodded. 'It seems so.' I grabbed a blank piece of paper and scrawled my mobile number on to it. I gave it to Ambrogio. 'Call me if you need anything or come up with any idea on how to stop Michael.'

He nodded and tucked the number into his pocket.

'I'll escort you back to the boundary.' Cobly volunteered.

'Still unsure,' Ambrogio smiled.

Colby grimaced. 'I'm sorry.'

'No no,' he replied. 'It's fine. I would do the same.'

'I was thinking it might be an idea for me to stay here,' Kai said suddenly. We all kind of looked at him instantly. The vampire looked at his father. 'I might be able to help Rya with these powers,' he said. 'It would work as a connection between the two of you if we need it and we need to learn how to work together anyway. Why not start here?'

I could tell that Colby wasn't all that keen on the spur of the moment decision that Kai had made but I could tell that he would support it if I thought it would work. I glanced at Harry, to be honest I was wondering if it was a good idea, I was all for introducing werewolves to a more friendly alliance with vampires but having one move into our house might be a bit confronting. Harry nodded at me. Apparently he approved.

'I think we can make some arrangements,' I said to Kai.

'Very well then,' Ambrogio said. 'We will be in contact.'

Colby led the two vampires out of the house before anybody had a chance to make any further decisions about vampires living in a house full of werewolves. 'What kind of food and sleeping arrangements should I organise for you?' I asked Kai once I heard the front door close behind them.

'Just a bedroom is fine,' he said. 'A bag of O positive a day is enough for me too.'

I nodded. 'I will make the arrangements,' I told him. 'Try not to push yourself onto the pack too quickly. Maybe hang back until they get used to the idea of you being here.' He nodded. 'Otherwise you're free to roam. Though I would rather you wear contacts if you go into town. I would prefer the humans didn't know you were here just yet.'

*****

That evening at dinner I had everyone gather in the rec room to talk to them about Kai staying with us and the discussions that were had about vampires and werewolves and the fallout of our alliance and how it was more of a way to cover up Michael in our history.

A lot of them were quite shocked about this news since it was how we were all raised and it was going to be strange trying to change the way we respond to a vampire's presence. I ended my discussion with them by telling them about Kai and explained who he was and that he would be staying with us for the time being to help our pack transition to this new mindset and also help keep contact with Ambrogio and his people while we strategised against Michael.

The reaction to him staying here was less than excitable, I kind of expected that, but I think they understood the need for the vampire presence, at least for the moment. By the end of it I was feeling more confident in my decision to allow Kai to stay with us and even went as far as introducing him officially to the pack as a whole. I think it went over very well to be completely honest. There was the flaring of nostrils as each of the werewolves took in the scent of the vampire but nobody growled and everybody's wolves remained relatively calm. I called that a win.

Kai didn't join us for dinner. Instead he went upstairs to the room I organised for him and grabbed a blood bag out of the bar fridge and had it upstairs, or at least I assumed that was what he did as that is what he told me.

We didn't do any more business talk that night. Instead we hung out in the rec room as a pack and Kai hung back but eventually Zac approached him and they started talking about what it's like being a vampire. I think Kai even let Zac in his mind so he could feel what it was like. Everyone had been a little edgy at first but otherwise they settled and we had an enjoyable first night together.

The next morning I went into work for the first time in a while. I felt confident leaving Kai at home. I felt like I could trust him after everything we went through together. The team at work was incredibly happy to see me. They hadn't seen me since before I made the message to Ambrogio. Stephen even pulled me into his office first thing in the morning after I arrived.

'Is everything okay?' he asked seriously. 'Anything we need to know about?'

I shook my head. 'Not at this point in time.'

'That message sounded serious though.' His tone seemed more worried than accusatory. 'What was it about?'

I shook my head. 'I'm unable to discuss it at the moment. I didn't want to resort to the public message, but I was left with no choice.'

'And it worked?' he questioned.

'Yes.' I answered. 'There are some serious matters at work at the moment and I would appreciate the time and the privacy to work through them.' I made this last part sound like an expectation. I did expect leniency for this until we got everything sorted out.

'As long as the work gets done, we can manage without you every so often,' he said. 'We mostly need input on studies and we have our meeting with the higher ups later this week. So we need to go to that too.'

'Great,' I said. 'If I organise my emails to forward home and pick up my jobs in the in tray each morning can I work from home temporarily?' I asked.

Stephen nodded. 'Yes, you can,' he confirmed.

Before I went home, he had me wandering around to talk to the other staff. Kelly was just about ready with the draft laws and guidelines for human and werewolf interactions. I asked her what we would do if we needed to add another race of supernaturals to the document. She replied by telling me that it would be best to sort out before it is published, otherwise we would need to organise an addendum or publish a brand new document.

I made a note to bring this up to Ambrogio when I next spoke to him. If we wanted this to work, then a truce between all three of our races would be preferable for sure. I hoped that he would make a decision earlier on than later because it would allow us to make the changes before it was published, and this was even if he wanted to go public anyway.

Next step was going into the science lab area and talking to them about the projects they were working on. Naomi was still trying to see if she could make a kind of healing serum by using werewolf blood. She had managed to make a few different serums based on some theories but was unable to get them to work. While I enjoyed the idea of using our blood to heal people, I also suggested she find another more achievable project to present to the bosses while she continues to work on this one.

Our tech guy was looking into making communicator chips that we could insert into werewolves that would allow us to communicate over a network system even if we weren't close by to each other. Almost like an internal cell phone that would be connected to other chips on the same server. I honestly really liked the idea. We would need a way to switch it on and off so that we could manage it properly but I think the idea had promise for the future and I'm sad I didn't think up the idea myself.

I finished making my rounds and updating myself on the tasks that my colleagues were doing but also catching up on a more personal level as well. This was mostly them asking me questions about everything that happened and me letting them know that I would be working from home for a while due to my pack duties at the moment. At least at home I could do both. At work I could only do work without giving the human government practically every detail about what was happening and we'd rather keep it on the downlow for now so Michael didn't find out what is happening too soon.

I didn't end up getting to go home until the end of the day, but that was with the instructions of how to link work emails to my home computer and everybody knowing to call or email me if they needed anything urgently. I would be going in hopefully every day to pick up anything from my tray anyway and return what I had already done.

Finally, at the end of the day, I informed the pack and Kai of my new work situation and how I would be spending the time trying to access my apparent alpha powers that I got from Lycaon himself. Crazy, huh? I went to bed that night thinking about the kinds of things we could try the next day to unleash the powers. To be honest I just hoped that I wasn't making a big mess of everything. I spent nearly an hour mulling over the things to come until I fell into an uneasy sleep.

The next couple of days were hard. Both Colby and Kai put me through my paces for several hours each morning trying to find any string of the power that had been unleashed several months prior, but nothing happened. Absolutely nothing.

I tried not to be discouraged. It took a threat on Zac's life to activate it last time and I tried to remind myself of that, but I couldn't stop thinking about this being the key to taking down Michael.

A few days into my new routine we got news from Ambrogio. Bad news. 'The Dallas coven isn't responding to communications,' he told us over the phone in the boardroom.

'What does that mean?' Harry asked. He was on the conference screen in a video call.

Ambrogio paused for a moment. 'It means that Michael might have taken another coven. This one had only old ones, but none of the original family. Still, they were trusted allies of mine.'

'If he's amassing stronger vampires then he's going to launch an attack,' Harry stated.

'With you being the new wolf in charge he's probably coming after you, Rya,' Kai told me.

I sighed deeply. 'I think I miss the old days of going to school and only having Erik to worry about.'

'No you don't,' Colby said.

'You're right, I don't,' I retorted. 'But this is just as bad, if not worse.'

'What do you want to do about it, Rya?' Colby asked me.

'We stand and fight him,' I said, sounding tougher than I felt. 'How many vampires were in the Dallas coven?' I asked the two vampires.

'Hundreds,' Ambrogio answered. 'It's a large city that werewolves haven't touched.'

'So we should expect a lot of vampires.' I sighed. There was no way we could fight off that many.

'I will send some of my own pack your way and will let Eddie know to do the same,' Harry said seriously. 'We aren't losing you, Rya. We aren't losing any more family.'

*****

Within twenty-four hours Wolfridge was home to hundreds of werewolves. We had to house them in the house and the bunker just to make room for them all. There were constant patrols in and around the larger territory and the small town of our immediate home. I think there were nearly twenty werewolves patrolling at all times. If Michael appeared anywhere, we would know about it very quickly.

When he finally did show his face it was as bad as we thought. Hundreds of vampires entered through the main road into town. We sent the word out and all the kids sprang into action and alerted the townspeople to get indoors and stay there. I had advised them that something might happen, so they were ready when the kids ran up and down the streets yelling out to everyone before they came to help us.'

Unlike our last big fight we knew they were coming. We were able to choose the turf we fought on. In the end we were on the school oval. It was the only large, wide, open space. It would provide us with plenty of room to fight on open ground and would allow for better visibility.

When Michael finally came into view, it took all of my will power, and the several werewolves standing in a protective circle around me, to not run straight at him. For the moment nobody moved except Michael as he walked closer and closer until he stood close enough to speak to me without yelling.

'I see you knew we were coming,' he said.

I smirked at him. 'We have our ears to the ground these days.'

He cocked an eyebrow at me. 'I heard you found out about what happened all those years ago.'

I nodded. 'I'm sorry for what my ancestors did to you,' I said. 'It wasn't right.'

'No, it wasn't,' he seemed oddly calm.

'I can't make what they did go away,' I said. 'But you can put aside your anger and your thirst for revenge.'

He seemed thoughtful for a moment. 'You would forgive everything that I've done, for peace, just like that?'

'Just like that,' I repeated.

He thought about it for several long minutes. 'No.'

As soon as he said it, everything started happening at once. The vampires ran towards us, werewolves stood their ground and waited for them to come to us. When they did… Oh, when they did it was huge. I had never seen or heard of a fight on this scale much less actually participated in it.

I tried to help but my protectors wouldn't let me past. They wouldn't risk losing me too. I hated it. So when a gap formed between the circle of werewolves, I dove into wolf form and darted out of the protective circle. I couldn't take it anymore.

I sensed two werewolves chase after me, both of them from Harry's pack. I leapt at a vampire in a fight with Mira and tore its throat leaving Mira safe for a few moments to catch her breath, then I continued onto the next one. The two werewolves that flanked me, helped kill vampires and protect my rear. I was glad that I wasn't being dragged back. I would rather have a couple of bodyguards to help me than sit out and let everyone else do the fighting.

I think I killed dozens of vampires that day. Most of them were fairly easy to kill, a few of the harder ones were older vampires and I can honestly say that I was reluctant to kill them before they attacked me, especially since I now knew they were being controlled by Michael.

I kept my eyes peeled for him. I was ready for him if he attacked me but he seemed to be hanging back behind his forces for the moment and surveying the scene in front of him. I slowly started making my way towards him.

Across the way I saw Zac manage to kill an older

vampire by himself. I cheered internally at his victory. He had come so far in such a short time. I was proud of the achievements he had made as a werewolf. Then I saw Michael look at him. Last time they had seen each other Zac had only just turned.

I started in that direction at the same time as Michael. Zac had been instantly taken up by another vampire and he was so busy defending himself against the new opponent that he hadn't noticed the danger he was in.

I had to fight my way through, vampires came at me from all directions. I wasn't going to get there in time. There was still so much distance between us and so many vampires. Too many.

Michael reached Zac at the same time as he killed his most recent opponent. I saw the glint of metal in his hand. 'ZAC!!' I shouted out and pushed through the vampire that attempted to stop me.

Michael glanced at me, smirked then stabbed with the blade in his right hand, the same one that had stabbed through my me and had since left a scar just below my ribs. Then he stabbed the blade forward and I watched as it plunged into his chest.

Michael pulled the blade back and Toby collapsed onto the ground. It had all happened so fast. Toby had come in from the side and pushed Zac out of harm's way. Zac was on the ground staring up at Michael as the hybrid towered over him.

I felt the anger well up in me as Michael turned his gaze to Zac and he started towards him. I felt a tug of energy from deep within my mind as electricity filled my body. The sky rumbled and lightning struck. It struck at Michael.

He jumped out of the way. Suddenly he was on the defensive. Another surge rushed through me and it struck the ground that Michael had been standing on only moments before. Around the field more lightning lashed out of the dark clouds and struck dozens of vampires across the school oval, leaving only scorched grass behind.

The anger continued to build within me, so did the storm that surrounded us. The clouds rumbled angrily and water began to fall from the sky. For the first time I saw fear in Michael's eyes as he stepped away from me even as I stepped towards him.

As if it was almost out of instinct, I raised my arm and I felt the next bolt of lightning strike me. I felt the raw energy of it channel through me and into my other hand that I directed at Michael.

My fingers glowed bright as the energy built up, when my whole hand was glowing with power, I felt a switch flip in my mind and the energy released in a large beam of light. It struck Michael and I heard him yell out in pain for only a moment before he disappeared. I knew he wasn't dead. The others had disintegrated on impact with the electricity, he didn't. He was just teleported away.

I could still feel the energy flowing through me as I walked toward Zac and Toby. I stopped next to Toby and looked down at his now lifeless form. I felt the energy leave me as I collapsed down to my knees beside him. Blood was still gushing from the wound onto the ground below his body, but he was gone.

I cupped his face in my hand and felt my eyes fill with

tears. Toby had been with me from the beginning, we were born on the same day we were best friends. I leaned over and rested my forehead on his chest. He was so still. There was no rise of his chest and no movement beneath his skin. There was no mind to reach out to. He was just gone. Toby was dead.

To be continued…